THE BIG DAY IN PAWNEE CITY . . .

It was the day Joe Jagger and Chad Morgan, partners, knew that their wild gamble was going to make them rich.

It was the day they sold the first business lots in Pawnee City, the town they had built out of raw prairie sod.

It was the day the first cattle cars were loaded in the town.

And it was the day of the lynch mob . . .

Morgan tried to protect the terrified victim. He threatened the lynch mob with his six-gun. But Jagger urged them on. "An eye for an eye!" he yelled.

The Big Land

Originally published under the title
BUFFALO GRASS

A Novel of Kansas
by
Frank Gruber

BANTAM BOOKS
TORONTO · NEW YORK · LONDON · SYDNEY

THE BIG LAND
A Bantam Book

PRINTING HISTORY

*Originally published by Rinehart & Company, Inc.
under the title* BUFFALO GRASS

Rinehart edition published September 1956

Bantam edition / March 1957

2nd printing . . . . . April 1957		*4th printing . . . August 1978*
3rd printing . . . . . May 1970		*5th printing . . February 1983*

ISBN 0-553-23378-5

Published simultaneously in the United States and Canada

Bantam Books are published by Bantam Books, Inc. Its trademark, consisting of the words "Bantam Books" and the por-
trayal of a rooster, is Registered in U.S. Patent and Trademark
Office and in other countries. Marca Registrada. Bantam
Books, Inc., 666 Fifth Avenue, New York, New York 10103.

PRINTED IN THE UNITED STATES OF AMERICA

H   14 13 12 11 10 9 8 7 6 5

THE
BIG
LAND
(Buffalo Grass)

Chapter One

The guns were stilled, the carnage had ended. Lee had surrendered at Appomattox Courthouse, Johnston had come to terms with Sherman and, in Texas, Kirby Smith had yielded the last armed force of the Confederacy.

The War was over.

Yet now, eight weeks after Appomattox, the gray-uniformed soldier lay on the ground in a canebrake in South Texas, the lifeblood seeping from a bullet wound in his chest. His pain-tortured eyes looked into the face of Sergeant Chad Morgan, of the Sixteenth Illinois Cavalry.

A few yards away, Sergeant Joe Jagger was searching the overturned army ambulance in which the Confederate had tried to outrun the two Union cavalrymen. Two dead horses were tangled in the harness. The broken wagon shaft had pierced the belly of one of the horses, a carbine bullet had taken care of the other.

Morgan dropped to one knee beside the wounded man. A quick glance told him the story.

"You've had it," he said soberly.

A faint gasp was torn from the dying man. "You— you're *sure?*"

"Whyn't you stop?" Morgan asked testily. "The war's been over for two months. Nothing would have happened to you."

The Confederate's mouth worked terribly. "Jo . . . Jo Shelby . . . needs . . ."

Morgan made an impatient gesture. "Shelby's a fool. He thinks he can go down into Mexico and enough Confederates will join him so he can come back and start the war all over. There's a civil war going on in Mexico. Juarez won't have Shelby and neither will Maximilian." He

1

scowled. "What's he got with him? A bunch of Missouri
bushwhackers who're afraid to go home, deserters, riffraff.
With *that* he thinks he can conquer Mexico. . . ."

"Chad!" suddenly called Joe Jagger. "Look . . . !"

Morgan sent a quick glance over his shoulder, saw that
Jagger was dragging a small, ironbound chest out of the
wreckage of the ambulance. He got quickly to his feet and
went over to join his fellow sergeant.

"Maybe this is why he wouldn't surrender," Jagger said.

Morgan gestured to Jagger to step aside. He pointed his
carbine at the lock on the chest and pulled the trigger.

The bullet smashed the lock and in a moment, Jagger
forced up the lid of the small chest. A cry was torn from his
throat.

"Gold!"

The small chest was filled, almost to the very top, with
bright golden eagles and double eagles.

Jagger's hands plunged into the golden mass, came up
with a double handful of coins. "Must be twenty-thirty
thousand here," he said in awe.

"General Shelby's war chest!"

Jagger shook his head. "Jo Shelby never saw this much
money." His eyes went beyond Morgan to the wounded
Confederate a dozen yards away. "Can he talk?"

"For a little while."

Jagger dumped the gold coins back into the chest. Both
men walked back to the wounded man. Jagger dropped to
his knees.

"We found the gold, Reb."

The wounded man groaned.

"Whose is it?" Morgan asked gruffly, then made a wild
guess. "Jeff Davis's?"

A spasm of pain contorted the Confederate's face. "So
that's lost, too!"

"They been lookin' for this money," Jagger exulted. "All
the way between here and Richmond, Virginia." He suddenly got to his feet and caught Chad Morgan's eye.

The two cavalrymen walked back to the gold chest.
"We're heroes, Chad," Jagger said. "They'll cite us in dis-
patches for this." He paused carefully. "In a few weeks

when they discharge us we can take those citations to the bank and cash them in."

Chad Morgan looked narrowly at the man who had been his closest friend for almost four years, the man who had twice saved his life and whose life he had himself saved; the man whose canteen he had shared, whose blankets he had often used.

"What you're thinking," he said deliberately, "is finders' keepers."

"Who owns this?" Jagger asked softly. "The Confederate States of America? There's no such thing. Jeff Davis? It wasn't his in the first place and anyway he's in prison now." His eyes went to the wounded Confederate. "It sure doesn't belong to *him* because where he's going he won't need any money." He cleared his throat. "It's *our* money, Chad. Yours and mine." He paused. *"Isn't it?"*

Chad Morgan rubbed his unshaven chin with the back of his hand. "Are you asking me, or telling me?"

They counted the gold as they stowed it away in their saddlebags. They found that there was an even twenty-five thousand dollars.

"I was looking forward to getting me a job in a store," Morgan said, "but now, I dunno. Maybe I'll read law for a couple of years. There'll still be some left over to set me up in a practice."

"And in five years you'll be earning just about enough to get by," said Joe Jagger. "In ten years you'll be able to support yourself and a wife, unless you're fool enough to get married before then. In which case you'll never get your head above water."

Morgan shrugged: "I don't figure to ever be a rich man."

"Well, *I* do," declared Jagger. "I want money, a lot of money, Chad. And I'm going to make it." He made a sudden sweeping gesture. "What's made the biggest impression on you about Texas?"

"The weather," said Sergeant Chad Morgan cheerfully. "It's hell."

Jagger scowled. "That's all?"

"The buffalo. There must be a million of them. . . ."

"And twenty million longhorns," snapped Jagger. "They

been roaming wild all these years. Every Texan's cattle poor. They've got no hard money—nothing, just longhorns."

"Well, they won't go hungry."

"They've got too much beef," Jagger went on, "so much that a longhorn is worth maybe two dollars. That's for the *hide and tallow*. But they're hungry for beef up North. A two-dollar Texas longhorn would fetch twenty dollars in Illinois."

"If you could get him to Illinois."

"They got them there before the war. I was in the livestock-feeding business in Bloomington. I saw two-three Texas herds brought in. Pretty ragged stuff, but not too bad after it was fattened up." He paused. "They've started to build the Union Pacific. It's moving out across Nebraska right now. And there's another railroad building out of Kansas City, across Kansas. It's going to be a lot easier to drive these longhorns to market than it was before."

"You're figuring on driving Texas cattle to Kansas?"

Jagger smiled. "Not me. Uh-uh. Oh, there's money in it, but not the kind of money I'm interested in. Not with a stake of twenty-five thousand——"

"Twenty-five?"

"You're going in with me."

Chad Morgan hesitated. "I was thinking of studying law. . . ."

"With the kind of money we'll have in two or three years you'll be able to hire a dozen lawyers. There're men in the East, Chad, who didn't have a quarter at the beginning of the war and now they're millionaires."

"You figure to be a millionaire?"

"A *rich* millionaire!"

Morgan looked thoughtfully at his friend for a moment. Then a sudden grin spread across his face. He walked to his horse and put the saddlebags on it. Then he turned to Jagger, a frown on his face. He nodded toward the Confederate.

"What about him?"

"He's dying, isn't he?"

"Sure, but it might be hours."

Jagger looked sharply at Morgan, then he went to the Confederate. He looked down at him and drew his revolver.

Morgan cried out in horror. "Joe! No . . . !"

Jagger's revolver roared. He looked coolly at Morgan and mounted his horse. "I'm in a hurry," he said, "for that million dollars."

Chapter Two

Joe Jagger and Chad Morgan didn't get started on their million dollars quite as soon as they had expected. Maximilian, down in Mexico, had been put on the throne with the bayonets of fifty thousand French soldiers under Marshal Bazaine.

During the bloody internecine strife north of the Rio Grande, no one had been able to do anything about the French troops below the border; but now the war was at an end and with a Union Army of six hundred thousand veterans, the Federal government remembered the Monroe Doctrine. They called it to the attention of the Lesser Napoleon in France. To point it up, General Phil Sheridan began massing troops on the Rio Grande.

The Lesser Napoleon got the idea and recalled his fifty thousand soldiers, leaving the sawdust emperor of Mexico to his fate.

It was the summer of '66, a full year after they had come into possession of twenty-five thousand dollars in gold, when the two cavalry sergeants, Chad Morgan and Joe Jagger, were finally discharged.

Each went to his own home for a short visit, Morgan to Wisconsin, Jagger to Illinois. In early September they met in St. Louis and proceeded to the offices of the Kansas & Colorado Railroad.

The suite of offices wasn't very impressive, for the railroad had only two crews of workers. One was laying track in Kansas and the other was out selling stocks and shares. The construction crew was doing a better job of it.

In the outer office of the railroad company was a girl who caused Chad Morgan to gasp. She was the most beautiful creature he had ever seen in his life. In her early twenties, she was dressed in a prim calico dress that should have made

6

her unattractive, but failed. She had golden brown hair, a marvelous complexion and her eyes were blue, with a light in them that would cause a lot of good men a great deal of trouble.

When Jagger and Morgan entered the office, she leaped to her feet and ran to Joe Jagger with outstretched arms.

"Joe!" she cried. "At last!"

For an instant Chad Morgan actually hated his friend. Jagger kissed the gorgeous one, then thrust her out at arm's length. "Why, damme," he said, "you're old enough to get married!"

"I was old enough when you went away," retorted the girl. She shot a quick look at Morgan. "You're Chad! Joe's written me about you." She held out her hand.

Morgan took the hand, found it warm and firm. "How are you, Miss . . . ?"

"Miss Ace-in-the-hole," chuckled Jagger. "My sister, Helen . . ."

A ripple of relief and exultation shot through Morgan. "You never told me about her. I—I mean, you talked as if she was a child. . . ."

"She was—once." Joe grinned maliciously. "She sent me her picture a while ago, but I didn't show it to you on purpose. . . ."

"Oh, you!" exclaimed Helen Jagger.

Jagger winked at Morgan. "I wanted him to make up his mind all by himself."

The door to a private office opened and a heavy-set man in a Prince Albert with a florid vest appeared. "Miss Jagger," he said, "if you'll come in . . ."

"Oh, Mr. Foss," exclaimed Helen Jagger. "This is my brother Joseph, and his partner, Mr. Morgan. You have an appointment with them."

For a moment Nathan Foss's face was blank. Then he grimaced. "Oh, yes, the Texas-cattle scheme." He drew out a massive gold watch. "I'm afraid I won't have time right now."

"You *have* the time, Mr. Foss," said Helen Jagger coolly. "I canceled Mr. Meyerson's appointment and Mr. Vandervoort's also, just so you'd have *plenty* of time."

Foss showed annoyance. "Now really, Miss Jagger . . ."

"I'm the man you've been waiting for, Mr. Foss," declared Joe Jagger. "The man who's going to save your railroad for you. Once you hear my proposition, you'll cancel every other appointment you've got this week."

Foss fixed Jagger with a dour look. "Frankly, Mr.—ah —Jagger, I'm in no mood for levity. . . ."

"Joe and his partner," Helen Jagger said clearly, "have twenty-five thousand dollars in gold!"

A strange new light came into Nathan Foss's eyes. "Come in, Mr. Jagger, come in. And you, too, Mr.——?"

"Morgan."

The two ex-cavalrymen followed Nathan Foss into his private office, a very fine paneled room that had impressed many a prospective investor in railroad shares.

Foss seated himself behind a huge desk, waited until his visitors had found chairs, then formed an inverted V of his hands by placing the thumbs and finger tips together.

"Gentlemen," he began, "railroad stocks today are the soundest of all investments. I can promise you, nay, I can virtually *guarantee* you, a profit of ten per cent on your money——"

"Whoa, wait a minute!" interrupted Joe Jagger. *"I'll* guarantee you a hundred per cent—and more, Mr. Foss!" A spot of red appeared on each of Nathan Foss's cheeks. It grew as Joe Jagger hurried on. "Your railroad's broke. You've got forty miles of track laid and you've had to shut down work until you can raise some more money. Oh, you'll probably be able to build a few more miles of track—and maybe a few more after that. But what's the use? There's nothing past Lawrence, nothing but prairie dogs. And *they* won't be shipping any freight on your railroad."

"Neither will you," retorted the railroad man. "This harebrained scheme your sister's told me about . . ."

"It's no scheme, Mr. Foss. We've got the plan all worked out and we've got the money for it. We're going to build a town out there, on your railroad. This town's going to have stores, a hotel, stockyards——"

"Stockyards!" snorted Foss. "Stockyards on the prairie . . . !"

"Stockyards," repeated Jagger firmly, "built with *our* money! It won't cost *you* a cent. All we want in return——"

"You just said it wouldn't cost me a penny!"

"It won't cost you *much*. I want your crew to build me a half mile of siding to facilitate the loading of the cattle onto the stock cars."

"That's nothing?" snapped Foss. "A half a mile of track costs twenty thousand dollars."

"It'll be the most important investment of your life."

"All right, suppose I said I'd build the siding . . . what else do you want?"

"Five dollars for every carload of cattle that is loaded at *my* loading pens, *my* stockyards . . ."

"Five dollars of nothing is still nothing. What else?"

"Land. Some of the drovers may want to fatten up their cattle before selling to the buyers."

"Land," said Foss, "is the one thing we have. Our grant from the government calls for every other section on both sides of the track——"

"From Kansas City to Colorado," said Jagger. "The land isn't worth ten cents an acre."

"All right, you can have a thousand acres . . . two thousand." Foss paused. "The moment you've built your stockyards and—and hotel!"

Jagger got up, crossed to the desk, picked up a pen, and dipped it into a well of ink. He extended the pen to Nathan Foss. "Put it in writing."

Foss scowled, hesitated, then took the pen.

Chapter Three

Little white stakes stuck into the ground stretched out for fifty miles beyond the end of track. Joe Jagger and Chad Morgan followed the stakes to their end and came upon a settlement that bore the name of Prairie Dog.

The place consisted of a sod-covered store that was also the horse relay station for the once-a-month stageline. In addition some dozen sod shacks were scattered about the landscape. Some rather miserable humans lived in them.

A man named Artie Puffpaff crawled out of one of the soddies as Jagger and Morgan rode up and dismounted. He was whiskered, wore trousers and a shirt that had seen their best days before the war—the war with Mexico. He was incredibly dirty and lice crawled over the patches of skin that showed through the rents in his shirt.

"Mr. Puffpaff," said Jagger, "we'll lay our cards on the table . . ."

Puffpaff blinked red eyelids. "What cards?"

Jagger made a gesture of dismissal. "You've squatted on a section of land. You've put out some boundary sticks and you may even have some claim to the land. Squatter's rights, perhaps. Whatever they are, I want to buy them from you."

Puffpaff regarded Jagger with an open mouth, the mouth becoming wider as Jagger went on. Then suddenly he closed his mouth and squinted craftily at Jagger.

"You want to pay me *money* for my—my homestead? Is *that* what you're getting at?"

"You're a very smart man, Mr. Puffpaff," said Jagger. "You guessed it right away."

Morgan drew a quart bottle of whiskey from his saddlebags. He held it so Puffpaff could get a square look at it. Puffpaff looked—and couldn't return his eyes to Jagger.

"You got money on you, Bub?" he whined. "Hard money?"

Jagger took a twenty-dollar gold piece from his pocket and tossed it into the dust at Puffpaff's feet. "Is that *hard* enough for you?"

Puffpaff's eyes fell from the bottle of whiskey, found the gold in the dirt. He picked it up and then his eyes went again to the bottle of whiskey.

"This is a valuable piece of property," he whined.

Morgan took a second bottle of whiskey from his saddle-bags. "You can squat on a brand-new piece of land, Puff-paff."

"Twenty dollars and two quarts of whiskey," snapped Jagger. He took a piece of paper and a pencil from his pocket and tossed it to Puffpaff. "Sign!"

Puffpaff was busy all of that day and the next, transferring the contents of the two bottles of whiskey to his stomach, so he was in no condition to do any work, but Jagger and Morgan found another squatter who was glad to earn five dollars.

He had a rusted old saw and cut up some lengths of wood into chunks about a foot long. He split these and in the course of a few hours provided quite a large supply of stakes, which he sharpened at one end with a hatchet.

He followed Morgan and Jagger around and drove a stake into the ground wherever he was told.

"This'll be the hotel," declared Jagger, after pacing off the ground. "It's got to be near the depot and stockyards, but it should face Main Street. Mmm, we'll make the street good and wide. Hate these towns with narrow, crooked streets."

"One street going to be enough?" asked Morgan cheerfully.

"One *main* street," replied Jagger. "Of course we'll need cross streets. Let's see now, we're going to need lots for business places. We'll figure it out in units of twenty feet. That's all the frontage a small shop'll need. Man needs a bigger place he'll have to buy two twenty-foot lots."

They worked their way down "Main Street," then turned back and crossed the stakes put out by the surveyors of

the railroad and paced off the distances for the stockyards
and loading pens, the railroad siding.

Finally, when the area looked like a field of growing
sticks, Jagger and Morgan paused to rest near a prairie-
dog mound where a prairie dog sat outside his hole watching them.

Jagger frowned at the animal. "Prairie Dog," he said,
shaking his head. "That's no good for a town name. Got to
have something more colorful." He drew a revolver from
his pocket, aimed at the prairie dog and fired. The bullet
kicked up dust four feet from the little animal, which
promptly jumped headfirst into its hole.

Morgan held out his hand to Jagger and Jagger handed
him the gun. Morgan waited a moment, until the prairie
dog stuck its head out of the hole. Then Morgan thrust
out the revolver and, seemingly without aiming, fired.

The stake man walked up to the prairie-dog hole and
with his scuffed shoe kicked out the headless prairie dog.
"That's shootin', Mister," he said.

Jagger grinned wryly. "Chad was the best revolver shot
in the Sixteenth Illinois Cavalry. Me, I couldn't hit a horse
at ten feet." He shook his head. "We still need a good name
for our town. Something colorful, easy to say and remember."

Morgan picked up a chunk of smooth, curved wood.
"Here's what's left of an old Indian bow. Might suggest a
name . . . Busted Bow, Broken Bow——"

"Not bad," said Jagger, "for a small town, but we want
something with more size."

"That's a Pawnee bow," volunteered the squatter. "There
was supposed to been a big battle around here with the
Pawnees some years ago."

"Pawnee!" exclaimed Jagger. "It's colorful. That's it . . .
Pawnee City."

Chapter Four

The tail end of a norther was still sweeping across the flat Texas country and Chad Morgan, hunched over his saddle pommel, hands thrust into his pockets, was cursing the Texan who had told him that there was a village only eighteen miles away. He had traveled at least twenty-five.

Something cold and wet plopped on his face. They said it didn't snow this far south. He raised his head and looked up at the overcast sky. If it wasn't snow, it was going to be an awfully cold thick rain.

Then he saw the man ahead of him. He was riding, like Morgan, hunched over. Morgan pressed his right elbow to his side. He felt the reassuring hardness of his Navy gun and then kneed his horse into a trot.

The rider heard him coming but did not slow his mount. He did, however, edge a little to one side of the rutted trail so Morgan could pass him without having to swing out.

Morgan eased his horse so it jogged beside the other one. "It's a bad day to be out," he said, to open the conversation.

The man looked sidewards at Morgan, but merely grunted a reply. He was unshaven and his lean features were weathered and hard. Morgan caught a mere glint of his slitted eyes and knew that the man was a hard case.

"My name's Morgan," he said. "They told me there was a town up ahead."

"A buffalo wallow," the other rider finally said, "two-three 'dobe shacks."

Morgan looked ahead. The twin ruts that were the trail curved off to the left and disappeared over a low ridge. "How far?"

13

Morgan's fellow traveler shrugged. "This damn country always looked the same to me. I been through before, and I never know where I am." He nodded. "My name's Alder."

"Alder," Morgan repeated. Then he looked sharply at the other man. "Tom Alder?"

Alder straightened a little in his saddle. "Yeah."

"You're a long way from home."

"You don't talk like a Texas man yourself," said Alder.

"Wisconsin," replied Morgan carefully. "I served in the Sixteenth Illinois Cavalry."

Alder said harshly, "I'm just back from Mexico. They told me the war was over back *here.*"

"As far as *I'm* concerned, it is," said Morgan.

"Yeah," said Alder. "I was with Quantrill and I went to Mexico with Shelby. He's still there, but he won't be for long. They got Max and there didn't seem to be any point in waiting around to be stood against a wall with him." He paused. "How's Missouri?"

Morgan hesitated, then shook his head. "Not good."

"Didn't think it would be."

"Some of the boys don't know the war's over. Been some bank holdups."

"Damn fools," snapped Alder.

He was about to add more, then suddenly thrust out his hand and pointed. "There she is!"

They had topped a small rise and down below, in a shallow valley, less than a half mile away, was a cluster of adobe buildings. Both men put their horses into a canter and rode into the tiny hamlet as the first snow flurries swirled around them.

Several horses were tied before a hitchrail in front of the largest of the adobe buildings. Alder and Morgan dismounted and tied their horses to the rail and went into the building, which turned out to be a combination trading post and saloon.

There was a short bar and two tables nearby. A poker game was going on at one of the tables. Four men, all wearing buffalo-skin overcoats, were in the game.

Morgan and Alder made their way to the bar.

"Bring the snow with you?" asked the bartender, a whiskered man who had not washed his hands in three months.

He set two unwashed glasses before them and filled them about half full with a brownish liquid. It had a pungent taste, but it sent a ripple of warmth coursing through Morgan's body.

He tossed a silver dollar on the rough counter. "One more."

"Take another dollar," was the reply.

Alder spun a coin on the bar. "How about a peso?"

The bartender shrugged. "It's good silver."

Alder took the bottle from the man's hand and poured the drinks this time, filling the glasses to the brims. The bartender scowled.

Alder raised his glass without spilling a drop. "A good trip home, Morgan."

Morgan drank, but when he set down his glass, he shook his head. "Not yet. I've got to cover a lot more territory." He opened his coat and took out a sheaf of folded handbills from an inside pocket.

"Mind hanging up one of these?" he asked the bartender.

The man unfolded one of the handbills, squinted at it and began to read aloud: *"The North Wants Beef."* He grimaced. *"Bring your steers to Kansas. Ready buyers waiting. Railroad loading pens. Grazing available. Accommodations for Drovers. Jagger & Morgan, Pawnee City, Kansas."* He lowered the handbill and regarded Morgan dourly. "You a Yankee?"

"Any objections?" asked Morgan.

One of the card players got up from the game and came over. "C'n I see that?"

He took the handbill from the bartender. "Fella was through here last week, said somebody's been puttin' out these things, but I didn't believe him." He read the bill. "You work for this Yankee outfit?"

"I'm Morgan," said Morgan, indicating the signature on the bill.

The man frowned. "I never heard of any Pawnee City."

"It's a new place. The railroad's building west and this is the end of track."

The Texan screwed up his face. "I got cattle. I got a lot of cattle."

"Then drive them to Kansas."

"And have the Jayhawkers take them from me?"

Morgan shook his head. "They operate out of Baxter Springs. You'll drive a hundred, hundred-fifty miles west of them. You won't see any Jayhawkers."

"These buyers—they'll pay hard cash?"

"Gold. Twenty dollars a head."

"What?"

The rest of the poker party came over. "Twenty dollars for a longhorn?" one of them asked.

"In trail condition," said Morgan. "Fatten them up and get more."

"How many head can they handle?" the first man asked. "A hundred? Two hundred?"

"How many have you got?"

The Texans exchanged quick looks. "We got more'n they can buy!"

"Five thousand? Ten thousand?"

"We got more."

"Can you drive that large a herd a thousand miles?"

"Will they buy that many?"

"There's a stockyard at Pawnee City," Morgan said, adding under his breath, "I hope." He cleared his throat. "We can handle five thousand steers a week, twenty thousand a month." He winced and said brusquely, "A hundred thousand a season."

The Texans again looked at one another. Then one of them said carefully, "What happens we drive a herd to this—this Pawnee City and there's nobody there with—with hard money?"

"*I'll* be there," said Morgan, then added quietly, "Anyway, what can you lose, except time? You got a market for beef in Texas?"

"Yancey," said one of the Texans to the bartender, "give the Yankee a drink. From the jug."

The jug was almost empty when Morgan's trail companion, Alder, said to him, "This Pawnee City you and this Jagger built . . . it musta cost you a lot of money."

Morgan regarded Alder thoughtfully. "Why?"

Alder shrugged. "I was just thinking. It was the Sixteenth Illinois that caught up with our rear guard last year when we were on our way to Mexico." He hesitated. "Shelby always said that they got Jeff Davis's gold that he had in an ambulance."

Chapter Five

Morgan heard the shooting before he saw the ranch buildings. There was a certain rhythm to the banging, the shots being spaced at fairly regular intervals, one every few seconds, then a pause of a minute or so and another series of spaced shots. Target shooting.

He kept his horse at an even lope and finally, when it crested a little rise, he looked down upon the ranch buildings. There was a narrow winding stream that was probably dry much of the year, but produced enough moisture to support a small growth of cottonwoods.

Among the trees he saw a sprawling house of unpainted clapboards, a long, low shed of peeled logs and three or four outbuildings. And a pole corral near the water's edge.

The shooting was coming from the corral and Morgan turned his horse toward it.

Two men were seated on the top pole of the corral, watching a man on the ground giving a boy gun instructions.

The boy, Morgan guessed, was probably fourteen or fifteen. He wore patched Levi's, rundown boots and a flannel shirt. His head, unlike those of the men, was uncovered. His hair had grown long and had been cut irregularly just below his ears.

A row of tin cans was set up on a bench some fifty feet from the shooters and these were the targets. They were not difficult to hit in straight shooting, but the boy, Morgan saw, was practicing the art of quick drawing and snap shooting. He wore a holster tied down to his thigh with a leather thong and the man giving him the instructions was demonstrating the quick draw.

Morgan stopped and watched.

"Forget the sights, Cass," the instructor was saying.
"You don't aim with this kind of shooting. You ain't got
time. You draw—you draw damn fast and you point.
Whatever you point at you shoot at. Watch——"

The shooting instructor turned toward the row of tin
cans. He dangled his hands at his sides, slouched so that he
was partly turned away from the targets. Then his right
hand darted for the gun in his holster. He drew so fast his
hand was a mere blur. The report of the gun came within
a fraction of a second and it seemed to Morgan, watching,
that it had been discharged before it even cleared the holster . . . but he saw a tin can jump into the air and land
on the ground twenty feet away.

"See, Cass!" the instructor exclaimed. "I didn't aim—I
just pointed. That's the way the Missouri boys did their
shooting and everybody knows they was the best shots in
the country. Why, I seen Tom Alder shoot like that and
hit his man at almost two hundred yards. . . ."

"With a pistol gun?" cried the boy.

"With a gun just like that there one in your hand."

The boy hefted the gun, shook his head and dropped the
weapon into his holster. He half turned away from the target in imitation of his mentor. "All, right, Sam, watch me
now——"

He let his hands dangle at his sides, then suddenly went
for the revolver. He brought it out smoothly enough, but
there was a slight pause before the gun was discharged.

A tin can jumped into the air, but the boy was not
through. He continued firing rapidly. He fired five times
altogether and three of the cans jumped.

"How's that, Sam?" he cried, turning to the instructor.

The gun teacher shook his head. "Fine for the last two
shots, but you aimed on the first. You're gettin' the hang of
it, but you got to do it in a single movement. Draw, point,
shoot."

The boy detached the little ramrod from the gun, swung
out the cylinder and began poking out the exploded caps.
"I'll load her up again." Then his eyes went beyond, saw
Chad Morgan, fifty feet away.

"We got company."

The three men turned, became alert. One of the two on the corral rail dropped to the ground.

"I'm looking for Mister Simcoe," Morgan announced.

"*Mister* Simcoe?" cried the boy. "You mean the general!"

He came running forward and Morgan saw then that he wasn't a boy at all, but a girl. She was lithe and swift as a boy, but she was not lean-hipped or flat-chested, for the flannel shirt, open at the throat, revealed the gentle swelling of young breasts.

"General Simcoe," Morgan corrected.

"He's around somewhere," the girl said, keeping her eyes on Morgan. "You can light and look for him"—her eyes suddenly narrowed in suspicion—"provided you ain't a damn Yankee!"

Morgan, starting to dismount, reseated himself in the saddle. "I'm afraid that's just what I am—a Yankee." He grinned. "I don't know about the damned part of it."

"All Yankees are damnyankees," the girl retorted hotly, although not with passion. "We-uns hate Yankees!"

"That's your privilege—ah—Miss——"

"My name's Cass. Cass Simcoe. It's really Cassie, but I hate Cassie." She looked at him sharply. "You call me Cass, y'hear?"

"I hear—Cass. I'm a Yankee; I've admitted it. But I'd still like to talk to Mis—to the general."

"Well, you can talk to him, but it ain't going to do you much good. The general hates Yankees even more'n me and the boys." She turned in the direction of the house, cupped her hands about her mouth and yelled, "Hey, General! There's a stranger man here wants to talk to you." She dropped her hands and cocking her head to one side, demanded, "What's your name, Mister?"

"Chad Morgan."

"You fit in the war?"

Morgan nodded.

"What were you—lieutenant, captain . . . major maybe?"

"Uh-uh. Just a sergeant—sergeant of cavalry."

"Cavalry, eh? Well, that's not so bad. Dad was a briga-

dier-general. Went in a major and they made him a colonel
after Shiloh. Kirby Smith promoted him to brigadier before
he sur—before he got his orders to quit fightin'.''

A man came out of the house, a tall, heavy-set man in
his early forties. He had a short spade beard and still wore
gray woolen trousers. The stripes had been removed from
the sides, but the marks of them still showed. He wore a
gray woolen shirt, with a black string tie about the throat.
A slouch hat was on his head.

"Here he comes," said Cass Simcoe. "Don't be surprised
if he runs you off the place. Hey—ain't you carryin' a
shootin' iron?"

Morgan opened his coat to show that he wore a revolver. Then he slipped off his horse.

The girl said suddenly, "How old are you?"

"Twenty-eight," replied Morgan in surprise.

"How old do you think I am?"

Morgan frowned lightly. "Fourteen. . . ."

"Fourteen!" she cried.

"Fifteen?"

She opened her mouth to shout at him in disgust, then
decided against it as her father came up.

"Dad, this is Mr. Morgan. He said he wants to talk to
you, although he wouldn't say why, but I got to warn you
right away. He's a damnyankee———"

"Cassie!" remonstrated General Simcoe. He turned to
Morgan, bowed stiffly, but did not offer to shake hands.
"How do you do, sir?"

Morgan nodded. "How are you, General? I'll get right
to the point. I understand you graze quite a few head of
cattle———"

A cloud seemed to pass over the general's features.
"That's about all I have these days, cattle."

"We're poor," interrupted Cass Simcoe. "You Yankees
took away everything we had and the general isn't even allowed to vote. They even made Mammy go away———"

"Please, Cass," said the general, "Mr. Morgan isn't interested in our problems."

"Perhaps I am, sir," said Morgan. He took a folded bill
from his pocket and opening it, extended it to General

Simcoe. The latter hesitated, then began reading the bill.
He shook his head.

"Is this why you've called, Mr. Morgan?" he asked. "Because if it is, I'm not interested. I tried to drive a small herd
north last year and some of your—ah—some ruffians——"

"Jayhawkers."

"Cutthroats," suddenly snapped the general. "Riffraff!
They weren't satisfied with cutting the herd of twenty-five
per cent, they stampeded the balance. We never got to
Joplin and I was out the expenses of the drive——"

"You wouldn't be going anywhere near Missouri," said
Morgan. "Pawnee City is a considerable distance west of
the territory in which the Jayhawkers are operating. The
drive would be quite safe—and ready money would be
waiting for you."

"Money!" cried Cass. "That's one thing we haven't got
any of. Golly, how I'd like to have some money. Even
your—" she wrinkled her freckled nose, "your Yankee
money."

Morgan reached into his pocket and took out a silver
dollar. He extended it to her. She started to reach for it,
shot a quick look at her father's frowning face, then shook
her head. "I'm too old to take money from men."

"Mr. Morgan," said the general, "I presume this is your
name on this bill."

"It is, sir. My partner, Mr. Jagger, and I are building
this town on the new Kansas & Colorado Railroad. It's approximately one hundred miles west of Kansas City. The
railroad has guaranteed us a siding, ample shipping facilities——"

"In other words, you do not yet have those facilities?"

"They are in the process of being built. As is the town
of Pawnee City."

"You're building an entire town?" asked the general in
surprise.

"A hotel, stockyards, some stores . . . we own the
townsite . . ."

"You own a whole town, Mister?" exclaimed Cass. "You
must be filthy rich!"

Morgan could not conceal a grin. "We have some capital, yes."

The general hesitated. "This puts an entirely new light on the matter. I have been in the cattle business most of my life and I drove some herds to New Orleans before the war. Even one to Joplin before—before the trouble. Nothing's been done with the stock in several years and we have a large increase, most of it unbranded, since we can no longer pay for help."

Morgan sent a look toward the three men by the corral. The general interpreted the look. "This is their home. I could not turn them out."

"They work for free," amplified Cass. "They're allowed to. But the Negroes ain't. That's why the Yanks made Mammy leave here. They said we had to pay her a—a salary. When we couldn't, they made her go away. She cried and cried and——"

"Please," said General Simcoe. Then he exhaled lightly. "As a matter of fact, I had freed her even before the war and when my wife—Cass's mother—died in sixty-two she —well, she became a sort of mother to Cassie. She was here until—until only a few months ago, when these damn carpetbaggers, I beg your pardon, sir——"

"It's all right, General. I share your views on the subject of carpetbaggers. They're scoundrels——"

"They're damnyankees!" spat out Cass Simcoe. "I hate them. . . . I hate *all* damnyankees!"

"Your manners, Cassie!" exclaimed the general. "You'll apologize to Mr. Morgan——"

"All right, I'm sorry, I apologize. But I don't mean it. *I hate you.*" She stuck out her tongue at Morgan, suddenly whirled and ran toward the house.

"You must forgive her," said the general gently. "This is a hard place to raise a girl. She was only fourteen when her mother passed on."

"Fourteen?" exclaimed Morgan. "But you said . . . you mean she's *eighteen?*"

"Almost nineteen."

"I told her I thought she was fourteen! No wonder she got mad at me."

The general smiled. "Cass considers herself a woman.
. . . Sometimes I think she's more man than woman, the
way she forks a bronc and shoots."

"She was practicing the quick draw when I rode up."

The general looked at the men by the corral. "Sam
Acres. I'll have to talk to him again."

"Oh, she shoots very well."

"I suppose so. Not exactly a woman's accomplishment.
But I wish . . ." The general frowned. "Perhaps I *will* try
another cattle drive, Mr. Morgan. I may *have* to. We can't
go on this way much longer. Cass needs some schooling.
And she's got to get out of those pants, into dresses!"

"Levi's look very good on her."

"Patches and all. . . . Mind if I keep this circular, Mr.
Morgan?"

"No, sir, that's why I'm here—distributing them. Think
it over, General. If you decide on a drive, the town of
Pawnee City will be ready for you . . . next spring."

"Very good, sir." The general suddenly held out his
hand. "Forgive me for being discourteous."

"Not at all, sir. You've been more than courteous."

Morgan nodded and turned away. He mounted his horse,
looked toward the house, then turned to ride toward the
crest, over which he had approached the ranch.

He was near the top of the ridge when he suddenly heard
galloping hoofs behind him. He turned in the saddle and
saw a wiry bronco coming swiftly toward him. It was rid-
den by Cass Simcoe.

Morgan pulled up his horse and waited for Cass. She
came up swiftly, jerking her mount to an abrupt halt, so
that it reared up. She quickly brought it under control.

"I'm sorry, Mr. Morgan. I—I *don't* hate you, really."

"Of course not," said Morgan. "And I want to apologize
to *you*. For saying you were fourteen years of age."

"Oh, Dad told you!" Her tanned features seemed to
turn a lighter shade—pink. "Dad's going to Kansas. I'll
make him. Will—will you be there?"

"I expect to be."

"Then I'll see you. It—it won't be so bad, knowing one
person at least."

Morgan exclaimed. *"You're* not intending to go with the trail herd . . . ?"

"What's wrong with that?"

"Why, I don't know. It just seemed like rather a—a hard thing for a girl, I mean, young woman."

"I can do anything a man can do. I can rope a steer, break a bronc, I—I can even cook." She stopped in some confusion, then went on. "Anyway, Dad wouldn't let me stay here alone, now that Mammy's gone."

"I'm sorry about that, Miss Simcoe."

"Miss? I'm not *that* old! Cass——"

"Cass." He smiled. "Well, then, we may meet in Kansas."

He gave her a half salute. A few minutes later he looked back and she was seated on her bronc, on the crest of the ridge. As she saw him turn, she waved to him.

Morgan waved back.

Chapter Six

The trail was a year and a half old. Many rains, snow and sleet had come and gone; the merciless Texas sun had baked the earth for two summers and the scavengers of the land had done their work. Yet there were traces of the rear-guard skirmish and Tom Alder had the time to study them.

He had nothing but time.

There had been casualties on both sides and he found the burial mounds, a long low mound and a shallow grave below, in which were buried the remains of eleven former Confederates and a more deeply dug, smaller grave in which five Union soldiers had been interred.

The bodies were badly decomposed, but Alder satisfied himself that none was that of his brother.

He crisscrossed the little valley in which the skirmish had taken place. He found the broken stock of a carbine, the metal parts of it a short distance away. He found scraps of clothing, disintegrating hats. He found cartridge pouches, the remains of a half-dozen broken wagons, the bones of horses killed in the battle.

It was too big a job for one man, even one as skilled as Alder in reading sign. He persevered by instinct alone.

He studied the lay of the land. The Confederates had been hard pressed. Pursuit had been dogged, unrelenting. The men of Shelby's command had been the hard-bitten ones, the desperate, to whom all was lost. Men like Alder himself. Many of them were from Missouri and knew they could never return to their homes. They fought to the bitter end.

Alder knew the hatred of the men on the other side for his kind. He had survived the aftermath of the Lawrence

26

massacre. He had fled Missouri, after the devastating Order #11 was put into effect.

He surveyed the ground. The rear guard had fought savagely. The two or three survivors who had caught up with Shelby had reported in full.

"Sure, we had the wagons," Alder recalled one of them had said. "We couldda formed a circle, but there was too many of them. They'd have got us in the end, so we kept movin' and they kept comin' and it was every man for hisself."

Had any of the wagons gotten out of the valley?

Alder widened the scope of his search and it was thus, after many long hours of riding and reading sign, that he came upon the overturned ambulance at the edge of the canebrake. The bones of two horses were still by the wagon.

The vultures and the coyotes had done their work, but even before he got down from his horse, Alder knew that this was it. Bleakly, he gathered together the scraps and shreds of cloth that had once been gray. He found a molded, rotted leather wallet and in it he found an illegible letter, and a few silver coins, a scrap of an old tintype.

He buried the bones, but not before he studied them carefully and found the chunk of lead in the skull, in a position which told Alder that it had been driven into the head while his brother, Jim Alder, had been lying on the ground.

A *coup de grâce*.

Alder gave his attention then to the ambulance. He found the iron-strapped wooden chest still in an excellent state of preservation. He scraped the inside with the sharp point of a knife, found enough bits of gold to know that the chest had once been loosely packed with gold. He even found a ten-dollar gold piece on the ground nearby, where it had been spilled in the hasty transfer of the currency to another receptacle.

The Sixteenth Illinois Cavalry.

The cattleman, Pete Mossman, wore Levi's, a patched woolen shirt and a hat that had once been gray. The sun had faded it to a neutral color, but there was a patch of felt on the front of the crown that had not faded as much as the rest of the hat, having been long protected by a metal ornament of crossed sabres.

He sized up Tom Alder carefully. "It's going to be a long, hard trip, Mister. Too much riding, too much herding at night. A lot of sun and a lot of wet rivers to cross."

"I've done all those things."

The cattleman nodded. "Thought you might have. All right, the pay's twenty dollars a month, paid up in Kansas. When I sell the herd. *If* I sell it."

"That's good enough for me."

"The grub'll be beans and steak, steak and beans. Coffee. And a little tobacco now and then." The cattleman paused. "What's your name?"

"I could tell you that it was Smith, or Vallandigham, but you'd find it out sooner or later, anyway. It's Tom Alder."

The cattleman whistled softly, almost soundlessly. "I've heard the name. The Union Army put out some dodgers on you, didn't they?"

Alder shrugged. "Maybe they've still got some out. I don't know."

The cattleman frowned. "I didn't wear a blue suit myself. I was with Ben McCullough at Pea Ridge. Some Missouri men helped us out. Maybe you were there yourself."

"I was."

"All right, Alder, you can come to Kansas with us. As far as *I'm* concerned, the war's over. Most of my boys went through it themselves and they won't hold anything against you. But they're Texas boys and they like to talk a bit. Some of them was born on horses and all of them cut their eyeteeth on guns. But they're not in your class, Alder, if what I've heard of you is true."

"I'll start no trouble."

"Good. That's all I ask. Don't *start* any gunplay, that's all."

Chapter Seven

Morgan went from the steamer that had brought him from New Orleans to the railroad depot and learned that the train for Kansas did not leave until the following morning. He checked into the Planters' Hotel and had a mint julep, then, seated in a cane-bottomed chair on the broad veranda, he scowled at the traffic seething back and forth on the dusty street.

He knew someone in St. Louis.

He went into the writing room and wrote four notes on the hotel stationery and tore them all up. Finally, he left the hotel and walked to the offices of the Kansas & Colorado Railroad.

Helen Jagger was even more beautiful than he had remembered. And she was delighted to see the partner of her brother.

"I've loads of questions to ask you," she exclaimed. "You—you've *got* to take me to dinner!"

That, of course, was why he had called and that evening in the dining room of the Planters' Hotel, he looked at her across the table and all of his misgivings and doubts about . . . about himself seemed to fade away.

"I had a letter from Joe only yesterday," she said. "The hotel is almost finished, the stockyards are ready and the railroad has built the spur siding." She grimaced. *"That* is my contribution. I didn't give Mr. Foss a moment's rest." She rested her elbows on the table and her blue eyes met his fully. "Now tell me, what reception did you get in Texas? Are things as bad there as the papers say they are?"

"Worse," replied Morgan. "The carpetbaggers are in full control and they've taken Texas away from the Texans.

A lot of good men have gone into the canebrakes and the country west of the Pecos."

"But the cattle!" exclaimed Helen. "Will they drive to—to Pawnee City?"

Morgan hesitated. "I think there'll be some drives. The drovers can get men just for their grub. And they don't have to lay out money for the stock. It's there for anyone to take. I didn't see many brands."

"They'll come, I *know* they'll come!"

A small frown creased Morgan's face, crinkled the edges of his eyes. "You're pretty keen on this scheme."

"Of course I am. Why shouldn't I be?" She looked at him sharply. "Scheme?"

Morgan shrugged. "I've still got my fingers crossed."

"But you went into it. Joe said you put up half the money."

"Joe can talk," Morgan said wryly. "And, besides, we've been together for quite a while. Joe saved my life."

"And you saved his!"

Now Helen was frowning and as she ate silently for a few moments, Morgan began to realize that Joe Jagger meant a great deal to his sister. The brother-sister relationship was a strong one. Morgan had no living kinfolk and had no gauge by which to judge such things.

He said, after a while, "What kind of life do you live here in St. Louis?"

"It's no life at all," she replied petulantly. "I'm a woman and it's a man's world."

"Isn't there a woman's world, too?" Morgan asked quietly.

"Oh, I suppose there is. But I don't want that kind of life." She flashed a smile at him. "What you're trying to find out is, is there a man in my life?"

He was disconcerted by her directness, but he nodded.

"There is," she said, "there *are!* Even my esteemed employer, Mr. Foss, has talked to me in a way that no married man with five children should talk to a woman other than his wife." She tossed her golden head. "I'm not ready. I had to go to work during the war to support myself. I've seen something of your man's world and I—like it. I want to *do* things. I want to build a railroad . . . or . . . a town——"

"A town?"

"That's what you and Joe are doing. I think it's magnificent. Joe wants a million dollars. Well, so do I. I want to go to New York, London, Paris. I want the things money can buy."

"Well, if this works out, Joe'll make money."

"And so will you!" She searched his sober face. "Or don't you care for money?"

"I guess I like it as well as the next man. Only—well, I've never had very much, so I don't really know."

"You've had dreams, haven't you? In your *wildest* dreams, Chad, what did you dream about?"

He could have told her that he had had many dreams and that they were, very often, of a woman such as Helen Jagger. He could have told her that, but it wasn't the moment. And perhaps she wasn't the woman, after all. Physically, yes, but——

Chapter Eight

The rails of the Kansas & Colorado Railroad had reached Pawnee City in early March. The framework of a depot was already up and part of it had even been boarded over, but there was no sign on it to identify Pawnee City. It wasn't necessary, of course. The almost completed stockyards and loading pens, the siding, were identification enough. And if that were not enough there was the gigantic structure on the south side of the tracks, that would be the biggest hotel west of Kansas City when—and if—it was completed. As yet the walls still remained on the lumber piles stacked up beside the tracks.

Chad Morgan was a passenger on the first train that went all the way into Pawnee City. It was actually a work train, consisting of a dozen cars carrying railroad ties, one freight car with supplies for the firm of Jagger & Morgan and a caboose at the end of it, in which Morgan traveled.

It was raining in Pawnee City, but a score of carpenter's hammers banged away at the soggy lumber. The buffalo grass, long since worn down by the treading of many boots and horses' hoofs, had exposed the earth and this was now a veritable sea of mud.

Carrying his valise, Morgan stepped down from the train and began to slough through the quagmire; there was a frown on his face, which had deepened to a scowl by the time he reached the partial shelter of the skeleton hotel. The veranda alone was roofed and here Morgan found Jagger, wearing a poncho and gloomily watching the work of the carpenters.

He saw Morgan and his face lit up. "Chad," he cried, "I was just thinking about you!"

"I imagine," Morgan said grimly. He nodded toward the

interior of the skeleton hotel. "I expected this would be completed by now."

Jagger groaned. "Why do you think we're working in the rain? They're behind, that's why. I had to offer every one of these men a bonus to come out here, from Kansas City."

"Can we afford that?"

Jagger turned, pointed down the main street of Pawnee City. "Some of the men are working on the stores. The general store's almost ready and that big place there, that's going to be The Longhorn Saloon." Jagger grimaced. "Fellow's put up a tent saloon already, and I'm having the devil's own time keeping the carpenters out of it."

"I asked," said Morgan, "have we got enough money for all this?"

"No," replied Jagger bluntly. "The stockyards and loading pens cost more than I'd counted on."

"They're twice as big as we need," retorted Morgan. "So's the hotel."

Jagger frowned. "I'm expecting a *lot* of cattle to come here. And drovers." He hesitated. "It didn't go well in Texas?"

Morgan shrugged. "How can you tell? I talked to a lot of people and I covered a lot of miles. If everyone I talked to brings as many head of cattle as he says he'll bring, the state of Kansas won't be able to hold them. But that was talk. I'll believe it when I see them here."

"They'll come," declared Jagger, "they'll come." He paused. "If they don't we're sunk."

"Why don't we stop building? The Texas men I saw can sleep on the prairie and they can drink their whiskey out of a barrel. Let's wait until they come before we go any further."

Jagger shook his head. "We can't stop. I—I bought a lot of stuff on credit. If we don't finish the buildings and sell off one or two, the creditors will grab the whole thing from us."

Morgan took a deep breath. "We're in debt?"

"Fifty thousand dollars. That's for lumber, equipment and supplies."

"How much cash have we got?"

"Enough to pay the carpenters for one more week."

"And then?"

"There'd better be some cattle here by then." Jagger suddenly grinned. "It's going to be a race."

A week went by and Jagger paid off the workmen. He had two golden eagles left and some small change. The roof was almost completed on the hotel and the saloon had a roof and half of a wall. The general store had a roof.

Jagger did not tell the workmen that they were through. He let them continue working, knowing very well that he had no money to pay them at the end of the week.

It was still raining intermittently, and Morgan was riding south of Pawnee City every morning to see if he could sight any Texas longhorns. He saw none.

A train came into Pawnee City bringing three frock-coated men. Cattle buyers.

"Bilked again," groaned one of them when he saw the incompleted hotel.

"The first herd will be here in two days," Jagger assured them. He winked at Morgan. "I've had word."

It was Saturday and the foreman of the carpenters came to Jagger. "It's payday, Mr. Jagger," he said.

Jagger groaned. "I expected the money on the train. It didn't come. It'll surely be here on next week's train."

"Mr. Jagger," said the carpenter foreman, "you haven't got any money coming on the train. You're broke."

"The cattle buyers are here," said Jagger, "the first herd's due any day. You'll get your money."

"When we get it, we'll work again."

"Get the hotel finished," said Jagger. "Move the men into the rooms. They'll be dry there, anyway."

The foreman went off and talked to his men. With the result that they were soon gathered around the saloon tent. An hour later Morgan, his Navy gun strapped about his waist, went to the tent saloon.

A balding man with a great scar down his right cheek was dipping tin cups into an open barrel of whiskey and selling them for fifty cents a cupful.

"Close up," Morgan said.

The tent saloon man glowered at Morgan. "What for?"

"Because I'm telling you."

"I paid Jagger fifty dollars for a license," snapped the whiskey seller. "I ain't sold enough whiskey yet to make that back."

"I said, close up."

The whiskey seller stooped behind his opened whiskey barrel. Morgan drew his Navy gun and sent a bullet into the barrel. The man behind it cried out and straightened up with a scatter-gun in his hand. But he looked into the muzzle of the Navy gun and dropped the shotgun. Meanwhile, whiskey trickled from the hole that Morgan had put into the barrel.

A half-drunken carpenter started to put his tin cup under the hole. Morgan kicked the cup out of his hand.

"When the first cattle herd comes into Pawnee City," Morgan said to the whiskey man, "you can open up again. In the meantime, you're not going to sell liquor to the workmen."

"Pay us our money and we'll go back to work," one carpenter shouted.

Morgan turned away and strode out of the tent. He found Jagger in the wet, dripping interior of the hotel.

"How much longer can you hold the cattle buyers?" he asked.

"Until the next train," replied Jagger; "there's no other way for them to get out."

"I'm going to ride south," Morgan said. "I'll be back before the train gets in and I'll know if any cattle are coming or not."

Jagger brightened. "I was thinking of riding myself, only there are so many things to do here."

"I've just closed down the whiskey tent," Morgan said. "Maybe the carpenters will get so bored, doing nothing, they'll go back to work." He frowned. "If we could only get the hotel finished!"

"It'll be finished by the time you get back."

Morgan got Jagger's horse, a rangy bay. He packed

some jerky in the saddlebags and, dropping a poncho over
his head and shoulders, started out of what he hoped would
one day be a real town.

The river, two miles out of Pawnee City, was swollen
and had spilled over its southern banks so that the prairie
seemed to be a lake. Morgan swam his horse across the
river and rode then for five miles through water a foot deep
and another foot of mud below it. It was hard going and
when he finally got onto comparatively solid ground, he
stopped his mount and looked ahead of him.

The prairie was lush and verdant. Soggy, muddy, close
up, but from a distance, a sea of green. The buffalo grass
had done well with the continual rains of the past two
weeks.

He rode on again.

Toward evening the rain stopped, but the clouds remained black and threatening. Morgan continued on in the
pitch-darkness until his horse began to stumble too often.
He came then to a coulee and halted. He hobbled the horse,
removed the saddle and saddlebags and huddled against a
bank, ate some of the jerky.

He was wet and miserable. A cold wind sprang up and
he wanted a fire badly but knew that he could build none.
Any wood that might be found in the darkness would be
too wet to burn.

Well, there had been nights like this during the war. And
frequently there had been a battle in the morning, a battle
during which both sides fought savagely, hating themselves,
the world and everything in it.

He huddled against the bank and dozed. He dreamed of
Texas longhorns and the lowing of a herd caused him to
grimace in his sleep. And then he awakened and still heard
the lowing of many cattle.

He blinked, shivered and then came to his feet.

He caught up his saddle, found the bay and saddled it.
Removing the hobbles, he vaulted into the wet saddle and
sent the horse southward up a slow incline.

As he neared the top, there was a rift in the clouds and
a bright three-quarter moon lit up the prairie.

Straight ahead, in the hollow of a gentle valley, Morgan saw the most wonderful sight on earth . . . grazing cattle.

Texas longhorns.

There was no fire in the Texas camp, but he found it by the chuck wagon and as he rode down, he was welcomed by the clicking of rifles and revolvers being cocked.

"Don't shoot!" he called. "I'm from Pawnee City."

"Pawnee City!" cried a man, running toward Morgan. He peered into the latter's face. "Damned if you ain't the man was down in Texas three-four months ago."

"That's right," said Morgan. "Your name's Hastings, I believe."

"Dan Hastings, with two thousand head of the wettest Texas cattle you ever saw. Whereinell's this here Pawnee City?"

"A day's easy ride," said Morgan, "maybe two days for cattle." He shook his head. "Two wet days."

"That's what took us so long," said Hastings, the Texan; "it rained all the way through the Indian nations." He reached out and caught Morgan's coat lapel. "Is it true, Mister? Has the railroad come into Kansas?"

"It's true enough. Rails reach into Pawnee City."

"What about the cattle buyers?"

"They're waiting."

Hastings whirled toward his trail riders. "Hear that, men? There's cash buyers waiting for us!"

A Rebel yell went up among the dozen trail hands. They crowded around Morgan, shaking his hand, exulting, declaring what they would do when they got into Pawnee City.

"You'd better have plenty of buyers and railroad cars," Hastings told Morgan. "There's a herd of four thousand head a day behind us and there are other herds, all the way from here to the Panhandle and down to San Antone. You're sure going to get a lot of longhorns in your town, Mister!"

Chapter Nine

The Drovers Hotel was completed. At least it was completely roofed over and had walls all around it and the rooms were partitioned into cubicles. Nothing had been painted, however, and the cracks between the boards gave suitable ventilation.

The carpenters were working on other buildings, the saloon, a general store, a livery stable. The sun was shining bright and in another day or two would dry out the lumber of the walls already put up.

But right now all work had ceased. The first longhorn herd was making the river crossing two miles south of Pawnee City and in a little while would be entering the city limits of Pawnee City. The tent saloon had reopened for business and both Jagger and Morgan had themselves partaken of a cupful of raw whiskey.

They stood now on the newly completed veranda of the Drovers Hotel, looking down Main Street, past the saloon and general store, down the line of stakes that marked out the street. Also standing on the hotel veranda were three very nervous cattle buyers. One of them looked at a huge gold watch.

"Two o'clock," he announced. "Time for me to take my stomick medicine."

"I'll go with you," promptly said the second cattle buyer.

"Me, too," cried the third.

"Gentlemen," declared Jagger, "you'll wait right here until the herd comes into town."

A gun banged somewhere in the distance, then another and another. A shout went up among the carpenters gathered around the tent saloon.

"Here they come!"

The first longhorn suddenly appeared a quarter of a mile

away. He was followed by a brace of steers, then a long, thin line of steers, charging along, three and four abreast. Gun firing continued as the Texas cowboys hazed the longhorns between the rows of stakes, toward the town of Pawnee City.

"We'll wait for them here!" cried Jagger.

His words were wasted. The cattle buyers charged down the stairs, began running up the street. They were blocked by the carpenters and laborers who also were surging forward.

The cattle came on, bawling and wild, and the humans gave way on both sides. Texas cowboys, almost as wild as their charges, came galloping down the street, keeping the steers in a tight group and turning them at the end of the street toward the stockyards and loading pens. It was savage work for the cowboys, but they forced a thousand head into the several pens, then drove the balance of the herd across the railroad tracks onto the lush prairie graze beyond. There the herd milled around and finally settled down to the grazing.

By that time, Hastings had already been besieged by the three cattle buyers.

"Give you twenty thousand for your herd," one of them cried.

"I'll make that twenty-two thousand," cried the second man. The third promptly raised the offer to twenty-five thousand.

"Double your offer," said Hastings, "and it's a deal."

The three cattle buyers looked at one another in consternation. "There're no cars here, Mister," one of them said. "Ain't no tellin' when there'll be any. One of us buys your steers, we got to take care of them."

"Gentlemen," declared Joe Jagger, "it's time we all had a drink." He sent a quick look around, seeking Morgan, but his partner was nowhere to be seen.

The invitation to a drink was received with a broad smile by the Texas cattle drover and the group adjourned to the whiskey tent, where two open barrels stood behind a plank set up on two sawhorses.

Morgan, coming from the lean-to railroad depot, sought

Jagger and the others and, guessing that they would be in the tent saloon, made his way toward it.

All work in Pawnee City had ceased. The carpenters and laborers were crowded into the tent. Morgan forced his way inside, saw Jagger with the cattle buyers and the Texas men, and caught his eye.

Jagger eased himself out of the group.

"The railroad agent just wired St. Louis about the cattle cars," Morgan told Jagger.

Jagger winced, took Morgan's arm and led him to one side. "I've been telling these people that they're already on the way. Be here tomorrow———"

"That isn't true," said Morgan. "The cars are actually in Kansas City, the agent tells me, but no order has been given to send them here."

"Damn that Foss," snapped Jagger. "I've been wiring him every day for a week. He should at least have had them started." He looked over his shoulder at the cattleman and the buyers. "We've got to stall them." He winked at Morgan, went back to the cattleman and the group around them. He said a few words to them. There was a quick exchange between Hastings, the drover and the cattle buyers and then Hastings let out a roar.

"Sold!"

Morgan joined the group. "What's sold?"

"My herd," said Hastings. "Mr. Palmer here, of Plankington & Armour, has bought the whole shebang for forty thousand dollars."

"But I don't take delivery until the stock cars are here," warned Palmer, the cattle buyer.

"They'll be here tomorrow," declared Jagger. He met Morgan's eyes. "The day after, at the very latest."

Chapter Ten

Helen Jagger carried the telegram into the office of the president of the Kansas & Colorado Railroad. She stood beside his desk while he read it.

"Interesting," he observed.

"Interesting?" exclaimed Helen. "It's wonderful!"

Nathan Foss smiled thinly. "Oh, I'll admit I'm surprised, Miss Jagger. Frankly, I had forgotten all about your brother. I've had so many harebrained schemes put to me——"

Helen's eyes glinted. "You consider the Pawnee City enterprise a harebrained scheme, Mr. Foss?"

The railroad president regarded his secretary thoughtfully. She was an attractive woman and if he hadn't been married to a woman who had put most of her fortune into the railroad venture and who was fat, middle-aged and jealous . . .

"After all, Miss Jagger," he said, "he's your brother. Naturally you're devoted to him. Of course, I've had reports of what he's trying to do out there. It's an ambitious project, too ambitious for a private individual."

"Two thousand steers reached Pawnee City today, Mr. Foss!"

"Pawnee *City,* Miss Jagger!" Nathan Foss smiled indulgently. "That's what I mean. A few half-finished buildings and he calls it a city." He shook his head. "Your brother's in debt. He owes more money right now than he can possibly recover. His creditors have shut down on him. I happen to know, because one or two have talked to me."

"Two thousand steers are in Pawnee City today, Mr. Foss," declared Helen. "Four thousand are approaching and there are herds all the way between Pawnee City and Texas. It says so in the telegram."

41

Foss glanced at the telegram again. "The operator's enthusiasm ran away with him. Perhaps it was induced by—ah—a few drinks of hard liquor, or . . . a small bribe!"

Helen Jagger's nostrils flared. She drew a deep breath. "You're sending the cattle cars to Pawnee City, Mr. Foss?"

Foss hesitated, then shrugged. "I'll risk that much. The cars are standing idle." He nodded. "I'll do it. I'll send all the available rolling stock . . . fifty cars."

"Fifty cars isn't enough."

"It's all we have. They'll *have* to do." Annoyance came over the railroad man's face. "Let's not go too far, Miss Jagger. Fifty cars will haul a thousand cattle."

"Can't you borrow some cars from one of the other railroads?"

"I suppose I could. The Missouri Pacific has at least fifty cars suitable for livestock hauling, and I think they're idle most of the time. The point is, I'd have to pay for those cars, once they're on our rails."

"You won't suffer any loss, Mr. Foss," said Helen earnestly.

"Miss Jagger," said Foss patiently, "I've been trying to tell you that your brother is bankrupt. His creditors are closing in on him. This whole venture will blow up within the next few days."

"You have an agreement with him. Five dollars for every car loaded at Pawnee City."

Nathan Foss hesitated, frowning. "If he does manage to load fifty cars, which I doubt, that'll be two hundred and fifty dollars. Which won't go far toward satisfying his creditors."

"Mr. Foss," said Helen Jagger, "I believe in my brother. So much so that I'm going out to join him in Pawnee City."

Foss exclaimed, "You'd quit your job here?"

"Yes!"

Chapter Eleven

The stockcars rolled into Pawnee City four days later, by which time nine thousand Texas longhorns were grazing on the lush buffalo grass both north and south of the railroad tracks.

Behind the stockcar train, came a special passenger train of two coaches. From it spilled a horde of people. Cattle buyers, laborers, carpenters, gamblers, thieves and a few speculators and businessmen.

And bill collectors.

A woman with an enormous bust and generous scaffolding, also got off the train. With her were six younger women. They were all very pretty young women, overdressed and overperfumed.

Morgan was in the ample hotel lobby when the train passengers began coming into the hotel. The only furniture in the lobby was a rough plank "desk." On it was a ledger in which Jagger had started to list the expenditures of the Pawnee City enterprise and given up when he no longer wanted to know exactly how much money he was spending.

A stout little man, in a sober business suit and wearing a derby, was the first arrival at the hotel.

He stopped just inside the door and looked around. "Aren't you open for business?"

"We are," said Morgan, "if you don't mind sleeping on the floor."

"The floor?"

"Our furniture hasn't arrived yet."

The stout man scowled. "Any other place around here a man can sleep?"

"Sure," said Morgan cheerfully. "The prairie. And it won't cost you a cent."

43

Two men came in from the street, then three in a group. All carried luggage.

Morgan said to the stout gentleman, "Rates are two dollars a day."

The man still scowled. "How about blankets? Sheets?"

Morgan shook his head.

"Washbowl?"

"Bare walls, that's all."

The man took two silver dollars from his pocket and tossed them on the "desk." "All right," he said with ill grace, "I was expecting to rough it out here, but——"

He was crowded aside by the new influx of potential guests. He fought his way back to the desk. "My key!"

"No key," said Morgan.

"What room?" bleated the first guest.

"Any room," said Morgan. "It's first come, first served." He turned to the waiting guests. "Two dollars apiece," he announced.

He had rented a half-dozen rooms before he remembered the ledger on the desk and turned it around so that the guests could register.

A whiff of strong perfume assailed Morgan's nostrils. He looked up into the face of a large, powdered and perfumed woman in her forties. She was surrounded by a half-dozen powdered, perfumed and overdressed young women.

"Seven rooms," the older woman said.

Morgan winced. "Uh—why—I don't know if——" he faltered.

"This is a hotel, ain't it?" the stout woman demanded. "Then you *got* to rent us rooms!"

"The hotel isn't finished," stammered Morgan. "That is, not for, ah—ladies."

"If it's good enough for menfolks, it's good enough for us!"

An eighth woman suddenly appeared. She was wearing a green traveling suit, a bonnet with a green feather and she carried a green carpetbag that matched her dress. She went around the crowd and stepped behind the desk.

"Hello, Mr. Morgan," she said coolly.

"Miss—Miss Jagger!" exclaimed Morgan. "Joe didn't tell me you were coming."

"He didn't know." She started taking off her hat and turned to face the large woman and her six charges.

"We're short of rooms, Madam," she said. "The young ladies will have to share rooms . . . Mmm, we can let you have a room for yourself and three for the young ladies——"

"I want seven rooms!" declared the big woman stubbornly.

"You'll take four. And the rate is five dollars a day—per room."

"Now wait a moment, young woman. I heard him charge those men only two dollars each for a whole room."

"Women require more service in a hotel," replied Helen Jagger sweetly. "I ought to know."

The leader of the female contingent sniffed, hesitated, then reached for the pencil. She scrawled on the ledger: *"Kate Clarke and girls."*

"Just one thing more," said Helen Jagger. "Members of the opposite sex are not permitted to visit in rooms. That's a house rule."

Kate Clarke glared at Helen. "Anything else?"

"Yes . . . payment in advance——for a week."

Kate Clarke opened her purse and fished out a handful of gold and silver. She counted out a hundred and forty dollars, threw a silver dollar on the counter. "There's your money—and a tip for you!"

Helen Jagger pushed back the dollar. "Hotel employees are not permitted to accept tips, money or otherwise."

Kate Clarke's eyes glinted, but she held herself in. She thrust out a meaty hand. "My keys."

Helen looked for the key rack, could not locate it. Morgan shook his head. "We haven't got any keys," he grimaced. "Or locks. The workmen haven't had time to put them on."

"This is an outrage!" shouted Kate Clarke. "How do you expect us to——" She caught herself, stopped and, glaring once more at Helen Jagger, suddenly turned away. "Come, girls!"

The girls, simpering and giggling, followed her to the stairs.

Morgan exhaled in vast relief. "Thanks for rescuing me," he said to Helen.

Helen smiled at him and turned briskly to the waiting guests. "Yes, gentlemen. Our rates are three dollars for single rooms, five dollars for double."

"I've been asking two," Morgan whispered.

She shook her head. "That isn't enough." She thrust the pencil at a guest. "Sign here, please."

The man shook his head. "Uh-uh. I'm here to see Mr. Jagger."

"I'm his sister," said Helen, "and this is his partner, Mr. Morgan."

"Morgan, eh? Guess you'll do." The man reached into his pocket and brought out a folded sheet of note paper. "I've got a bill here against you. Nine thousand, six hundred and forty-three dollars and eighty cents."

Morgan blinked. "You must be crazy!"

The man shook his head. "Lumber. I'm with the Kansas City Lumber Company." He drew out another folded paper from his pocket, a legal-looking piece. "If you don't pay up, I hand you this. An attachment."

"Let me see that," exclaimed Helen Jagger.

The man held it away from Helen. "Just Mr. Jagger. Or his partner."

"Jagger," said Morgan. "*He* takes care of the bills."

"Well, let him take care of this one."

A second derby-hatted man moved forward with a piece of paper in his fist. "He can take care of me at the same time. Allington Hardware Company. Two thousand, three hundred——"

"Six thousand, six hundred for me," a third man sounded off. "And *I* got a judgment."

"I'll go and find Mr. Jagger," said Morgan.

"We'll go with you," one of the bill collectors volunteered promptly.

"Gentlemen," interposed Helen Jagger, "we've only a few rooms left and there's no other place within fifty miles where you can sleep indoors. The train doesn't go back to

Kansas City until tomorrow. Now, do you want these rooms, or would you rather sleep out on the prairie with the prairie dogs and rattlesnakes?"

The bill collectors were city men. Helen's description of the physical discomforts was enough to turn them away from Morgan and the latter was able to slip out of the hotel. He went to the whiskey tent, saw that the whiskey seller was broaching a new barrel of whiskey, with a crowd of men waiting anxiously.

He found Joe Jagger up the street, trying to sell a twenty-foot lot to a red-faced, perspiring man. "Five hundred dollars!" the man was saying. "That's too much for a measly little piece of ground."

"City lots come high, friend," said Joe Jagger easily. "What kind of business were you thinking of starting here?"

The man hesitated, "Well, I ain't quite decided yet."

Joe Jagger nodded. "In that case, the lot will cost you seven-fifty."

The real-estate buyer glowered at Jagger. "Now, look here, Mister."

"You're a speculator," Jagger said coolly. "I own the townsite and I figure to do all the speculating round here. I want legitimate businesses right now——and the price of this lot is five hundred if you get started building a store here right away. If you're not building, the price is seven hundred and fifty . . . and going up."

"Mister," said the red-faced man angrily, "I ain't liking it—but I'll give it a whirl. . . . I'll take these two lots here."

Jagger shook his head. "Two lots to one buyer brings the price up . . . to two thousand——" He winked at Chad Morgan.

The red-faced man started to bluster, suddenly closed his mouth and took a fat billfold from his pocket. "Here's your money. Just give me a receipt."

Jagger searched into his pockets for a piece of paper, found an old envelope and with a pencil borrowed from Morgan, wrote on the envelope: *"Received from bearer two thousand dollars, full payment for Lots #5 and #6."*

The man snatched the receipt from Jagger, gave Morgan

a scowl and turned to walk briskly back toward the hotel.

"There he goes, looking for a quick turnover at a profit," chuckled Jagger.

"At the hotel," Morgan said bluntly, "are three bill collectors with bills totaling eighteen thousand dollars. One of them has a judgment."

Jagger, instead of being disconcerted, chuckled. "What good is a judgment going to do him? There's no sheriff here to serve it, no judge to make out a writ of attachment."

"We still owe the money."

"Sure, sure, but you just saw me make two thousand, didn't you? Well, I'm going right up the street and make a few thousand more. Pillsbury's been wanting to buy some property from me, but I didn't know how much to ask him. Now, since a price has been established——"

"Wait, Joe! One thing more. Your sister's here."

Delight spread over Jagger's face. "She wrote me that she was thinking about moving out here after we got going, but I didn't expect her nearly so soon——" He turned abruptly away from Morgan and started running back toward the hotel. Morgan, having no desire to encounter the bill collectors again, stayed where he was.

A heavy-set man of about fifty headed toward him. "Know where I can find Mr. Jagger?"

"He just passed you. I'm Chad Morgan, his partner."

The man brightened. "I understand you and Mr. Jagger own all of Pawnee City. I just got off the train and I—well—I thought I'd kinda like to locate here. Open a little store."

"What kind of store?"

"Hardware, farm tools, implements."

"You'll need more than one lot, then," Morgan said. "The lots are only twenty feet."

"That all? Mmm, I'll need about four-five lots."

"How about the corner over here? Give you an entrance on both sides. And plenty of room in back for wagons to drive in."

"I had in mind something like that." The man frowned. "How much for the five corner lots?"

"A hundred feet?" Morgan frowned. "Well, my partner just sold two lots for two thousand dollars . . ."

"All right, I'll take them. Ten thousand."

Morgan swallowed hard. "Uh, no. I meant Joe sold the *two* lots for two thousand . . . a thousand each."

The buyer smiled at Morgan. "I was prepared to pay the ten."

"Five thousand is enough."

"You're an honest man, Mr. Morgan." The corner lot buyer held out his hand. "My name's Buffington, Mr. Morgan. We'll get better acquainted in time."

"Chad!" called Joe Jagger from up the street. He was running toward Morgan and Buffington. "Don't sell those corner lots. I got a buyer."

"It's too late," Morgan said. "I've just sold them to Mr. Buffington for a hardware store."

Joe Jagger came up, frowning. "How much?"

"Five thousand—for five lots."

"It ain't enough," complained Jagger. "Pillsbury just offered me ten thousand for the three corner lots."

"The whiskey seller?" Morgan looked sharply at his partner. "Isn't that the saloon we're building back there?"

"That's *our* saloon," Jagger said easily. "Mr. Pillsbury wants to build one, too." He shrugged. "Pawnee City's big enough for two saloons." He looked at Buffington. "Care to resell your lots?"

Buffington promptly shook his head. "I'm satisfied with the deal."

Jagger scowled. "Nothing's been signed."

Morgan said promptly, "I gave my word."

Jagger hesitated, averting his eyes from Morgan's. Then he shrugged. "I guess the town needs a good hardware store. I'll sell Pillsbury the corner across the street."

Chapter Twelve

With the advent of the Texas men and the trainload of cattle buyers, speculators, gamblers and riffraff, the population of Pawnee City had swelled to over one hundred. There was food enough for all, but no one to cook it, no one to dispense it.

The cook for the laborers recruited an assistant or two and took care of some of the hungry ones that evening. Hastings, the cattle drover, accommodated the overflow and it was here that Chad Morgan found Helen Jagger shortly after dark. She was seated on the ground near the chuck wagon eating a plate of beans and gnawing at a chunk of beef that had been broiled to a crisp.

"Best food I've ever tasted in my life," she declared.

"The service is good, too," grinned Morgan, as a cowboy handed him a tin plate full of food. He squatted down beside her. "Where's Joe?"

"Making money," said Helen. "He's been selling town lots all afternoon. I saw him an hour ago and he was talking to a man about opening a bank."

"A faro bank, or a regular bank?"

She almost choked over a mouthful of beans. "That's what Joe asked. It seems that a faro bank has a better chance of succeeding in Pawnee City."

She put down her plate on the ground beside her. "Everything I dreamed of back in St. Louis is coming true. We have a town and we're making money. We'll be rich. There's just one thing more to settle." She paused. "Us."

Morgan exclaimed, "What?"

"I saw you looking at those girls of Kate Clarke's." She regarded his profile in the flickering campfire light. "You're a handsome man, Chad. Hasn't any girl ever told you that?"

Morgan knew that his face was reddening and he was too far from the campfire for the heat to have done it. "I haven't had a great deal of time for that. The war and since——"

"We're all going to be pretty busy for some time," said Helen. "But there's no reason we shouldn't settle things right now. Women are going to be swarming into Pawnee City and I might as well put my brand on you right now." She smiled impishly. "I learned that from one of the Texas men."

Morgan put down his plate and stared at the fire a few yards away. Helen watched him. "I like a shy man because —because I'm not shy myself. Look, Chad, there's no reason for you to pick an outsider. And *I* certainly don't want any of our money going away. We can keep it in the family. My mind's made up. Of course, if you want to shilly-shally around awhile——"

"I don't," said Morgan hoarsely.

"Then it's understood! As soon as a preacher comes to Pawnee City . . ." She paused, then added in a low tone; "Let's walk back to the hotel. I—I'd like you to kiss me."

He got to his feet swiftly, reached down and, catching her hand, drew her to her feet. He was still holding her hand when the sharp, spiteful crack of a gun split the night air.

Morgan let go of Helen's hand and looked toward the tent saloon, a hundred yards away. A couple of lighted lanterns hung outside the tent and in their fitful light, Morgan saw men spewing out of the place.

"Something's happened," he said.

And then he left Helen Jagger and was running swiftly toward the tent saloon.

A man was backing away from the tent when Morgan pounded up. He caught the man's shoulder and whirled him around.

"What happened?"

"Somebody's shot somebody."

"Who?"

"I dunno," said the man, one of the carpenters. "We was playin' faro and all of a sudden this cowboy called the dealer a crook and then, bang, before anybody knew what was happenin', the dealer had a gun in his fist and the cowboy was dead."

Morgan released the man and went into the saloon.

Pillsbury and a half-dozen men were standing in a small semicircle, looking down at the crumpled body of a Texas cowboy. One of the men, whom Morgan had never seen before, was holding a revolver in his hand. He was a lean, pasty-faced man in a Prince Albert, dark trousers and a gaudy vest.

Morgan's eyes went to him at once.

"You killed this man?"

The gambler lifted sullen eyes at him. "Nobody calls Buckley Thorne a cheat."

"Give me that gun," snapped Morgan.

The gambler's eyes narrowed. "Why?"

"Because I'm telling you, that's why."

Buckley Thorne's eyes flickered to the tent-saloon-keeper. Pillsbury growled, "Him and Joe Jagger own this townsite."

"So?"

Morgan said evenly, "You'll give me that gun, or——"

"Make me give it to you."

Three cowboys came into the saloon behind Morgan. They started to brush past Morgan, but Chad Morgan threw out his hand. "Hold it."

"Mister," said one of the cowboys, "this tinhorn just killed Curly Meeker. We aim to put a rope around his neck."

The gun in the hand of Buckley Thorne came up. "Nobody puts a rope on me," he said hoarsely. "I'm getting out of here."

"Not alive you ain't," said one of the cowboys.

"Take more'n a bunch of Johnny Rebs to stop me," snarled the gambler.

At that moment Chad Morgan hit him. It was a savage blow and caught the gambler flush on the point of the jaw. He went down, his revolver flying from his hand.

The cowboys swooped down on Thorne. Only semiconscious, he was brought to his feet and was being dragged from the tent, when Chad Morgan found the gambler's revolver.

He thrust it skyward and pulled the trigger.

The blast caught the cowboys unprepared. They let go of Thorne, who managed to retain his feet and turned on Chad Morgan.

"You're not hanging him," said Morgan evenly.

The cowboys exchanged quick looks. "Mister," said one of them, "make up your mind whose side you're on."

"I'm not on anyone's side," said Morgan. "If he killed a man he's going to pay for it, but he's going to get a fair trial."

Joe Jagger came striding into the saloon. "Here, what's goin' on?" he demanded.

Morgan indicated the dead cowboy on the ground. "Pillsbury's card shark killed him."

"What for?"

"What's a man gonna do when somebody calls him a crook?" interposed Pillsbury. "Anyway, the cowboy went for his gun first."

Jagger hesitated, then nodded. "Sounds like self-defense."

"Self-defense or not," snapped Chad Morgan, "he's going to stand trial."

"Wait a minute," said Jagger. "What're you going to do, arrest him? We haven't got a jail in Pawnee City. For that matter we don't have a sheriff or marshal, a judge."

"He can be taken to Kansas City."

"Who's going to take him?"

"*We'll* take him," volunteered one of the Texas men. "We'll take him to the nearest tree and you can save yourself a lot of fuss and trouble."

Dan Hastings, the Texas cattle drover, came into the saloon. At his heels were three more Texas men. He pushed through until he came to the body of the dead man.

"Curly Meeker," he groaned. "Just a kid. I promised his ma I'd look out for him." He looked around and picked out Thorne. "You're the man killed this boy?"

"He pulled a gun on me," snarled Thorne. "It was him or me."

"You killed him," said Hastings.

"He ain't gonna kill nobody else," shouted one of the cowboys.

Joe Jagger nodded enthusiastically. "Mr. Hastings, I'm sorry about the boy. This is a new town and things are still pretty unsettled, but one thing we can't have here is somebody going around killing people. I say we make an example——"

"Joe!" cried Chad Morgan, aghast.

Jagger bared his teeth. "An eye for an eye, Chad!"

Morgan started to protest, but a sudden shout went up among the cowboys and his words were drowned out. And then it was too late. Hands grabbed at the gambler-killer. Fists smashed into his face. Guns came out and struck him. Screaming and babbling, he was dragged out of the saloon.

The gun in Chad Morgan's hand was useless. The press of men in the small space was too great. They were too angry, too violent to be stopped. Outside the tent, there were more cowboys and once the mob was in full cry, it was joined by laborers and others of the new citizens of Pawnee City.

This was the day that the first cattle cars were loaded in Pawnee City. It was the day when the first town lots were sold, when the promoters of Pawnee City, Joe Jagger and Chad Morgan, late of the Sixteenth Illinois Cavalry, knew definitely that their wild gamble was going to succeed and make them rich.

It was also the day when the first man was killed in Pawnee City.

And it was the day of the first lynching in Pawnee City.

Candles were at a premium in the Drovers Hotel, but when Morgan came into the hotel lobby late, he saw the candlelight in the room beyond the desk and he turned in that direction.

The door was open and he saw Joe Jagger and Helen in the room, Helen seated on a stool behind a rough plank desk and Jagger pacing back and forth.

"It wasn't our fault, Joe," Helen was saying. "Stop worrying about it."

"I could have stopped it," Jagger said, "but word would have gone out that I favored a gambler over a Texas man. This town, this entire venture is built upon the good will of the Texans and——"

He stopped as Chad Morgan appeared in the doorway. Helen came off the stool. "Chad! Where've you been?"

"Walking."

"In the dark?" She came to him, looked earnestly into his face, then turned and, slipping her hand under Morgan's arm, faced her brother. "I've told Joe."

Jagger swooped forward and gripped Morgan's hand. "This is the one thing I wished would happen, Chad. You two . . ." With his free hand he gripped Morgan's shoulder hard.

There was some talk of the event, which for some minutes pushed into the background the differences between Jagger and Morgan that had occurred that day, but they had to be faced before any of them could call it a day and it was Jagger who finally had to broach them.

"I took care of the bill collectors."

"You got in eighteen thousand in cash?" Morgan asked.

"No-no, I gave them each a thousand dollars. That'll hold them for a while. They know now that their bills are going to be paid. Pawnee City is a success."

"Is it, Joe?" Morgan asked quietly. "Two men were killed today."

Jagger scowled. "This is the frontier, Chad. It's rough, it's wild. There's no law and men settle their differences with the knife and the gun."

"And the rope?"

"Joe," Helen Jagger said, "do we have to go into this now? I'm tired. I've had a hard day and I want to get some sleep." She turned to Morgan. "*You* can use it."

Jagger said to Morgan, "I thought I knew you, Chad.

We went all through the war together and I never saw you squeamish about anything."

"That was war."

"So is this," retorted Jagger. "It's you and me against the world."

"It's *us*," said Helen Jagger. "The three of us." She turned to Morgan. "Isn't it?"

With only a trace of hesitation, Morgan nodded.

Chapter Thirteen

Where were the prairie mounds? Where were the little rodents who had held domain over this country from time immemorial?

Where was the little soddy that had once been home to Artie Puffpaff?

Puffpaff was here. He stood in the middle of the dusty street as shabby and dirty as ever. He had lived here, right on this very spot, that was now churned into dust by the boots of men, by the hoofs of cattle and iron-shod horses.

Owlishly he looked toward the huge hotel, straight ahead at the cattle pens beyond, where the bawling of cattle never ceased.

He turned slowly and surveyed the buildings on his left: a saloon, a restaurant, a photographer's shop, a general store, a barber shop, a hardware store, another saloon, buildings on beyond.

He turned back, shifted to his right and groaned aloud. A third saloon and Puffpaff needed a drink more than he had ever needed anything in his life.

A bank.

Banks had money and Artie Puffpaff had none.

The bank belonged to Jagger and Morgan, who had swindled Artie Puffpaff out of all this. It had been his. They had taken it from him by force. They had been two to one and they had had guns.

Well, Artie Puffpaff had a gun.

It was an old dragoon pistol that had seen much service. It had no trigger guard; it was big and cumbersome and kicked like old Ned, but it could still fire a very loud and very lethal charge of lead.

Artie raised the gun and pointing it at the sky, pulled the trigger.

The report was still ringing in his ears when Artie looked up and down the main street of Pawnee City. Not one single soul was looking at him.

Gunfire in Pawnee City was as common as the yelling of a drunken Texas cowboy. The two, in fact, were synonymous. Drunken cowboys yelled and they fired their guns. They also galloped their horses up and down the street.

Puffpaff reloaded and aimed the old horse pistol at the window of the bank. He pulled the trigger again. The bullet almost missed the window, but managed to score near the upper left corner of the rather large glass pane and to Puffpaff's ears came the pleasant crash and tinkle of glass.

Joe Jagger happened to be in the bank and he came dashing out, his Navy gun in his fist. He saw Puffpaff and strode toward him.

"What do you think you're doing, you drunken fool?" snapped Jagger.

"You cheated me," said Artie Puffpaff. "You robbed me and you cheated me out of this here prop'ty."

"I bought this land from you," snapped Jagger.

"Yuh gimme a bottle of whiskey," whined Puffpaff. "Got me drunk and made me sign it away."

"I paid you hard cash," Jagger said. "The land wasn't worth a damn and you had no real claim to it, anyway. I could have taken it without giving you anything."

"That's what you did . . . didn't, I mean. You took 'er away from me by force, that's what. It ain't right. You got a town here now. And it's supposed to be mine. All mine."

"You fool," said Jagger, "go and get yourself a drink. Here——"

He took a silver dollar from his pocket, Artie Puffpaff's hand went out automatically, but Jagger threw the dollar into the dust of the street. Puffpaff went down to his knees and searched for the dollar and could not find it. He was still on his knees, sifting the dust through his fingers when Chad Morgan entered The Longhorn Saloon and said to the bartender, "There's an old man out in the middle of the street. He's on his hands and knees——"

"Old Puffpaff," said the bartender. "I threw him out of here an hour ago."

"Give him a bottle of whiskey," said Morgan. He pointed to a quart bottle on the backbar. "Take that out to him."

The bartender frowned, hesitated. "Who's going to pay for it?"

"Who owns this saloon?" asked Morgan coldly.

"Mr. Jag . . ." the bartender winced. "I guess you and Mr. Jagger——"

"Then take the whiskey to Puffpaff."

But Puffpaff was already entering The Longhorn. He clutched the silver dollar that he had finally found, and bore down on the bar.

"I got money," he whined to the bartender. "You can't throw out a customer with money." Then he saw Chad Morgan. "Mr. Morgan, please, is it all right for me to buy a—a drink here?"

"Of course, Artie," said Morgan. "And your credit's good, too. Up to a point, Artie, up to a point." He made a gesture to the bartender and went past Puffpaff to the door.

He went outside and stood on the sidewalk a moment before turning right and going to a store on which was a sign: *Jagger & Morgan, Real Estate.* A wagon loaded high with furniture, boxes and barrels stood in front of the real-estate office and inside Morgan found a blond giant, a big-boned woman with two half-grown boys.

The clerk who took care of the office saw Morgan with relief. "Ah, Mr. Morgan, I didn't know what to tell this—this man. He says he wants to buy a farm and I told him we didn't exactly deal in farm lands."

"Why not?" asked Morgan. He turned to the farmer. "How big a farm did you have in mind?"

"I think maybe eighty acres," the farmer replied in a heavily accented tone. "If the price be right, maybe a hundred and sixty acres."

"How much money have you got?"

"I sell my farm in Wisconsin, but it is not a good farm. I have only maybe five thousand dollar."

Morgan pursed up his lips. "To tell you the truth, Mr. . . . ?"

"Turnboom, Axel Turnboom."

"Mr. Turnboom, I don't know if this is good farming

land. There's plenty of rain in spring, too much sometimes and there's a lot of it during the fall and winter, but
the summers get pretty hot. And there isn't a lot of rain
after March or April. Sometimes none, the old-timers say."

Axel Turnboom nodded. "I am a hard worker. I make
crop grow. My boys they big enough to help. I like buy
farm."

"All right," said Morgan. "I'll sell you a hundred and
sixty acres." He hesitated. "You'll need money to put in
your crops and maybe you'll have to dig a well or two to
carry you through the summer. Suppose we say ten dollars
an acre."

The farmer showed surprise. "On'y ten dollars acre?"

"Yes, we want good people around here. I'm sure most
of the stores will give you some credit and if they don't
you come over to the bank and we'll take care of you."

There were two maps on the wall. One was of the square
mile that constituted Pawnee City proper, with the lots
marked off and colored, some of them—the majority—in
red, indicating that they belonged to the townsite owners,
Jagger & Morgan. The other map showed the land owned
by the two partners, some deeded to them by the railroad
and some representing their original purchase from Artie
Puffpaff.

Morgan took a pencil from his pocket and marked off
one quarter of a square on the map. "Show Mr. Turnboom
this quarter section," he said to the clerk.

The farmer studied the map a moment, then nodded.
"No need to show, I take it."

"Good," said Morgan, "and welcome to Pawnee City,
Mr. Turnboom."

A few minutes later he left the real-estate office. A Texas
man sat easily on a horse by the hitchrail. When he caught
Morgan's eye, he gave him a half salute.

"Hello, Morgan."

The man was Tom Alder.

Morgan said, "Getting a little close to home, aren't you?"

Alder dismounted and tied his horse to the tie rail. "I'm
all right in Kansas." He hesitated briefly. "I think."

"As far as I'm concerned," Morgan said, "I told you in Texas: the war's over."

"Your word's good enough for me." Alder glanced around, making a small gesture. "Quite a town you've got here. Wouldn't think you could do it with only twenty-five thousand . . . ?"

"What?"

Adler regarded him thoughtfully. "Seems to me I heard somebody say that you started this with twenty-five thousand."

"We spent seventy-five," said Morgan, only slightly accenting the word "spent." Then, to change the subject: "You came up with a trail herd?"

"Thirty-five hundred skinny longhorns. Just got in yesterday and got my pay today. Care to join me in a drink?"

"Not now. I've some business to take care of. I'll catch up with you later."

Alder watched him go off, then strolled to The Longhorn Saloon.

Chapter Fourteen

Morgan, walking toward the hotel with bent head, was aware of a horse galloping swiftly behind him. But that was a common sound these days in Pawnee City. So was the sudden bang of a gun.

Then a voice yelled, "Hey—Yankee!"

Morgan whirled just as the horse behind him was pulled up violently. Cass Simcoe, still wearing Levi's and a man's shirt, her hair only a little longer than it had been the previous fall in Texas, bounced down from her bronc.

Morgan chuckled. "Hi, Reb!"

"Reb?" cried Cass. "You damnyankee!"

He extended his hand. She hesitated only briefly, then caught it. Her hand was small, but calloused. There was strength in the grip she gave him, in the way she clung to his hand.

"So you made it," Morgan said. "Well, what do you think of Kansas?"

She shot a swift look around. "I haven't seen much of it yet. We only just got in. As a matter of fact, Dad and the men are still crossing the river. I—I rode ahead." She wrinkled her nose. "You call this a town? We've got better towns in Texas."

"Of course," said Morgan. "Come—come to the hotel with me. I want you to meet my fiancée."

"Your fian—your what?"

"Fiancée. The woman I'm going to marry."

Cass drew her roughened hand out of his grip. "You never told me you had a Yankee sweetheart."

"I didn't have one last fall," replied Morgan. "She's my partner's sister and when I was in Texas I had met her only once. But she's here now and we're going to be married . . . in a little while."

Cass Simcoe uttered a sudden, rather high-pitched laugh. "Well, good for you, Yank! I'm going to get married myself . . . one of these days."

"Of course you are. Your Texas men aren't going to let you roam about much longer. One of them will be putting his brand on you soon." Morgan chuckled.

"The trouble with Texas men," flashed Cass, "is that they're all so poor." Her hand shot out and caught his arm in a hard grip. "Is it really true—*can* we sell our herd for hard money?"

"Every herd that's come in so far has sold readily."

"For how much? We—we've got fifteen hundred head, but they're awfully thin. We lost a lot of weight on the way."

"The price will depend on the condition of the steers. Perhaps your father may prefer to graze them awhile before selling——"

"No, I'm sure he doesn't. He said we'd sell as fast as we could and—and go home. We met some cattlemen going home. They said they'd gotten over twenty-five dollars per steer, but you know how men are, they just can't help piling it on a little. Brag-talk."

"They didn't lie, Cass. Some steers have sold for as high as thirty dollars, but if your cattle's poorly—well, you may have to take eighteen or twenty dollars."

"For each steer? Golly, twenty times fifteen, that's— that's thirty thousand dollars." She winced. "There isn't that much money in all the world!"

"There is, Cass," Morgan said gently. He took her arm. "Come now, I want to take you over to the hotel."

She started to go with him, then drew back. "Golly, this —this sweetheart of yours. I can't let her see me in these overalls. Patches and all."

"She won't mind."

"But *I* mind. Couldn't I—couldn't I wait to see her until we've sold the herd and bought some clothes for me? A—a dress."

"How long is it since you've worn a dress?"

"Not since I was a girl! No use at home. I—I've tried on

some of mother's dresses, though. They didn't fit me—
too big, but I——"

"Perhaps Helen will——" Morgan stopped.

"Helen? Is . . . that her name?"

"Helen Jagger."

"Is she very pretty?"

"She's the most beautiful woman in the world," said
Morgan with a note of fervor.

It was not lost on Cass. Her enthusiasm dropped several
degrees. "I'm going back to Dad and the boys."

She started to pull away, but Morgan clung tightly to her.
"You come along," he said with mock sternness.

He led her to the hotel, into the lobby, where she again
tried to pull away from him, then on behind the desk, into
the office, where Helen Jagger was working.

She looked up. "Chad!" She started to rise, sent a sharp
look at Cass's face. "Why, she's a girl!"

"Cass Simcoe," said Morgan. "General Simcoe's daughter . . . Cass, this is my fiancée."

"*General* Simcoe?" asked Helen, puzzled.

"Late of the Confederate Army. He's brought a herd
up the trail. Cass came along. I stopped at their place in
Texas last fall."

"I see," said Helen. Then suddenly she smiled and held
out her hand to Cass. "Hello, Cass. Welcome to Kansas!"

"Golly, Miss—Miss Helen," exclaimed Cass. "You're
beautiful!" She flashed a look at Morgan. "You didn't tell
me she was *that* beautiful."

"You've discussed me?" asked Helen.

"Just a few minutes ago," grinned Morgan. "When I
told her I wanted her to meet you."

"You've checked into the hotel?" Helen went on.

"Check—checked in?"

"Registered," said Morgan. "No, they haven't registered.
Cass came on ahead. The herd was still crossing the river.
I imagine the general will be coming in before evening. In
the meantime, Cass has mentioned that she'd like to do
some shopping."

"Oh, I can't," cried Cass. "We haven't got any money
to spend. Not yet, anyway."

"You'll have enough when your father sells his cattle. Which won't be long. The stores will trust you until then."

But she shook her head. "I can't spend any money until we got it."

Helen suddenly understood. "You'd like to clean up, though, wouldn't you?" She came away from the desk and took Cass's arm. "Come along to my room. I have a dress that I think you'd like. I'll *lend* it to you."

Cass gave Morgan a desperate look, but he shook his head and Cass allowed herself to be taken away by Helen Jagger.

Morgan was in the hotel an hour later, when General Simcoe came in. He was accompanied by Joe Jagger.

"Chad," exclaimed Jagger. "You remember General Simcoe? He said you stopped at his place last fall."

"Of course. How are you, General? I'm glad you decided to make the drive."

"So am I—if everything I heard about the cattle business is true."

"Oh, it's true, all right," chuckled Jagger. "We've stockyards, a railroad siding and most important of all, cattle buyers!"

"Good. I'm ready to sell for a fair price." The general sighed wearily. "It's a long time since we've had any money in our household. Like most Southerners, we lost everything in the war."

"You'll make it all back and more," promised Jagger. "Now, I imagine you'd like to get a room, General——"

"Two rooms," replied the general. "I've my daughter with me, Mr. Morgan, she rode in ahead. You haven't by any chance seen that girl of mine, have you?"

"I have," said Morgan, looking past the general at the stairs that led to the second floor.

Cass Simcoe was coming down to the lobby. It *had* to be Cass Simcoe, he gasped.

She was wearing a dress, a pink and white checked gingham that was rather full at the breast. Her face shone from recent scrubbing and Helen had done something to her cheeks to redden them. She had also done something to Cass's hair, for it was shiny now . . . almost glowing.

"Dad!" called Cass.

The general turned, started to bow as he saw his daughter, then exclaimed as full recognition struck him.

"Cass!" he cried hoarsely.

She came running across the hotel lobby, into his arms.

"I didn't recognize myself in Miss Jagger's mirror!" she cried hysterically.

The general held her off at arm's length. "For a moment I thought I was looking at your mother twenty years ago."

Helen Jagger came across the lobby. She was smiling. "She's very pretty, General."

"Helen," said Morgan, "General Simcoe."

The general bowed with elaborate grace. "Delighted, ma'am." Then, "Jagger?"

"My sister, General," said Jagger. "Chad and she are engaged to be married."

"Congratulations, sir," murmured the general. "And my best wishes to you, ma'am." Then his eyes went back to his daughter and he continued shaking his head.

Morgan found Helen in the office behind the hotel desk. There was now a full-time clerk on duty at the desk, and Helen spent most of her time in the office.

"She's very pretty, Chad," she said.

"Cass? The first time I saw her she was practicing drawing a gun and shooting. I thought she was a boy, a fourteen-year-old boy."

"She doesn't look like a boy in that dress of mine."

"No, she doesn't," admitted Morgan. "It was very nice of you to lend her the dress."

"I was glad to." Helen got up, came to him and, putting her arms about him, kissed him soundly. "I don't see enough of you, Chad. Seems to me I never see you more than once or twice a day."

"I'm around," said Morgan, "but you're always working."

She sighed wearily. "There's so much to do. You know Joe, details bore him. Somebody's got to keep a record of what's going out—and coming in."

"Well, what *is* coming in—and going?"

She hesitated a moment, pursing up her red lips. "The Longhorn Saloon's doing well, the hotel is making money, and the bank is losing a little. The real estate——"

"I sold a farm today."

"A farm? Who'd buy a farm around here?"

"A farmer," said Morgan. "I tried to tell him that there wasn't enough rain for crops, but the man insisted he'd make out."

Helen was frowning. "How much land did you sell him?"

"A hundred and sixty acres."

"That's only a drop in the bucket. How much did you get for it?"

"Ten dollars an acre."

"Do you think that's enough?"

"It's land we got for nothing—practically nothing."

"That's no way to look at it, Chad." Helen sighed. "If land is worth *anything,* it's worth fifty dollars an acre. You're too easy, Chad."

"Is one thousand per cent profit being too easy?"

"You're not making one thousand per cent. There's our overhead, remember. The fact that we got something cheap doesn't mean that we should sell it cheap. We've a large over-all investment."

"We've earned that back."

"That isn't enough. We took a risk. We have a right to be paid for that risk. Of course, our prices are high, but this is a boom town, Chad. Things are always high in a boom town. And we *are* selling tangible things. Not just blue sky, like Mr. Foss when he started the railroad. All he had to sell were some pieces of paper—railroad shares. There was no railroad, no rolling stock. All of it was bought with the money paid in by the shareholders. *We* sold tangibles right from the start, real estate, property, a town——"

Morgan shook his head. "How does your pretty head hold all those things?"

She flashed him a smile. "I'm a good businessman."

"Businesswoman."

A cloud flitted across her features. "You still refuse to concede that a woman can do things as well as a man?"

"As far as this business is concerned, you can do them better than either Joe or I." Morgan hesitated. "But I happen to be in love with a woman, not a business *man.*"

She came to him and gave him a quick kiss. "When I'm with you, Chad, I'm glad I'm a woman. Now, clear out of here, I've work to do."

A sense of strange unease settled over him as he left her in the office. He stopped in the lobby. There were chairs and even a sofa in it now, although the floors were still bare. So much mud and dust was tracked in that a carpet would have been impractical.

He stepped out upon the veranda and was about to start down the street when he sighted Joe Jagger coming out of The Longhorn Saloon, headed for the hotel. He looked around quickly, saw a guest seated on a chair at the far end of the veranda and went down to meet Jagger.

"Joe," he said, when Jagger came up, "I've been meaning to tell you. Tom Alder's in town."

Jagger grimaced. "He introduced himself to me in The Longhorn."

"He say anything more than just introduce himself?"

"What do you mean?"

"He knows that we got the Confederate gold."

"He said so?" Jagger demanded sharply.

"He isn't that blunt. He dropped it, like a casual thing he'd picked up . . . as if it was general knowledge."

"So what? Nobody can prove a thing on us—not at this date."

Morgan hesitated. "I don't think it's a matter of proof, Joe. It's—it's Alder."

Jagger looked at Morgan, surprise lighting up his eyes. "If I didn't know better, Chad, I'd say Alder was—was bothering you."

"Doesn't he bother you?"

"Why should he?"

"We spent some time in Missouri, chasing Quantrill.

Surely you must have heard of Tom Alder during that time?"

"Of course I heard of him. He was one of Quantrill's worst, one of his lieutenants, or captain or something."

"He held himself in better than Bloody Bill, or George Todd, but he was a tougher man than either. Even the guerillas said he was the best shot in the outfit."

"You're a pretty good shot yourself, Chad."

Morgan shook his head dubiously. "I'm not a killer."

A glow came into Jagger's eyes. "Meaning?"

Morgan winced. "Not what you think I mean."

"No?" There was a bite in Jagger's tone. "A horse breaks its leg, you put it out of its misery, The Reb was dying, he was in pain. You've been thinking of that, Chad. *Haven't you?*"

"I'm not going to quarrel with you."

"I asked you a question!"

"I gave you my answer at the time, down in Texas. It's done, Joe, no use raking it up."

"You brought up this Alder."

"He's here, Joe. I figured we ought to talk about him. He went to Mexico with Shelby."

"Because he was afraid to go back to Missouri!"

Morgan hesitated a moment, then shook his head. "I have a feeling that Alder isn't very much afraid of—of anything. It's pretty certain that he was at Lawrence with Quantrill and Kansas is about as dangerous to a Quantrill man as Missouri ever was. Yet, he's here."

Jagger frowned, then suddenly shrugged. "What happened down in Texas is between you and me, Chad. There were no witnesses. I'm not worrying about it. And I'm not worrying about Alder." He paused. "What makes you think he knows about the gold?"

"He said we built quite a town with twenty-five thousand dollars."

"I don't see anything wrong with that. Our creditors know by now that we didn't have any more than that when we started Pawnee City."

"It was the way he said it. He tied it in with a similar

remark when I met him down in Texas—Shelby's gold having been captured by—by the Sixteenth Illinois Cavalry."

"Doesn't mean a thing. Everybody knows it was the Sixteenth caught up with Shelby's rearguard. You worry too much, Chad." He suddenly smiled. "Isn't it about time you and Helen took a little trip?"

"She's too busy."

"We're *all* busy." Jagger shook his head. "Beats me how she takes to this. I went off to war and she was in pigtails. Now she's a businesswoman."

"Yes," said Morgan, "she's that."

"You two have words?"

"No-no, Joe!"

Jagger hesitated a moment. "That Texas tomboy's rather pretty, don't you think?"

Morgan smiled. "I'll admit I was caught flat-footed when I saw her in Helen's dress. Down in Texas I'd thought her"—he suddenly looked sharply at Jagger—"now wait a minute, Joe! You're not thinking——"

"No?"

"She's a child."

"A child of nineteen or twenty." Jagger grinned.

"No," said Morgan. Then he repeated it. "No."

Jagger nodded. "I'm one to talk about my sister when I can't handle her myself. Still, if I were you, I'd *make* her quit this work awhile. Get her on a train and run up to Kansas City. Get it over with." Jagger gripped Morgan's arm. "Nothing'd please me more than to have you for a brother-in-law."

Chapter Fifteen

Helen Jagger was putting away the books when her brother came into the office. He studied her for a moment before speaking, then: "You look tired, Sis."

"There's a lot of work here."

"It's time we brought in a bookkeeper. I should think you'd be able to find one in Kansas City."

"I'd rather do the work myself, Joe. I *like* it. And I like being tired, when I know I've been doing something worthwhile."

"I think you ought to take a rest. Go to Kansas City, find a bookkeeper and send him out."

"*Send* him?"

"Why, I thought you and Chad might want to go together."

"This is Chad's idea?"

"No," said Jagger. "It's mine. It isn't natural, two people in love, too busy to take time off to get married. Especially, if it's the woman who's too busy."

A tiny frown creased her forehead. "Has Chad talked to you?"

"About you? No. But I know Chad. At least, I *think* I do. He's got an odd—I don't want to use the word 'puritanical,' because that isn't just right. Mmm, he's old-fashioned. Doesn't believe in women working."

"He said that?" A sharpness crept into Helen's tone. "That Texas cowgirl works. She's got hands as rough as a man's. She rides and she shoots."

"Chad isn't in love with Cass Simcoe. He's in love with *you*." Jagger grimaced. "I just said what *I* thought. Chad doesn't discuss you, not even with me."

Helen was silent a moment. Then she said, "I think

71

you're wrong about him. He knows how much there is to do here."

But the frown remained on her face.

The dining room in the hotel had been opened a month before. It was patronized by cattle buyers, drummers who stayed at the hotel and by the cattle drovers who came there to carry on negotiations with the buyers.

Morgan came into the hotel shortly after six, looked into the office behind the desk and saw it deserted. He crossed to the dining-room door to see if Helen were eating and was surprised to see Cass Simcoe seated at a table by herself. She was still wearing Helen's dress.

Morgan went to her. She sprang up as she saw him approaching. "Mr. Morgan!"

"Chad," he smiled. "I also answer to the name of damn-yank."

She grimaced. "Dad says I can't say that as long as we're up North."

"Then I can't call you Reb." He looked over his shoulder toward the door. "Is your father coming down to supper?"

"He's gone out with the boys. Said he wouldn't feel right sleeping in a bed when they're out there. I tried to go with him, but he made me stay here." Worry came over her face. "I'm scared."

"Of what?"

"Eating here, dressed—like a lady."

"You *are* a lady, Cass."

"But I—I don't know how to eat with all these forks and knives and spoons. We ain't—we haven't had anything at home for so long, ever since the damn—since the war." For an instant her face looked as if she was going to burst into tears, but then she made a quick recovery. "I'm hungry—that's the only reason I came down."

"Then let's eat!"

He stepped around, pulled out her chair to help her. She gave him a quick, stunned look, then seated herself.

Morgan took the chair opposite her and signaled to a

raw-boned woman of about fifty, who had been impressed into duty as a waitress in the dining room.

Morgan and Cass were halfway through their meal when Helen Jagger appeared in the doorway. She looked around, saw Morgan and Cass Simcoe at a table. A sudden look of pique crossed her face, but she erased it quickly and came forward.

"Here you are," she said sweetly to Cass. "I went up to your room to ask you to have supper with me, but——"

Morgan was already on his feet, drawing up a chair. "Sit down, Helen."

She shook her head. "No. I can't right now. Joe wants me to go over something with him." She started to turn away, then stopped. "That dress becomes you, my dear."

"Th-thank you," said Cass in a strange, choked tone.

Helen gave her a bright smile and walked off. Morgan looked after her.

"She's mad," said Cass.

"Helen? What makes you think that?"

"I know. She—she doesn't like you eating with me."

"That's absurd, Cass. Helen's a very busy woman."

"What does she do?"

"Why, she handles all the details of our business. The bookkeeping, the bills, the receipts. Actually, she's doing more work than either Jagger or myself."

"She doesn't like me."

Morgan looked at her in surprise. "Why should she *dis*like you?"

Cass dropped her eyes to her plate. Morgan regarded her a moment, then said gently, "You're a very pretty girl, Cass."

Her eyes came up. "You thought I was a boy—a fourteen-year-old boy!"

He grinned at her and after a moment she could not repress a slow, shy smile.

Chad Morgan came out of The Longhorn Saloon and stood on the wooden sidewalk. Horses lined both sides of the street. Men were clomping along the sidewalks, were churning up the dust of the street. It was a busy street, even though it was past midnight.

A gun banged and a cowboy's "Yip-Yip-Yay" split the night air.

Chad Morgan turned to the right and walked along the sidewalk. He passed a couple of stores that were closed, looked through the window of Buffington's hardware and equipment store and saw a small light on in the rear.

On the opposite corner was The Texas Saloon, the establishment of Pillsbury, the pioneer whiskey-dispenser of Pawnee City. It was quite an elaborate place. Built later than The Longhorn Saloon, the owner knew that he had to compete against The Longhorn Saloon and had built accordingly.

Morgan stopped on the corner and a woman came out of the shadows. "Hello, big boy," she said.

Morgan turned and the woman recognized him. "Sorry, Mr. Morgan," she said.

"What are you doing out here?" Morgan asked gruffly.

"Getting some air. That's all, Mr. Morgan. Honest." The girl hurried away, crossing the street and entering The Texas Saloon.

Yes, Pawnee City was a town now.

Morgan started to turn away and heard boots coming along the sidewalk. A short, stocky man in a sack suit came up—Harlow Tarbox, owner of The St. Louis Store.

"Hot, isn't it?" he said to Morgan.

"We need a good rain."

"That's all hell needs," chuckled Tarbox. "A good rain now and then. They tell me it might not rain until November or December. Well, at least, there's no farmers around here. They need rain more than town folks."

"I sold a farm to a man today," Morgan said. "I tried to warn him that there wasn't enough rainfall, but he said he'd make out." Then he added as an afterthought, "Seemed to know his business."

Chapter Sixteen

Withers was a gaunt, beetle-browed man from East Texas, who would not be going back to his home territory. He had killed a Negro there and the carpetbag politicians of the county were voting the Negroes to keep themselves in their lucrative elective offices. Withers had served with Nathan Bedford Forrest and had no vote in Texas.

He had not gone out of his way to pick a fight with Tom Alder on the drive from Texas, but there was no liquor along the trail and Withers had not reached the depth of his depravity.

There was plenty of liquor in Pawnee City, however, and Withers was averaging about three shots for every time the faro dealer went through his deck.

He was standing beside Tom Alder and the press of players was crowding him against Alder. As the dealer shuffled for a new run of the cards, someone on the left jostled Withers and he snarled at Alder on his right.

"You're crowding me!"

Alder looked at Withers and pushed gently against the man on his right. He got an inch of space, which eased him away from Withers. The dealer put his cards into his box and said, "Place your bets, gentlemen."

Alder switched his dollar and put it on the jack of diamonds. The queen lost, the jack won.

"Damn the luck!" swore Withers.

He fished a crumpled greenback out of his pocket, raked up all his silver and sweeping aside the two dollars that Alder had set on the queen of hearts, dumped his own money on the card.

Alder said, "Put my money back on the queen."

"I'm playing the queen. Keep your damn money off mine."

Alder looked at the dealer. "I'm playing the queen."

The dealer hesitated, noting the condition of Withers, then nodded. He leaned across, gathered up Alder's two dollars and put them on the table just inside the queen, not touching Withers's money, but clearly indicating that it also was bet on the queen.

Withers reached out and swept Alder's money away, scattering it to the far side of the table. One of the dollars rolled to the floor.

"You're not jinxing me with your two-bit bet," he snarled at Alder.

"Mister," said Alder, "get down on the floor and pick up my money."

Withers jerked back violently. "What's that?"

"You've been trying to pick a fight with me," said Alder evenly. "You've got it, unless you pick up my money."

"Why, you dirty bushwhackin'———" Withers began.

Alder hit him in the face with the back of his open hand. It was a hard, raking blow and sent Withers reeling back. He bumped into a man seated at a poker table, caromed away from him and almost went to the floor. He recovered and stood, eight feet from Alder, his feet planted wide apart on the floor.

"Reach for your hardware, you bushwhackin' bastard!" he said through his teeth. "I been listenin' and hearin' about you all the way from Texas. You're so goddamn handy with a gun, let's see you use it now."

"Let it go," Alder said, "while you're still on your feet."

"Draw!"

Alder held up his right hand, palm turned outward, as if to placate Withers. Or ward him off.

"I'm warning you, Withers. Force me and you're a dead man."

Withers's hand snaked down for the Colt in the holster slung low on his right thigh. He was three-fourths drunk and his speed was presumably not as good as if he had been sober, but Alder gave him all the best of it. His gun hand was up, palm turned out. It did not go for Alder's own weapon until Withers's hand had touched his revolver, was drawing it from the holster.

Then the hand moved—so fast that it was a mere blur. Only one gun spoke. Tom Alder's.

Withers's gun was clear of its holster, but it clattered to the floor in the instant of dead silence that followed the explosion of Tom Alder's gun.

Then Withers was gasping, choking. "You—you dirty . . ." he sputtered. Then he folded forward, his face hitting the floor of the saloon even before his knees.

Alder held his gun loosely, his eyes going easily around the ring of faces.

"Was it fair?" he asked softly.

No one spoke. Pillsbury came out of his office, pushed his way through the crowds. His eyes went to the dead man on the floor, to Tom Alder, then to the dealer at the faro table.

The dealer said, "It was a fair fight."

Chapter Seventeen

When Tom Alder killed the Texan, Withers, the town of Pawnee City was officially two months, plus three days, old. Two men had been killed on the first fateful day, one of them lynched. There had been violence in Pawnee City right from the start. Drunken cowboys rode their horses up and down the street and fired at the sun and the moon and the stars. Occasionally their exuberance was a little more obstreperous and they sent a bullet through a windowpane of one of the numerous stores along Main Street. Now and then a man rode a horse into a store or saloon.

This was in the nature of sport. The Texans were proud. They had fought a war and lost and did not take well to the rule of the North. They hated the Union Army, the North and everything pertaining to it. They hated Kansans especially.

Yet they brought their trail herds to Kansas and received there the only hard money most of them had seen since doffing the gray. That did not mean that they liked it. Money enabled them to buy liquor and then all their subdued, simmering rage was fanned into a blaze.

They cut loose.

Yet, in spite of the violence, there had been no deaths in Pawnee City after that first day. Not until the gun duel between Alder and Withers, in which Withers had died.

No one blamed Alder, no one castigated him. He was not a Texas man, but he was a Southerner. He had fought for the South even longer than the Texans themselves, for he had gone with his command into exile in Mexico. He had fought in battles there which did not help the cause of the South, but he had been one of the unconquerables. He had not "come in," he had not received the official amnesty of the victorious North. He was therefore a Southerner of unimpeachable quality.

Yet Alder's killing the Texan, Withers, seemed to set the torch to the tinder that had been smoldering for more than two months.

Texas humiliation.

Texas pride.

Texas rage.

A dozen Texas men rode into Pawnee City in mid-morning, following the night of the gun duel. They were quiet, sullen, when they rode into town. They stopped at The Longhorn Saloon, had three or four drinks apiece. They spoke only among themselves and in low, tense voices.

They left the saloon, mounted their horses and rode in a body to The Texas Saloon. The whiskey was beginning to work by this time and they had some more.

Then one of the Texas men, a towheaded, hard-faced man, said to the bartender, "Where's the lop-eared Yank who had the nerve to call this place The Texas Saloon?"

Pillsbury, coming out of his little office at that moment, knew his drinking men. He came forward, smiling amiably. "Not me, boys. Uh-uh, I'm no Yank. Mississippi's my state, Natchez my city."

"The hell you say," sneered the towhead.

"Mississippians is folks," chimed in another cowboy. "Prove it."

Pillsbury knew how to do that. He gestured to the apron behind the bar. "One on the house, Ab, from the bottle with the red label." He smirked at the Texans. "My best, gentlemen."

The apron set out a fresh bottle. The towhead grabbed the bottle, tilted it to his mouth and took two huge swallows. He lowered the bottle and scowled at it.

"It ain't good, but it ain't bad." He handed it to the hellion beside him. "See what you think, Pesh."

The man called Pesh took a huge swallow of the whiskey, gasped and took a second swallow. "Hog swill," he said. Then, to the bartender: "Let's try another bottle."

The bartender looked at Pillsbury. The saloon man's smile was a frozen one, but he nodded. Pesh drank deeply, handed the second bottle to the towhead, who sampled about a gill of the whiskey.

"Our friend may be from Mississippi," he said, "but this is Yankee whiskey. It just don't taste right."

"I'll find some Southern whiskey," volunteered a third cowboy. He strode behind the bar, reached for a bottle at random and shoved it across the bar. He took down a second bottle and handed it to another Texas man.

"Who're you boys riding for?" asked Pillsbury. "Dan Hastings?"

"Hastings?" sneered the towhead. "Who's he?"

"Mossman?" pursued Pillsbury. "He came in day before yesterday with a herd."

"Never heard of him," growled the towhead. He held out a hand to one of the cowboys behind the bar. "Let me try that-there square bottle."

"Sure thing, Brog," replied the happy cowboy behind the bar.

The bottles were now being opened freely. Each was sampled copiously, handed around for others to sample and new ones started around the group.

Pillsbury stood nearby, adding mentally the value of the several bottles.

And then he added the price of the backbar mirror to his mental bill as one of the cowboys, disgusted with the quality of the whiskey, heaved a bottle at the mirror.

A few minutes later one of the cowboys slumped to the floor in front of the bar. The others, made of sterner stuff, carried bottles out to their horses with them, to better their conditions should there be danger of the liquor wearing off.

They mounted their horses and galloped up the street, Yip-Yip-Yaying and firing their revolvers. They were well gone, past the stage where they fired at the sky.

They fired now in any direction, up, down, sidewards. Glass crashed in store windows. Pedestrians scurried for shelter in the business houses. A frightened horse burst loose from its tie at a hitchrail, tore pell-mell up the street. The cowboys began firing at it, wounding and maddening the animal so that it jumped the hitchrail and pitched headlong into a glass store front. A dozen bullets peppered the horse then and it expired, half in, half out of a store.

The cowboys galloped up to the railroad tracks, sent a round of bullets into the flimsy hotel structure, wheeled their horses and galloped back up the street.

Inside The St. Louis Store, Cass Simcoe was looking at some dress-goods material when the shooting began on the street. She did no more than look over her shoulder toward the windows. The proprietor of the store, Harlow Tarbox, however, showed alarm.

"Those drunken Texas men!" he exclaimed apprehensively.

"I'm a Texan," Cass said, instinctively defending anything Texan.

A bullet crashed through one of the windowpanes. "They'll kill somebody," cried Tarbox. "Get down——"

Cass continued examining the bolt of the material. Glass crashed again and a wild bullet tore the bolt of material from Cass's hands. "Now wait a gosh-darn minute," she said angrily. "This is going too far——"

She turned and started for the door.

"Miss!" cried Tarbox. "Don't! Get down!"

"For somebody that shoots that bad?" retorted Cass. She went to the door, opened it and looked out. The Texan men had passed the store, however, and were headed toward the hotel. Cass closed the door and turned back to the store proprietor.

"You got a gun, Mister? I'll show them some shootin'!"

Tarbox stared at her in astonishment. Cass made an impatient gesture with her hand. "A gun, Mister. You got a shootin' gun?"

"I don't carry them. The hardware store——"

"Darn this dress," said Cass, looking down at Helen Jagger's dress. "A person can't rightly carry a gun they're wearin' something like this." She winced. "Here they come back!"

Tarbox ducked down behind a counter, but Cass remained at the door. The galloping horses approached, the yelling and shooting became closer—and then a bullet smashed out glass a foot from Cass's head.

"Dammit!" she swore.

In The Longhorn Saloon, the half-dozen customers were sheltered behind the bar. With one exception. Chad Morgan. He stood by the broken window looking out upon the street. The cowboys were receding up the street and Joe Jagger took the occasion to come out of the bank across the street and rush for The Longhorn.

He tore into the saloon.

"They've gone wild!" he cried. "They're shooting up the whole town."

Blake, the manager of the saloon, came out from behind the bar. "There's ten-twelve of them," he said. "They were in here, liquoring up a half hour ago. By now they've got skinfuls."

Morgan looked steadily at Jagger. "Well, Joe?"

Jagger returned Morgan's steady look with scowling eyes. "All we can do is lay low until they get tired of it—or sober up."

"And what if they destroy Pawnee City by that time?"

"They're not going to do that . . ." Jagger signaled to the bartender. "Recognize any of them?"

Blake nodded. "They're Pete Mossman's men."

"Somebody's got to find Mossman!"

"Who?" asked Morgan.

Jagger sent a quick look around, picked out a man wearing a dirty white apron, the swamper of The Longhorn. "You, Mose, or whatever your name is, get a horse and ride south of town. Find Pete Mossman and tell him his boys are cutting up."

The swamper began taking off his apron. "Mr. Jagger, I just quit my job."

Jagger strode up to the man and rocked him with an openhanded slap and caught him with the same hand as it swept back. "I'll tell you when you quit!"

The swamper dabbed the back of his hand to his mouth, saw blood on the hand. He shook his head. "Slap me some more, Mr. Jagger," he said. "It ain't as bad as a bullet in my gizzard. I know. I was shot at Pea Ridge, right smack-dab in the gizzard. I ain't never got over it, so go ahead, slap me."

Jagger raised his hand again, but Morgan sprang forward and caught Jagger's arm. "Stop it, Joe. You can't ask

a hired man to go out there. It's your job, Joe, and mine.
We own this town—remember?"

"Give me a dozen troopers of the old Sixteenth," Jagger
raged, "and I'd give them hell for breakfast."

"There's only two men from the Sixteenth here," Morgan
said coolly. "You and me . . ." He signaled to Blake, the
manager. "Have you got a gun, Mr. Blake?"

"On'y a scatter-gun," replied the manager of The Longhorn. "And a Navy gun——"

"Give me the Navy gun!"

But then it was too late. The cowboys had shot up the
south end of town and were coming back—at a full gallop.
Yelling and shooting. The penned-in customers of The
Longhorn again took refuge behind the bar. Jagger headed
for it, reached the rear of the bar and cried to Morgan,
"Get down, Chad!"

Morgan stepped aside so he would not be in direct range
of bullets fired through the window. The racket outside
was at its peak. The cowboys were galloping past the saloon.
A bullet shattered a piece of glass remaining in one of the
windows, plunked into the bar. Behind it a man cried out.

The cowboys were past the saloon then. But they had
only a short distance to go, to the hotel that faced the dead
end of the street. They milled around there, sending a dozen
or so bullets into the hotel. Morgan, peering through the
window, exclaimed aloud. He whirled, rushed for the bar.

"Blake! The gun!"

Blake raised his head tentatively above the bar level. He
held a Navy Colt in his hand. Morgan caught it, turned for
the door.

Jagger came up. "Chad! Don't be a fool. You can't go
out there!"

He was too late.

Morgan stepped out of The Longhorn Saloon onto the
wooden sidewalk. A hundred feet away, the Texas men
were assembling to make another murderous charge down
the main street.

Morgan stepped to the edge of the sidewalk, his right
hand grasping the Navy gun dangling at his side. He stood
there, waiting.

A sudden step on the wooden sidewalk caused him to shoot a quick glance over his shoulder. Tom Alder was coming out of the barbershop next door to The Longhorn Saloon.

He said, as he came up, "They'll kill you, Morgan."

"One or two of them will die first," retorted Morgan.

"That's going to do you any good? You'll be just as dead as if you hadn't killed any of them."

Morgan said, "It's not your fight, Alder."

"I'm not fighting. My gun's in my holster and it's going to stay there. Besides . . . I'm one of them."

"You killed a Texas man last night. That's what started them off."

"It was only a matter of time." Alder shrugged. "Maybe that's why I'm out here now." He became alert. "They're ready to come back now."

The drunken Texas men had gotten into some semblance of a formation and were formed in a rough phalanx. They were starting their horses back for another run.

And now Helen Jagger stepped out of the bank across the street. She took a quick look toward the hotel, saw the Texas men bearing down on her and panicked. Instead of whirling back into the bank, she started across the street . . . running.

A roar went up among the Texas men. The riders swerved to cut her off.

Yells went up.

"First man grabs her, has her!"

"Lookit the Yankee sweetheart!"

"I seen her first!"

Helen saw she could not make it across the street and stopped dead in her tracks. A skidding horse being jerked to a violent stop almost knocked her over. Another horse went past her, was stopped so violently it reared up. A third horse did strike her, knocking her to her knees.

Before she could get up, Brog, the towhead, had hit the ground and was reaching for Helen.

"Damme," he cried, "if you ain't the best thing I've seen in Yankeeland." He grabbed her arm, jerked her toward him. "Here, give us a kiss!"

Behind the towhead, a gun roared and a bullet whispered past the Texan's ear.

He let go of Helen, whirled, his hand going automatically for the gun he had holstered. It froze in mid-air.

Chad Morgan was striding toward him. His gun was in his hand; it was raised, but the muzzle was pointed only carelessly in the towhead's direction. It could be swiveled quickly toward any of the Texas men.

Helen had distracted all of the Texas men. Several of then still had their guns in their hands, but they were caught flat-footed, as were those who had put away their guns.

Of course they could draw . . . if anyone wanted to draw against a man who had come out deliberately into the open against a dozen wild, drunken Texas men.

Morgan said to the towhead, "Climb on your horse and get out of town."

"Mister," said Brog thickly, "you got about five seconds to live."

"You've got less than that," retorted Morgan.

A sudden hush fell upon the Texas men. The towhead was their obvious leader. He it was who had brought them to town, he it was who had led the taking over of Pillsbury's saloon and the street. And it was he, too, who had led the charge to cut off the Yankee girl who had foolishly wandered out upon the street.

The eyes of the Texas men were upon the towhead. The cowboy knew it, even though he never once took his eyes from the bleak face of Chad Morgan.

Brog started to bluster. "Never saw the damn Yankee yet I couldn't lick."

"You'll never lick me," said Morgan, " 'cause I'll kill you at the first move *anyone* makes."

The towhead was suddenly more sober than he had been in more than a half hour. He saw something in Chad Morgan's eyes, something he had not seen in many eyes before. Death.

The Yankee had no chance, of course. The cowboys would riddle him with bullets . . . but the towhead would not be alive to see it. He knew that. His eyes finally tore themselves from Morgan's face, flickered to the drunken face of the man named Pesh.

"Pesh," he said thickly, "you know I never backed down to anyone in my life . . ." He waited for an assuring word from Pesh. None came. Agony spread over the towhead's face. "We fit together all through the war," he went on. "Nobody never had to call me——"

"Make up your mind," Morgan said harshly. "Back down, or fight!"

A shudder ran through the towhead's long body and Morgan knew that he had won. The man would not fight; he was not drunk enough to be heedless of his danger and he was too drunk to reason it out.

He half turned, stumbled toward his horse.

The muzzle of Morgan's gun came up. The move was being made. The followers of the towhead could become reckless. It was best that they see the positive result of such recklessness . . . the gun pointed directly at their leader.

"Get out of town!" he cried. "Ride!"

The towhead was in the saddle. Without looking again at Morgan he kneed his horse forward. Morgan half turned so he could continue to follow the man with the muzzle of his revolver.

A second Texas man started after the towhead. That was all that was necessary, the others following swiftly, those afoot vaulting into their saddles.

Their horses went fast, but there was no more Yip-Yip-Yaying. And no more shooting.

"Chad!"

Helen Jagger's poignant cry brought Morgan back to her. He turned, looked at her.

"Get off the street, Helen," he said tonelessly.

She looked at him, her eyes wide in shock. Then she turned and walked back toward the bank.

A hundred feet away, Cass Simcoe stood in front of The St. Louis Store, from where she had watched the entire episode between Chad Morgan and the Texas men. Her mouth was slightly open, her eyes were shining.

"That's a pretty good man," she said, "for a damnyank!"

Faces began to appear in broken windows along the

street. A door or two opened and a merchant ventured out tentatively.

Morgan, going back to The Longhorn Saloon, saw Tom Alder standing in front of it, leaning carelessly against one of the supports of the overhanging roof.

"Guess you don't figure on being an old man," Alder remarked casually.

Morgan gave him a sharp look and went past him. In the doorway of the saloon he encountered Joe Jagger about to come out.

"That was a damnfool grandstand play!" Jagger exclaimed.

Morgan stopped and looked squarely at his partner. "You think I did that for fun?"

"Those men were drunk. A wrong move and they'd have gone berserk. Somebody would have gotten killed. Helen might have been hurt."

A heavy-set little man with long walrus mustaches came running up. "Mr. Morgan!" he cried. "I'd like to talk to you."

"Some other time," said Morgan, turning away.

The little man caught at his arm. "Wait—I'm Charles Fesler, the publisher of *The Pawnee City Lance*. Our first edition's coming out tomorrow and I'd like to use this for my lead story. I didn't see all of it. I'd like to know just what happened."

Morgan indicated Jagger. "Mr. Jagger can tell you," he said, and walked off. Both Fesler and Jagger looked after him in some surprise. Then Jagger grunted.

"Now, what's the matter with him?"

"Reaction," said the newspaperman. "He bluffed down those Texas men and I guess it's just hit him the big chance he took."

Jagger gave his full attention to Fesler. "Now, wait a minute, get it right. That isn't exactly what happened."

"You *saw* it, Mr. Jagger?"

"I saw as much as anyone. Let's not go insulting the Texas boys. We need their trade. The boys got a little out of hand, but they'll be sorry for what they did when they sober up."

"Will they pay for my window?" asked the news-paperman.

"If they don't, I will," snapped Jagger.

"And suppose somebody was hit by their shooting? Will they pay the doctor's bills?"

Jagger regarded the newspaper publisher coolly. "Mr. Fesler, who sold you the building in which you've set up your shop?"

"You did."

Jagger nodded. "You've been in Pawnee City a week or so. I'm sure you've learned by now that every business-man on this street bought his property from me. *I* built this town, Mr. Fesler."

"Yes, I guess you did, Mr. Jagger. You—and Mr. Morgan."

Chapter Eighteen

Chad Morgan's room in the hotel was very much like all the others; it was nine by twelve feet in size and furnished with a cot, a washstand on which was a pitcher and bowl and a straight-backed chair. Nails in the wall held Morgan's changes of clothing.

The room, however, was one of the choice ones in that it was at the front of the house overlooking the street. This might also prove a disadvantage if future invasions of Texas men shot up the town indiscriminately. Fortunately, Pete Mossman's exuberant cowboys had missed the window of Morgan's room.

Morgan lay on the bed, the fingers of his hands interlaced under his head. He stared sightlessly at the ceiling and did not hear the steps coming along the hall.

Knuckles rapped on the door.

Morgan came back to the present. "It's open," he called.

Jagger pushed open the door and came in. "Been looking for you."

"Sit down."

Jagger picked up the straight-backed chair and turned it around. Straddling it, he sat down, bracing his chin on the high back of the chair.

"We haven't had much time for talking lately," he began.

"Hasn't been much to talk about."

Jagger exclaimed almost petulantly, "What's got into you, Chad?"

"Nothing, Joe. Why?"

"Dammit, can't you even sit up?"

Morgan sat up, swinging his feet to the floor. He looked inquiringly at Jagger.

Jagger said, "I still say it was a fool play. That white-headed cowboy, he's killed two men. If you hadn't gotten the drop on him, he'd have killed *you!*"

"Good thing he didn't."

Jagger got to his feet and kicked the chair aside, breaking a rung. "I can't get through to you any more. What's eating you?" He grimaced. "Helen?"

"You're Helen's brother, Joe," said Morgan, "but let's keep her out of this."

"Can't," said Helen Jagger from the open doorway. "I'm here."

She came into the room, closing the door and standing with her back against it. "You probably saved my life," she said. "I shouldn't have come out on the street, but I—I saw you and Joe in The Longhorn and I wanted to get over to you. I—I lost my nerve when they charged down on me." She smiled wanly. "Thanks, Chad."

"I want to talk to Chad alone," growled Jagger.

"You *were* talking alone," Helen said sweetly, "and you broke that chair."

Morgan got to his feet. "What's there to talk about? A bunch of drunken cowboys shot up the town. It's done. Only thing is to see that it doesn't happen again."

"It's not as simple as that," said Jagger testily. "Seems we got a newspaper starting up. Nosy little beggar. The way he talked he wants to make something of this business." He grunted. "I told him a thing or two and when he thinks it over he'll know which side his bread's buttered."

"What'd you tell him?" Morgan asked carelessly.

"I reminded him of who owned this town——"

"Joe," Helen Jagger said suddenly. "I'd like to talk to Chad alone a little while. We never seem to get a chance. Do you mind?"

"Of course not. But . . ." Jagger hesitated, then made a gesture of annoyance. "A thing or two I want to straighten out with Chad——"

"Later, Joe!"

Jagger glowered at his sister, then turned and jerked open the door. With his hand on it he hesitated, unsatisfied, but finally went out. He left the door open and Helen closed it.

She turned to Morgan. "Tell me something, Chad," she said quietly.

"Yes?"

"Do you love me?"

Without hesitation, Morgan caught her arm, drew her into a savage embrace. It was a long moment before he released her. "That answer your question?"

"It answers one question," she replied tauntingly. He reached for her again, but she evaded him. "I know now that a man's hotel room, with the door closed, is no place for—for a lady."

She made a small gesture to keep him at arm's length. "Maybe we ought to take that trip to Kansas City that Joe suggested." She winced then, realizing she had made a slip. "We don't get enough time together. Tonight, right after supper, why don't we rent one of Amos Goodman's buckboards and take a ride?"

"I'll put in a standing order for the buckboard."

She seated herself on the edge of his bed. "I'm tired."

"You're working too hard."

"I know," she admitted. "I didn't mind it as long as it was just work. But"—she looked up at him—"it's you and Joe. You're snapping at each other lately."

He sat down beside her, but did not touch her. He leaned forward, locking his hands together. "When Joe first suggested this scheme to me down in Texas, he said he wanted to make a million dollars in a hurry."

"And you, Chad? Aren't *you* interested in making a million?"

"I'd be a fool to say I wasn't. Only—well, maybe I'm not in quite as much of a hurry as Joe is." He paused. "You, Helen?"

It was her turn to be quiet a moment, then she said, very low, "I want money, Chad. I want a lot of money. But I want more than that!"

"You want what money can buy . . . power?"

She shook her head petulantly. "You make it sound like a dirty word. I want to *be* somebody." Her voice rose a little. "We were poor, Chad. Very poor. I—I wore underwear made of floursacks until I was fourteen years old."

"I'll bet it looked good on you!"

"Stop it, I'm serious. You've seen Nathan Foss. What kind of wife do you think he's got?"

"Fat?"

"Fat and ugly. But she's wearing diamonds. Even when he couldn't pay his construction workers, his wife still wore the diamonds. She came into the office now and then and she—she acted like a queen. When I knew her husband could hardly pay me my salary. She's used to money. She's had it and it's given her something."

"She's still fat and ugly. Diamonds can't hide that."

She got to her feet. "Well, I'm not fat and I'm not ugly. I—I know how I look to men. And I know that diamonds would look awfully well on me. And one day I'll walk into the opera in St. Louis, or Chicago or New York, and I'll have so many diamonds that every woman in the place will be envious of me. But I don't want to be an old woman when that happens."

"You won't be," said Morgan quietly, "not at the rate we're making money in Pawnee City."

"That's it, Chad!" exclaimed Helen. "That's why I'm working so hard, why I'm driving—why I'm encouraging Joe. We've an opportunity here that few people have ever had in their entire lives. A chance to become rich and powerful in an amazingly short time. Only one thing can beat us—dissension. You and Joe *must* be friends, Chad. Do you hear?" She reached down, took his head between her hands and turned up his face. "Darling . . . please . . . !" She bent down and kissed him on the mouth.

"Make it up with him, Chad!"

"Of course," he said.

But he did not get up and after looking at him again, searchingly, Helen went out.

Morgan was still sitting on the bed five minutes later, when timid knuckles rapped lightly on his door.

"Come in," he said wearily.

The door opened and Cass Simcoe entered tentatively a step or two. She was wearing her Levi's and man's clothing. Morgan exclaimed and came to his feet.

"Cass!"

"Is it against the rules for a girl to come into a man's room?" she asked worriedly.

"It is," replied Morgan, "but it's all right."

"I—I wouldn't have come," said Cass, "only I heard her——"

"Helen?"

She nodded. "My room's right across the hall. I—the doors are pretty thin and I couldn't help hearin'. Not everything," she added quickly. "Just some of it between Mr. Jagger and you . . . and her."

"I'm sorry," Morgan said. "I guess we talked too loud." He shook his head. "We've got problems. Business problems . . ." Then he looked sharply at Cass.

"What happened to the dress?"

"I'm going to give it back in a few minutes. We—we're headin' back home first thing in the morning."

"Already?"

"Dad sold the cattle today and he's in a hurry to get home."

"I hope he got a good price."

"Twenty-nine thousand dollars, Mr. Morgan!" cried Cass. "Golly, we're rich. There ain't—isn't—that much money in all of Texas. We bought a lot of stuff and we're going to send for more. Dad says he can pay the taxes and get the damn—I mean, the Yankee carpetbaggers—off our necks. We can pay our menfolk and"—she paused —"Mammy."

"That's fine, Cass," said Morgan. "We're going to miss you around here."

"Me?" she exclaimed in surprise. "You're going to miss *me*?"

"Of course."

Her eyes fell from his. "Next time I see you, you'll be married."

"Probably," replied Morgan. Then: "Next time? You're coming again?"

"We got ten times as many steers as we brought. Maybe twenty-thirty times, the general says. We don't even know how many head we got. But now that we're rich again"—

she smiled brightly—"Dad says why not get *real* rich? Rich enough to buy up the state of Texas. We'll be making lots of drives, Mister Morgan."

"Chad, I told you."

"Chad," she said, and held out her hand. "Goodbye." He took her small, calloused hand. "Goodbye, Reb."

"Damnyank," she smiled and turning, stepped out quickly, closing the door behind her.

Chapter Nineteen

Pete Mossman rode into town the next morning, accompanied by a sober and subdued towhead, his trail boss. He found Joe Jagger at the hotel.

"Mr. Jagger," he said, "seems my boys got a little liquored up yesterday and busted a window glass or two." He looked at the cowboy with him. "Go ahead, Brog, say your piece."

"We was drunk," offered the cowboy reluctantly.

"That's the understatement of the year," exclaimed Joe Jagger. "I've had more complaining about what you boys did yesterday than for anything that's ever happened in Pawnee City."

"I said we was sorry," snapped Brog. "And I'm only sayin' it 'cause Pete insists on it."

"You're damn well going to pay for the damage, too," growled Pete Mossman. "You figure twenty dollars'll cover it?"

Jagger hesitated. "Pillsbury of the Texas Saloon says they drank up sixty-two dollars' worth of his whiskey—and broke his mirror for which he paid ninety-three dollars, including freight."

The cattleman frowned. "Sounds pretty steep, Mr. Jagger."

"They also broke about thirty, thirty-five windows around town."

Mossman turned on Brog. "You told me two-three windows."

"That's all I saw," snarled Brog. "You ask me, they're pilin' it on. I told you they're a bunch of damn Yanks who'd——"

"Wait a minute, Brog," interposed Jagger swiftly. "I've

pretty well squared things around town. It took a bit of talking, but no one holds a grudge——"

"I don't give a damn if they do."

"Brog," said Mossman, "least you can do is listen. Mr. Jagger's a reasonable man. He wants us Texans to bring our herds to Pawnee City. He makes money offa us."

Jagger looked sharply at the Texan. "That's right, Mr. Mossman, but without me *you'd* be skinning your steers down in Texas and selling the hides for shoe leather. What'd you get for that herd you brought up?"

"Not what it was worth, but it's all right, I made a deal. I'm not complaining."

"You'll be coming back with another herd, I imagine."

"I ain't hardly thought about it. Not much. Maybe I will, maybe I won't. That's beside the point. But I'm a fair man. The boys did some damage and I figure they ought to pay for it. A fair price, the amount of the damage they did, not no profit."

"All right," said Jagger. "I'll go along with that. I'll even pay half of the damage out of my own pocket. What do you say to a hundred dollars for your share of the business?"

"You can go take a running jump at——" began Brog, but stopped as Mossman hit him in the side with his elbow.

"It's a fair price, Mr. Jagger," Mossman said. "The boys had their fun, they can pay for it. Ten dollars apiece ain't too much."

And while Jagger was talking to Pete Mossman at the hotel, a dapper little man, the clerk for Buffington, the hardware man, came into the real-estate office where Chad Morgan was studying the little squares on the wall map.

"Mr. Buffington says he'd appreciate it if you'd step over to his place," the clerk said.

"Right now?" Morgan asked.

"Five-ten minutes. I got to ask some more people."

A few minutes later Morgan entered the store of Buffington. He had himself sold the hardware dealer the land on which the store stood and Buffington had had a crew of workmen throw up a shell of a store. It was a well-stocked store, containing just about anything a person could require on the frontier. Morgan noted that there was a considerable quantity of farming tools.

He found Buffington at the rear of the store with Harlow Tarbox, the proprietor of The St. Louis Store.

"Quite a thing you did yesterday, Mr. Morgan," said Tarbox.

Morgan made a deprecating gesture of dismissal. "I did what had to be done."

"That's what I told the boys," declared Buffington. "We had a sort of get-together last night."

Fesler, the editor and publisher of the new *Pawnee City Lance*, came into the store. He was carrying a damp sheet of newsprint. "My front page," he said. "I'll be going to press with it in about an hour."

He started to hand the sheet to Buffington, then diverted it to Morgan. "What do you think of it?" he asked.

Morgan looked at the page proof. A headline ran across the page:

"Drunken Mob Shoots Up Pawnee City"

Morgan gave the newspaperman a quick look and began to read the two-column article on the right side of the page. It began:

A mob of drunken Texas cowboys yesterday took over Pawnee City and for a brief period held complete power of life and death over the residents of our city. The drunken men galloped up and down the street, shooting at anyone and anything with an appalling disregard for life and property. That the ruffians were finally subdued and driven from town was solely due to one of the most heroic deeds it has ever been our privilege to witness. Mr. Chad Morgan, one of the founders of Pawnee City . . .

Morgan lowered the proof of the newspaper. "It's a little strong, don't you think?"

"Absolutely not," declared Fesler. "Gentlemen, it is true that we are living in a frontier town, but there have been other frontier towns. Lawlessness had to be stamped out in all of them before the towns could prosper. *We must put down lawlessness in Pawnee City!"*

"How?" asked Harlow Tarbox. "Two of my windows were broken yesterday and the bullets did considerable damage in my store. One of them went through a bolt of dress goods, ruining it completely, and almost striking a customer."

"Mr. Morgan," said Buffington, the hardware man, "we talked this over last night, the three of us along with John Thompson and Oliver Wakeman. We've come to a definite conclusion—Pawnee City needs some law——"

Morgan hesitated and nodded. "That would require a town government."

"Exactly!" exclaimed Fesler. "That's why we asked you and your partner to come here."

"You've sent for Joe?"

"Yes," said Buffington, "and if I'm not mistaken, he's coming in now."

Everyone turned to the door, which was opening. Buffington's clerk was entering. He left the door open and in a moment Joe Jagger appeared. He was frowning when he came in and the frown did not leave his face as he approached the group at the rear of the store.

"What's this," he asked, "a town meeting?"

"You might call it that," said Fesler.

"Eh?" The scowl became deeper and Jagger focused his eyes on Morgan. "I just had a visit from Pete Mossman. He's paid for the damage his men did." He took a sheaf of greenbacks from his pocket. "Two hundred dollars, but a hundred of that goes to Andy Pillsbury for the whiskey and mirror."

"A hundred dollars wouldn't pay for the damage to *my* store," said Harlow Tarbox.

"You won't get a hundred," snapped Jagger. "I think it was damn decent of Mossman paying anything. You've got to expect a certain amount of what happened yester- day——"

"Why, Mr. Jagger?" asked Fesler.

Jagger glowered at the newspaperman. "You again! I thought we talked this over yesterday."

"We didn't discuss it," retorted Fesler. *"You* told me your views, but you didn't ask for mine, or let *me* tell them." He suddenly extended the newspaper proof to Jagger. "That's my front page today."

Jagger took the newspaper sheet and exclaimed instantly. "What the devil!" Then he read for a moment. Not more than two or three paragraphs. He lowered the sheet.

"You're not figuring to print this?"

"It goes on the press in an hour."

Jagger had himself under momentary control. He looked around the group. "All right," he said, "you called me here for a reason. Spill it."

Tarbox looked at Buffington, but the latter kept his eyes on Fesler. The fiery newspaperman nodded, accepting the assignment. "A group of businessmen in this town have decided that we need law and order in Pawnee City."

"Who?" said Jagger. "Who, besides you three?"

"John Thompson, Oliver Wakeman—others."

"Andy Pillsbury? Did you talk to him?"

"Mr. Pillsbury runs a saloon," said Tarbox, relieving Fesler of some of Jagger's attack.

"I own a saloon," said Jagger. He suddenly pointed an index finger at Chad Morgan. "You haven't said a word, Chad."

"I got in only a few minutes before you did," replied Morgan. "They were just saying that we needed a town government when you came in."

"And?"

"And what?"

"What did you tell them?"

"I didn't have time to express an opinion."

"Good," snapped Jagger. "I'll tell them, then." He drew a deep breath and exhaled it in a rush of wind. *"Mind your own goddam business, the bunch of you!"*

"This is our business," cried Fesler.

Jagger fixed the newspaperman with a cold eye. "You've been in this town a week, Fesler. You're here because I let you come. I sold you the property in which you're holed up. And I'm carrying your note at the bank."

"Which I'll pay in six months, when it's due."

"You hope, because if you don't keep your mouth shut around here, you won't last six months. I started this town and if it needs any kind of government, I'll install a government."

"No, Mr. Jagger," said Fesler doggedly. "You can't do that."

"Why not? I own this town——"

"Do you?" lashed out Fesler. "I thought the people owned it—the people who live here, who bought property —yes, from you, Mr. Jagger. But we do own the property. Thirty-six of us. . . ."

Both Buffington and Tarbox nodded agreement. "We paid you what you asked," said Tarbox. "And it was pretty high, too."

"You're making money, all of you."

"Yes, Mr. Jagger," said Buffington quietly, "but what good is money if a man's afraid to step out on the street for fear some drunken cowboy rides him down . . . or if bullets come through his windows at all hours of the day and night?"

"That happened once. It won't happen again."

"Can you guarantee it?"

Jagger exclaimed irascibly, "Of course I can't. These cowboys who come here have been on the trail for six or eight weeks. They've lived on beans and bitter coffee. They've swum rivers, eaten dust and chased longhorns. They've worked hard and long. They've got to have some fun when the trip's over. So they do a little damage. But they bring money to this town—money that you people get from them."

"The saloons get most of it," said Tarbox, then added pointedly, "And none of us own saloons."

"Maybe," said Jagger grimly, "there shouldn't be any businesses here except saloons!"

"You don't mean that!" cried Fesler.

Jagger glowered at the newspaperman. "If I say I do, you'll print it in your paper."

"Perhaps I will."

"There's no use talking to you people. I'm wasting my time." Jagger caught Morgan's eyes, jerked his head toward the door. "Coming, Chad?"

"I'll stay awhile."

"Stay!" snapped Jagger, and headed for the door. No one spoke until the door was closed behind him, then Fesler said to Morgan, "Your sentiments are the same as his, I suppose?"

"Not necessarily."

"You're his partner."

"His business partner, yes."

"Then I would say *our* interests are opposed to yours."

Buffington said, frowning, "I don't think you can jump to that conclusion."

"Why not? Even though Jagger does all the shouting and keeps talking of *his* town, *his* views, Mr. Morgan shares in the profits of Joe Jagger."

Morgan said, "Perhaps I'd better leave you gentlemen so you can go ahead with your discussions——"

"No," said Tarbox. He pointed at the sheet of newsprint in Fesler's hand. "You're forgetting the piece you just printed 'bout Chad Morgan's putting down the riot yesterday. . . . You saw it, Mr. Fesler, and you didn't see anyone else on the street, not you, not me. Mr. Morgan was the only man in this town with the courage to go outside—and do something."

Fesler nodded reluctantly. "Perhaps you're right. Very well, Mr. Morgan, stay, but we trust you will treat as confidential anything that transpires here."

Morgan shook his head. "I don't feel that I can make that promise at present. I had better go. If you feel inclined to tell me anything later, I will listen, but I cannot guarantee to keep it confidential."

He nodded and started for the door. The three businessmen watched him go, reluctance on the faces of Buffington and Tarbox, the newspaperman frowning.

Chapter Twenty

Jagger was in the Drovers Hotel, chewing an unlighted cigar, when Morgan entered.

"Well?" he asked.

"I didn't stay."

"What do you mean, you didn't stay?" growled Jagger. "You were still there when I left."

"They wanted me to keep confidential anything they said. I didn't feel that I could do that."

Jagger gave Morgan an odd look. "You're a queer duck, sometimes. Confidential . . . ha!" He took out a match, lighted the cigar. "They've got a hell of a nerve."

"I think they are going to form a town government."

"They wouldn't dare!"

"Don't count on that, Joe. They've gotten together and they've talked it over."

"I'll run them out of town. They're a bunch of weasels, the lot of them. Not one of them can stand up on his own hind legs——"

"Individually, perhaps not, but they've got the strength of numbers."

"But they can't start a government, Chad. Dammit, the two of us own this town. We'd be fools to let them say so-and-so's mayor, so-and-so's a judge."

"I don't know the business of forming a town government, Joe, but it's been done in other places. I never heard that any one or two people stopped the majority."

"Majority, hell. *We're* the majority. We own this town."

"Are you sure, Joe? We *did* own it. But we sold a lot of property. The merchants came in, they brought in workers. If it came to a vote, we'd be swamped."

"Who said anything about voting?"

"Isn't that the way people are elected to—to office?"

"How should I know? I'm no lawyer." Jagger grunted. "*You* were going to study law. Maybe you should have." He grimaced. "I never had any use for lawyers myself and that's one thing we can do without in this town, lawyers." He looked toward the office behind the desk. "Let's hear what Helen's got to say about this government business."

Helen Jagger had already heard them in the lobby and was coming out of the office toward them.

"Helen," began Jagger, "Chad and me've just been to a little meeting up the street. Seems like some of the businessmen want a government for Pawnee City——"

Helen looked at him sharply, then suddenly shifted to Chad Morgan. "I don't understand——"

"The merchants objected to what happened yesterday," said Morgan. "Although it seems they've been talking about this even before. They want law and order in Pawnee City."

"Nobody got hurt yesterday," growled Jagger. "Nobody's going to *get* hurt."

"Tom Alder killed a man night before last," reminded Morgan.

"That was a fight—a fair fight. It didn't concern anyone else."

"Two men were killed the day the first herd came into town," Morgan went on. "One of them was lynched by a mob."

"Dammit!" cried Jagger. "Whose side are you on, anyway?"

Morgan stiffened. "You've asked me that before. I'm on the side of what's right. This isn't your town any more, Joe."

"Your town?" snapped Jagger. "*Our* town!"

"You keep saying it's *your* town——"

"Dammit, so that's what's in your craw? I make a slip of the tongue."

"You make that slip a good many times."

"Chad's right, Joe," interposed Helen. "I've heard you say it. It's always you, not Chad—us. *You're* going to do this, that, not *we!*"

"A man can't think of what he's saying every damned minute," snorted Jagger. "All right, Pawnee City was my idea. But we've been partners from the moment I told you about it. I haven't held out anything. All the money that's come in is *ours*. Fifty-fifty, even Stephen. You can go into the bank any time and help yourself to half of whatever's there——"

"I can't, Joe. I may not be a lawyer, but I know that much. The bank money *isn't* ours."

"Why not? It's our bank."

"The money belongs to the depositors. Except perhaps the amount we put in to start things. That ten thousand——" A sudden frown came over Jagger's face and Morgan looked sharply at his partner. "It's still there, isn't it?"

Jagger's response was almost too quick. "Oh, sure, sure!"

"Our financial position is excellent," Helen Jagger added. "Our original debt will soon be liquidated, and——"

"What original debt?" asked Morgan.

"The fifty-some thousand we spent that we didn't have last spring," Jagger growled. "I told you we went into the hole."

"I thought that had been paid off."

"We've been paying it, two-three thousand every week. It's down around thirty thousand now."

Morgan looked at Jagger, then at Helen. "Just what is our financial position right now?"

"You can look at the books any time," replied Helen with a note of acerbity. "I'll be glad to explain things to you."

Jagger said nastily, "We weren't talking about money. Let's stick to the subject—this town-government business. I don't like your attitude about it."

"I don't like yours, Joe," Morgan suddenly flared back. "I've listened to you talk about *your* town, *your* hotel, *your* bank, *your* this and that. I haven't said anything. But I'm saying it now. I'm fed up."

"Chad!" cried Helen in sudden panic. "Don't!"

She was interrupted by her brother, who threw up a desisting hand.

"All right," he said harshly, "you've had your say. Now I'm going to have mine."

"Stop it, Joe, stop it," cried Helen almost hysterically. "You mustn't fight. You'll ruin everything."

"He's making the fight," continued Jagger hotly. "He's gotten a little too big for his britches and I'm going to cut him down to size." To Morgan: "Just because you ran a shindy on some drunken slobs don't think you can scare me."

"Cut it out, Joe!" warned Morgan tonelessly.

Helen sprang forward, caught Morgan's arm and tried to turn him away from her brother. "Chad, don't—don't do something we'll all be sorry for——" She tugged at him. "Please . . . for my sake . . . !" There were tears in her eyes and she was sobbing. "Don't, Chad, please . . . for me."

And Chad Morgan let himself be pulled away.

They were at the door before he was able to disengage her grip on him.

"All right, Helen," he said. "It's over."

But Helen, seeing her brother following them toward the door, gave Morgan a sudden push that almost knocked him off balance. "I'll talk to you later!" she cried and whirling, rushed toward her brother.

Morgan, looking over his shoulder as he went out of the hotel, saw her struggling to hold back Joe Jagger.

The man who held down the real-estate office had gone for the day. Morgan sat alone behind the desk, staring gloomily at the broken window, which had been patched with a sheet of cardboard. A buggy pulled up outside but Morgan was only vaguely aware of it. Then the real-estate office door was pushed open and Helen Jagger stood in the doorway.

"Something," she said clearly, "was said to me about taking a buggy ride out into the country. I've got the horse, I've got the buggy. I need the driver."

Morgan got to his feet. "I'm sorry, Helen——"

"You'll be sorrier if you don't come out and climb into the buggy. It's costing me fifty cents an hour."

Morgan went to her, started to reach for her, but she drew away. "Not here," she said archly. "And maybe not when we're alone in the buggy. I'm not that kind of a girl.

Which reminds me, what's the name of the little blonde at Kate Clarke's place?"

"I wouldn't know," grinned Morgan.

"Next you'll be asking me, who's Kate Clarke?"

"I'm not *that* blind."

She looked at him tantalizingly, then turned and went out of the door. Morgan followed. He helped her into the rig, backed the horse and they rolled swiftly down the street in the direction of the river, two miles away.

Helen sat very close to him and Morgan was quite conscious of it, but there was still in him the memory of the scene at the hotel that morning. Both remained silent until the last building of the town was behind them, then Helen said, "Do you know, I've never seen the river."

"It's not much of a river right now, but last spring when I rode this way to see if the Texans were coming, it wasn't a river—it was a lake, a lake more than ten miles across."

Morgan reached for the buggy whip and touched the flank of the horse. It broke into a swift trot that caused the buggy to bounce and jolt. Helen was thrown against him and he threw out a hand to support her. She leaned against him and he kept his arm about her, even when the horse began to ease off.

"You've a strong arm," Helen observed, after a moment or two.

"And a weak mind?"

"No!" Helen turned partly to look into his face in the fading light. "I didn't bring you out to quarrel, Chad. To make up."

"I know," he said. Then, after a pause: "I don't like it when we quarrel, Helen."

"Neither do I. I—I've felt terrible all day."

He suddenly turned to her and held her close. Her lips found his and they clung together in a tight embrace. When he finally released her, she exclaimed in chagrin.

During their embrace, the buggy had been taken by the horse into the camp of a half-dozen Texas cowboys, all of whom were now on their feet, watching Morgan and Helen.

"Oh!" cried Helen.

Morgan caught up the buggy whip, applied it to the horse and the buggy raced away. Yells and whistles followed them.

There were two or three more herds of longhorns between them and the river. There were several thousand Texas longhorns grazing and Morgan noted that the buffalo grass which had been so rich and green in the spring had now turned to a golden brown. It also seemed to have curled itself down close to the earth. The grass, he knew from having listened to the cattlemen, was extremely nutritious to the Texas longhorns as well as the buffalo. Trail-thin cattle could add a hundred pounds per steer in a little more than a week's peaceful grazing.

Dusk was falling when the buggy reached the river. A three-quarter moon appeared pale in the eastern sky. Morgan twisted the lines around a pole on the dashboard of the buggy. When he turned from the task, Helen was waiting for him, slipping easily into his arms.

Neither spoke for a few minutes, then Morgan, knowing it was his turn to open the "peace talks" said, "When are we going to take that trip to Kansas City?"

"I've been thinking about it all day," Helen replied. "Saturday."

"What's the matter with tomorrow?" he prodded.

"I can't, tomorrow. Joe wants the books——" She stopped, catching herself.

"All right," he said after a moment, "what does Joe want done with the books?"

"Chad," said Helen, "let's not talk about Joe now."

"You brought up his name."

"All right, I'm also telling you now I don't want to talk about him."

She kissed him lingeringly, but it was a forced kiss. She drew away, lowering her head for a moment. "It's no use, is it?" she asked, low.

"I wish," Morgan said, "that Joe wasn't your brother."

"But he is."

"I know."

"Chad," said Helen poignantly, "we're not children.

You had a quarrel with him, but is that any reason *we* should quarrel?"

"Tell me just one thing," he said. "Did Joe suggest this?"

She stiffened. "If that's what you think——"

"It isn't, Helen," he said quickly. "I guess I shouldn't have asked that question."

"It was *my* idea, Chad!"

He reached for her, but her body was unyielding. She said, with a note of bitterness, "It's that Texas tomboy, Chad. She's come between us."

"That's ridiculous!" he exclaimed.

"Is it? Then why did you never talk about her?"

"Because she meant nothing. She was—just someone —I had met in Texas. I don't believe I ever mentioned Tom Alder to you, although I had met him in Texas and he was of much more importance to me—and Joe—than Cass Simcoe."

"Tom Alder? That's the man who killed another man the other night? Why should he be important to you and Joe?"

Morgan realized that he had made another mistake and could have bitten off his tongue. "Alder's a former Confederate."

"So's everybody else who comes from Texas."

"Alder's a Missourian—a former Quantrill man."

"A guerrilla?"

"One of the best—or worst—of them. He's reputed to have been the best shot in Quantrill's outfit."

"But how is he important to you and Joe?"

"Joe and I were in the last fight of the war—after the war was already supposed to be over. The Sixteenth Illinois caught up with Shelby's rearguard—mostly former Missouri guerrillas. We gave them a mauling."

"Alder was one of them?"

Morgan hesitated. "I have an idea he was, although he has never said so. He doesn't say a lot."

Helen exclaimed, "You think he's dangerous—to you and Joe?"

"No, I don't think so."

"We don't want men like Alder in this town. Can't you get rid of him?"

"How? You forget, there's no official authority in Pawnee City. If we had a peace officer, a marshal, or sheriff——"

Helen exclaimed in annoyance. "Now we're back on that subject! Chad—what's wrong with you? Or is it me? We come out here to take a ride and—and watch the moon—and we're at each other's throats."

"We talk too much," Morgan said harshly. He caught her roughly and drew her into a hard embrace.

Later, when it was very dark and the lights of Pawnee City were twinkling like bright stars, as they approached them, Helen once more got back onto the dangerous subject—Joe Jagger.

"You'll make up with him, won't you, Chad?"

"Of course," said Chad Morgan. "We're in this together, for better or worse." He chuckled. "And *you'll* be saying that to me next Saturday."

Chapter Twenty-One

The train, which now came to Pawnee City every other day, deposited at the depot three passengers who were to have an important effect upon the lives of Joe Jagger and Chad Morgan, as well as on the prosperity and development of Pawnee City.

One of the men was none other than Nathan Foss, president of the Kansas & Colorado Railroad.

The second man was the most famous man of the trio. He was a tall, lean man with the coldest blue eyes. He wore his light yellow hair extremely long; his mustaches were also long, the ends of them drooping down over his jaws. He had large, strong white teeth from which his lips peeled back whenever he essayed a frosty smile. His name was Jack Mason, but he was universally known as Wild Jack.

He wore striped trousers, a Prince Albert and a florid vest. He looked like a gambler and indeed spent much of his time gambling, but his fame came from another art . . . he was reputed to be the greatest revolver shot in the country. His speed of draw, his amazing marksmanship were already legendary west of the Missouri River.

He had fought the war on the side of the North, although his activities were somewhat irregular, having been attached to a company of soldiers who called themselves Kansas militia, but had been known even before the war as Jayhawkers. (Not to be confused with the Jayhawkers of southwestern Missouri, who were in reality nothing more or less than border ruffians, thieves, and cutthroats.)

The third man of the trio was Judson Drake and his name was known to only one resident of Pawnee City, Charles Fesler, who had written the letter that had brought Drake to Pawnee City.

Nathan Foss, having left his luggage on the train, where it was quite properly being watched by the conductor, strolled easily to the Drovers Hotel.

He found Joe Jagger behind the desk, counting the cash in the till.

"Mr. Foss!" cried Jagger. "It's a pleasure to see you."

Foss grunted. "You call this a city? Why, it's nothing but a collection of claptrap buildings."

"But it brought *you* here," chuckled Jagger. "Or was it the two thousand carloads of cattle that I've shipped on your railroad since April?"

Foss grunted again. "That's one of the reasons. I've lost money on those shipments."

"What?"

"Cattle make poor freight. They've got to be tended, they damage the cars. The railroad loses several dollars on each car of cattle we handle."

"I find that hard to believe," Jagger said indignantly.

"Nevertheless, it's true and we simply can't continue, not at the present freight rates."

"In other words, you want to raise your rates? The commission houses and the meat packers won't like it."

"I know they won't. And—ah—as a matter of fact, I *can't* raise their prices. We have agreements with them, contracts . . ." Foss paused as the scowl grew on Jagger's face. "The money will have to come from another source. You, Mr. Jagger."

"Now wait a minute," Jagger said truculently. "I have an agreement, too, an agreement signed by you. Five dollars for every carload of freight shipped from Pawnee City."

"The railroad is canceling the agreement."

"The railroad!" gasped Jagger. "*You're* the railroad!"

"I happen to be the president. But I am responsible to a board of directors and they have advised me that we can no longer honor the agreement."

"You can't do that!" shouted Jagger. "I'll sue you!"

"That is your privilege, Mr. Jagger."

"It'll be my privilege—and pleasure!"

"Of course," Nathan Foss went on, "the moment you start suit, the railroad will close down the depot at this—ah—point."

"You wouldn't dare!" gasped Jagger. "You're doing too much business with the merchants of this town."

"Oh, they wouldn't be too inconvenienced. They can freight their things over from the depot we will erect five miles east of town, or the other one we are thinking of building five miles west. . . ." He smiled wolfishly. "You knew, of course, that track construction is being resumed next week?"

"I didn't know it," Jagger said in a strained voice.

"Oh, yes, the construction crews will be coming along in a day or two. And we'll be needing most of our rolling stock to transport ties, rails, supplies and equipment."

"Mr. Foss," said Jagger thickly, "what would happen if I waived that five-dollar-a-carload fee?"

Nathan Foss pursed up his lips. "Why, that's very generous of you, Mr. Jagger. It really is and I am sure my board of directors would appreciate it greatly." He shook his head sadly. "You have no idea of the tremendous amount of money it costs to build—and operate—a railroad. Sometimes I scarcely know where to turn for money. Yes, Mr. Jagger, your generous offer would certainly be appreciated by my colleagues. Mmm, I have a suggestion . . . I believe you are charging the cattle drovers—ahem—one dollar per—ah—cow, for the use of the stockyards. The stockyards are a great convenience to the drovers and I know that they do not object to paying that trifling fee. They probably would not even object to paying—ah—a dollar *and a half* per head. Do you think so?"

"They'll *have* to pay it!" snapped Jagger.

"Quite so. And—ah—if you could see your way to giving, or shall we say, paying that extra fifty cents to—ah—me . . . ?"

Jagger groaned. "You, or the railroad?"

Nathan Foss laughed mirthlessly. "Didn't you say just a moment ago that I—ah—was the railroad?"

"I guess you're the railroad, all right. You'll want it in cash, I suppose? Not a check, or a draft on the bank."

"Ah, yes, the bank. I had forgotten that you also have a bank. You've been fortunate here, Mr. Jagger, very fortunate. This magnificent hotel, your own bank and—ah—the townsite."

"I waive the carload fee," Jagger said tightly, "and I'll pay you fifty cents for every head of cattle going through the stockyards. But that's all."

"Yes, Mr. Jagger, admirable. A good arrangement for both of us." He coughed gently. "Only one thing more ——"

"No!" roared Jagger. "Not one cent more."

"It's the land, Mr. Jagger," Foss pursued. "We have so much of it and the—ah—my board of directors has complained that we've been able to sell so little of it. They've complained bitterly and if you—ah—could see your way clear to purchasing a few sections——"

"How many sections?"

"Well, let's say five thousand acres."

"At how much an acre?"

"Ten dollars."

"It isn't worth ten cents an acre!"

"Oh, but it is, Mr. Jagger. Perhaps, when it was just wild prairie, it wasn't worth ten cents an acre. But now—now there's a town here. Values have gone up. This land you bought right here for—what was it?—two bottles of whiskey?—why, someone told me you've been selling twenty-foot building lots for a thousand, even two thousand dollars."

"Mr. Foss," said Jagger desperately, "I haven't got fifty thousand dollars."

"Dear me, with a bank of your own, a hotel, a saloon, the shipping yards—all that money rolling in every day of the week . . . why, I should imagine fifty thousand would be but a trifle to a man of your means."

"It's a shakedown, Foss. I won't pay it."

"I'm sorry to hear that, Mr. Jagger, because you've been so reasonable about everything else. Dear me, here I have been offering you a—a virtual partnership, so to speak, a sort of you-help-me, and I-help-you proposition, and you reject my offer." He shook his head sadly. "And

I did promise my wife that I—ah—would repay her some
of the money she had loaned me. She will be very disap-
pointed." A sudden note of hardness came into the railroad
man's voice. "And so will I, Mr. Jagger!"

At the moment that Nathan Foss was putting the squeeze
on Joe Jagger, Charles Fesler, the newspaper publisher,
was introducing the second new arrival in Pawnee City to
Harlow Tarbox, the proprietor of The St. Louis Store.

"Mr. Judson Drake of Kansas City, Mr. Tarbox," Fesler said proudly. "Or perhaps I should have said, Judge
Drake."

"No, Charlie," protested Judson Drake. "I'm merely
Mister Judson Drake, attorney at law. I haven't been on
the bench in over a year now."

"I'm very happy to make your acquaintance, Judge,"
said Tarbox fervently. "I guess Fesler told you about our
problem."

"He outlined it in some detail in his letter. You want
to establish a government in this community—and a very
thriving community it seems to be—and you want my ad-
vice on how to do it. It's really quite simple, Mr. Tarbox.
You petition the legislature to create a new county of a
certain amount of territory surrounding this community,
naming Pawnee City as the new county seat. You then hold
elections and elect a sheriff, a board of supervisors——"

"Whoa, wait a minute!" cried Harlow Tarbox. "You're
way ahead of us. We haven't even got a town government
here. That's the first—and most important thing."

"Of course, sir, but that's a comparatively simple matter. You merely elect your local officials and then——"

"How? How do we do that?"

Fesler exclaimed, "They don't know a thing, Judge.
You'll have to spell it out. Right from the very beginning.
One—there's no law here of any kind, no supervisors, no
nothing. No organization of anything. Two men think
they own this town—consider it their private property.
They think they have the right to make the laws and rule
this town——".

"Oh, my dear Charles!" exclaimed Judson Drake. "Not in this day and age. Feudalism passed with the Middle Ages. Tut-tut, I see where we'll really have to start at the beginning."

"You'll do it for us, Judge?" asked Tarbox. "You'll stay here long enough to get it started?"

"As it happens, Mr. Tarbox," the judge said, beaming, "I have been rather tired of city life and when I received Friend Charlie's letter, it occurred to me that this might be just the sort of thing that would interest me. A brand-new community, a growing town. Of course, I would lose by it financially, but the idea appeals to me very much. I might just decide to settle down here, open a law office and call this my home."

"You won't be in a law office long, Judge," said Fesler. "You get us a county and you'll be the judge—or maybe you'd rather go to the legislature—"

The third arrival on the train that day did not bother to stop at the hotel and engage a room. He walked from the depot, past the hotel and entered The Longhorn Saloon. He had a drink, surveyed the games that were played even so early in the day and in a little while produced some money and proceeded to play faro.

He played for five minutes and then said to the dealer, "Mister, I don't like that card box of yours."

The dealer stared at the new player in astonishment. "Who the devil do you think you are?"

"My name," said the new player, "happens to be Jack Mason——"

"Wild Jack!" exclaimed the dealer in a tone of awe.

"Yes, sir," said Wild Jack, "and I've played a bit of faro in my time, never liked a card box that showed so little of the cards. I like a nice, open box." Wild Jack smiled coldly. "I am not suggesting that you are dishonest, but it makes me feel better to have everything open and above-board."

Tom Alder, who had been having a quiet drink at the bar, came over and watched the dealer replace his regular faro box with a new one from his bag, which was constructed more along the lines of what Wild Jack had suggested.

Alder's eyes remained on Wild Jack and the latter suddenly turned to him.

"You're staring at me, sir!"

"Cost anything to look?" asked Alder mildly. "You're a famous man. I've heard about you."

"My pleasure, sir. And your name . . . ?"

Alder shrugged deprecatingly. "Alder."

"Not . . . Tom Alder?"

"Yes."

"Well," said Wild Jack, somewhat at a lack for words, "I must admit I have heard of you, too. Although not favorably." He essayed a weak smile. "We were on opposite sides during the recent conflict."

"Once or twice," said Alder. "We gave you hell a couple of times, I believe."

"Not in a fair fight," snapped Wild Jack. *"We* fought in the open and you, sir, you belonged to a gang of bushwhackers."

Alder smiled, but there was no warmth in the smile. "And a good day to *you*—sir!" He nodded and turning, walked out of the saloon.

Wild Jack looked after him.

"Bushwhacker!" he said again.

Chapter Twenty-Two

Nathan Foss left Pawnee City the following day. In one of his fine leather valises he carried a parcel containing fifty thousand dollars.

"We can't tell Chad," Joe Jagger said to his sister who, of course, had to know about the transaction with her erstwhile employer. "He'd raise an unholy row about it."

"I don't see how we can withhold it from him," Helen said worriedly. "What if he decides to look at the books?"

"You've got to keep him from doing that."

"That horrible man!" exclaimed Helen. "Foss, I mean. He'll be buying that fat wife of his some more diamonds."

"You'll be buying diamonds, Helen," her brother assured her. "It's a hard blow but we'll weather it. The money's coming in and we just need a little time. And we've got to sell some more property. Lots." He grimaced. "I'll persuade Chad to sell some more of that farmland. Ten dollars an acre, eh? Well, it's only cost us a dollar an acre. That's a thousand per cent profit."

Helen suddenly groaned. "I promised to go to Kansas City with Chad on Saturday."

"To get married?" Jagger frowned. "I wish you two *were* married, but"——he hesitated——"I'd feel safer if the books were taken care of. You'll want a honeymoon of a week or two—and you should have it—but what'll I do with the books while you're gone?"

"I know," said Helen reluctantly. "The wedding will have to be postponed for a few weeks. Chad won't like it."

"He'll have to like it," said Jagger.

Helen sighed.

On the surface, things between Chad Morgan and Joe

Jagger were as they had been before the quarrel. Less demonstrative than his partner, Morgan was able to resume his daily contacts with Joe Jagger with no outward display of hostility. Jagger greeted him and talked to him with a note of restraint, intermingled with bursts of overfriendliness.

Morgan, of course, did not know of what had passed between Nathan Foss and his partner. He had seen Foss, had spoken to him briefly, but he had left the railroad magnate in the hands of Jagger and his sister.

Morgan was not aware of the arrival in Pawnee City of Judson Drake. Strangers were coming to Pawnee City almost every day of the week. Some came by train, some rode in on horseback, some came in carriages, buggies and even muleback.

Some of the strangers, the more affluent ones, stayed at the hotel, others camped out on the prairie, or shared the chuck-wagon food and blankets of the trail drivers.

The advert of Fesler's newspaper created only a mild flurry. Everyone in town already knew what had transpired the day the Texans "treed" the town of Pawnee City. Morgan himself had already been one of the outstanding citizens of the town, one of the "owners" of the townsite. The real old-timers of Pawnee City, those who had been there when the town officially opened two months before, already knew of his physical prowess. The reports of his quelling of the first killer in Pawnee City and his subsequent attempt to prevent the lynching, even though it had failed, had lost nothing in the telling and retelling.

Morgan was a formidable man; everyone in Pawnee City knew that.

Things were moving behind the scenes. Morgan was aware of that. He would enter The St. Louis Store and find Tarbox in discussion with Buffington, Fesler, Wakeman or another Pawnee City businessman. There would be a brief, awkward pause, then they would talk casually to Morgan of trivial matters.

Morgan was no longer in the confidence of the businessmen and they kept the account of their machinations pretty well undercover, until the second issue of *The Pawnee City Lance* came out.

It was all there:

"PAWNEE CITY TO FORM CITY GOVERNMENT," read the headline. The three-column article told the entire story. Under the guidance of the noted former judge of Kansas City, Mr. Judson Drake, papers of incorporation had been drawn up. Pawnee City would be a city. Business establishments would be taxed to bear the expense of governing the city. A temporary board of five supervisors was offering a slate of candidates to the voters of Pawnee City, in an election to be held August first—a bare week from the announcement.

On the slate were seven names:

For Mayor:

Charles Fesler

For Justice of the Peace:

Judson Drake

For Supervisors:

Alfred Buffington
Harlow Tarbox
John Thompson
Oliver Wakeman
Chad Morgan

There was only the one slate. Election of all the men named on it was a certainty.

Newspapers, fresh off Fesler's press, were distributed among the business houses by Fesler himself. Morgan, in the real-estate office when he received the paper, seated himself at his desk and waited for the explosion.

It came within ten minutes, Joe Jagger having received his newspaper at the hotel. It took about eight minutes for Fesler, on his rounds, to reach the hotel from the real-estate office.

Jagger came storming into the real-estate office, the newspaper crushed in a savage grip.

"Damn you, Morgan, for a dirty double-crossing bastard!" Jagger raged.

Morgan kicked back his chair and sprang to his feet. "Now, hold it, Joe! I didn't know a damn thing about this until just ten minutes ago."

"You lie like hell!" snarled Jagger. "You've been conniving with these bastards behind my back. Your name's on the list of candidates."

"They didn't ask me."

Savagely, Jagger threw the crumpled newspaper into Morgan's face. He followed through with a smashing blow that caught Morgan flush on the jaw and knocked him backwards over the chair.

Morgan hit the floor heavily, rolled over and got to his knees. In that position he shook his head to clear away the haze before his eyes and stared up at Joe Jagger.

"Get up!" yelled Jagger. "Get up and take the beating I should have given you long ago."

The man who took care of the real-estate office stepped into the breach. "Mr. Jagger," he began, "you can't——"

Jagger gave the man a backhanded blow that sent him spinning. He stepped in swiftly to meet Morgan as the latter came to his feet. Another savage blow caught Morgan squarely in the mouth, crushing his lips. He tasted blood, gasped as Jagger's left caught him in the stomach and bent him forward.

A roaring filled Morgan's ears. He had as yet landed no blow on Jagger and it was doubtful if he would be able to do so; Jagger's sudden, murderous attack had virtually incapacitated him. He was only vaguely aware that he had thrown up his hands instinctively, but a sharp pain suddenly shot up his arm into his shoulder. He was not even aware that he had lashed out at Jagger, but there was a moment's respite of Jagger's savage attack and Morgan gasped in great lungfuls of air.

Then Jagger was back at him. A jolting blow struck him in the stomach, a fist crashed him on the side of his head. He staggered against the wall, ricocheted off it into another crashing fist.

Then he was down again on hands and knees. Whether he would have been able to resume the fight was doubtful, had Jagger stopped his attack at that moment, but so great was Jagger's fury, so intent was he on crippling Morgan that he overdid it. Not content with smashing Morgan to his knees, he now used his boot to kick him in the ribs.

A gasp was torn from Morgan. He fell over sidewards, rolled over and, calling upon his last resources, came up to his feet. He was unsteady, but his eyes were suddenly clear.

He saw Jagger closing in on him; he struck out, knew that he had reached Jagger's face and hit again—and again. Jagger gave way before him and Morgan was suddenly doing the crowding.

Jagger was still strong, however. The blows delivered by Morgan were bruising, but were delivered by a weakened man. Jagger retreated a few steps, then with his back almost in the open doorway, he made a sudden stand. He took a blow in the face, then suddenly threw out both hands and wrapped them about Morgan, trying to wrestle him to the floor.

Morgan knew that he had already taken too much of a beating to match his strength against that of Joe Jagger. He gasped as his partner's grip tightened about him. By a tremendous pull, he got one arm free, thrust the heel of his palm under Jagger's chin and pushed with all his strength.

Jagger's breath began to labor. With a sudden cry he released Morgan and lowering his head, tried to butt him. He did not know that he had turned Morgan completely around in the struggle, that it was now Morgan's back that was toward the open door.

Morgan, trying to leap aside, took the butt upon his hip. It was a staggering blow, but delivered with Morgan moving aside. Jagger caromed from him, went out through the open door headfirst.

He landed heavily on the wooden sidewalk in front of

the office. Morgan followed and as Jagger climbed to his feet, he sent a smashing blow into Jagger's face that sent the man back against the hitchrail. He came away from the rail, ran headlong into Morgan's fists.

Jagger was down then on both knees. Morgan, neglecting to step back, found his knees suddenly grabbed by Jagger and then he, too, crashed to the wooden sidewalk. Jagger swarmed over him. Morgan squirmed out from under, took a knee in the pit of his stomach and rolled aside. Jagger followed him and again caught Morgan. Clinched together, the two rolled over and over under the hitchrail, out into the dust of the street.

Both men were using everything now: knees, elbows, fists, their heads.

The struggle was too savage to last much longer, however. Morgan, tearing loose from Jagger, found he was so weakened that he could not rise to his feet. On his knees, he waited for Jagger to rise. Jagger came up, lurched toward Morgan and the latter hit him with his last ounce of strength.

Jagger went over sidewards, kicked once and lay still.

The fight was over.

It was another moment or two, however, before Morgan could raise his head. He saw then that at least fifty citizens of Pawnee City had crowded around and were silently watching him.

It was Fesler, the newspaperman, who stepped out of the crowd. "Here," he said, "gimme your hand."

He reached down, caught Morgan's hand and helped him to get to his feet.

"Nice fight," he commented laconically.

"Your fault," panted Morgan. "That damn newspaper of yours—"

"I take it your friend didn't like the piece about the city government," chuckled Fesler.

"I didn't like it either," snapped Morgan, "using my name as a candidate without telling me about it."

"Oh, that!" said Fesler.

Fesler was a much smaller man than Morgan, but the

latter was in no condition to turn on him. He had beaten Jagger, but he had licked himself in the struggle.

He turned, saw that Jagger was moving. A groan came from him and Morgan dropped to one knee to try to turn Jagger over on his back. He was in that position when Helen Jagger came rushing up. Her face was white, drained of all blood, her eyes were flashing like the eyes of a cornered bobcat.

"Get away from him!" she said savagely. "Take your dirty hands away from him."

Morgan rocked back on his heels. "He started the fight, Helen——"

She gave him a look of utter loathing and contempt. *"I hate you!"* she said through clenched teeth.

She dropped to her knees, slipped one hand under Jagger's head and raised him to a sitting position.

"Joe," she sobbed, as Morgan turned away.

Chapter Twenty-Three

It was an hour before Morgan was able to go to the Drovers Hotel and get his few belongings from his room. He carried them to the real-estate office and set them down on the floor in the rear. After a while he went to Tarbox's store and bought a cot and some blankets.

A clerk sold him the things, Tarbox being away from the store.

It was Tarbox, however, who visited him at the real-estate office shortly after six, when Morgan was alone.

Tarbox pretended not to notice the half-closed eye on Morgan, the welts and bruises on his face. "Charlie Fesler tells me Jagger didn't like the piece in the paper."

"Why didn't you come to me before you ran it?" exclaimed Morgan. "You had no right to put up my name for supervisor——"

"You're saying you won't take it?"

"How could I? My interests are opposed to yours."

"Are they, Mr. Morgan?" Tarbox asked quietly. "You've had a fight with Jagger——"

"A fight that you brought on."

Tarbox hesitated, then shook his head. "A fight that had to come sooner or later. Unless I misjudge you badly, and I don't think I do. You and Jagger are of different breeds."

"Don't be too sure of that. We were together all through the war. We shared the same blanket many a time."

Tarbox continued to shake his head. "We're holding a meeting this evening," he said, "in Buffington's store. We'd like you to come."

"And Jagger? You've asked *him?*"

"No." Tarbox looked at him worriedly. "You intend to make it up with him?"

"Mr. Tarbox," said Morgan quietly, "you knew that Joe Jagger and I were partners. But did you also know that his sister and I are going to be married?"

"Some talk about it."

"I suppose," Morgan said angrily, "that the talk is we're being married because she happens to be my partner's sister. That's true—but it's also *not* true. Helen Jagger and I happen to be in love with each other."

"I was in the crowd when she came up. You'll forgive me, Mr. Morgan, but I couldn't help hearing what she said to you—half the town heard it. She didn't ask who was right or wrong, she sided with her brother."

"What else could she do?"

"I don't know, Mr. Jagger. I don't know the young lady." Tarbox nodded brusquely and went out of the real-estate office.

A Chinese had come to Pawnee City a week previously and for two thousand dollars, paid to Joe Jagger in bright, shiny double eagles, had purchased a twenty-foot claptrap shack. He had opened a lunchroom only the day before.

Morgan, although still somewhat sick at his stomach, decided shortly after Tarbox left the real-estate office that some soup might help to ease his queasiness.

He went to the lunchroom and ordered a bowl of soup. He spooned in half of it and felt worse. Leaving a quarter on the counter, he left the lunchroom and stood outside for a moment. He was about to cross the street when he saw Fesler, the newspaperman, going toward Buffington's store.

He grimaced and crossed the street. He was a dozen feet behind Fesler, when the newspaperman reached the door of the hardware store. Fesler saw him then.

"Ah, Mr. Morgan," he said cheerfully. "You're coming to the meeting."

Morgan nodded and they went into the store. With Buffington at the rear were Oliver Wakeman, who ran a dry-goods store, Tarbox and Judson Drake, although Morgan did not yet know Drake.

Tarbox hurried forward to meet Morgan. "Glad you

decided to come, Mr. Morgan," he said. "I don't believe you've met Judson Drake."

"The new justice of the peace?"

"A little premature," Drake said. He extended a flabby hand to Morgan. "Delighted, Mr. Morgan."

John Thompson, one of the early settlers of Pawnee City, who ran the livery stable, came into the store.

"Well, gentlemen," Fesler began, then, "shall we get to the business?"

"One moment," interrupted the lawyer, Drake. "I would like to have it established clearly that Mr. Morgan's presence here signifies that he is—ah—sympathetic to our group."

"I take that as a fact," quickly said Buffington. He looked anxiously at Morgan.

Morgan said, "I came here for one reason—and one reason only. I want to know why you put my name on your slate of candidates without asking my permission?" He sent a quick look around the group.

No one answered.

"I'll narrow it down," said Morgan. "*Who* suggested that I would consider being a candidate?"

Fesler drew a deep breath. "Very well, Mr. Morgan, I guess I'll have to answer that. *I* forwarded your name."

"Why?"

"You want the truth?"

"I intend to get it."

"Very well, you and your partner, or is it ex-partner? have a certain nuisance value. Your election to the board of supervisors—I am giving it to you bluntly—is a sop to the firm of Jagger & Morgan." He added hastily, "Mind you, we do not recognize your claim to having a voice in the government of this city——"

"We don't want trouble," interposed Buffington worriedly. "That's why we feel that we need a government. To stop trouble, trouble that——"

"You think Jagger's going to take this lying down?" snapped Morgan. "Why do you think he and I fought this afternoon? He thinks I'm siding with your group against him."

"Gentlemen, gentlemen," said Judson Drake loudly. "Let's not start this meeting with recriminations. It is apparent that Mr. Morgan is *not* in sympathy with the aims of this group. I therefore request that he leave and permit us to get on with the business at hand."

"If I walk out now," Morgan said grimly, "I'll fight you to the last ditch—and I assure you, you won't like the way I fight."

"Morgan," snapped Fesler, "I don't scare worth a damn."

"A moment!" Buffington said loudly. "I think I know Mr. Morgan better than anyone here. At least, I know him longer. He's a fair man. I *know* that. I believe he has something to say and I would like to hear him—before we wind up wrangling among ourselves. Mr. Morgan!"

"All right," Morgan said, "I think you've gone about this thing too fast and I think you've handled it badly. I could have brought Jagger around. Now I don't know. As far as I'm concerned, I believe this town needs a government. I, myself, would support the government—if it was a proper government. But let's not forget one thing. Not one of you—or me—would be here tonight if Joe Jagger had not conceived the idea of establishing a town at this spot. If he had not put up his own money . . . and persuaded me to go in with him, there would be no Pawnee City today."

"We'll give him a vote of thanks," snapped Fesler.

"You'll do more than that. You'll elect him mayor."

Fesler's roar drowned out the sudden hubbub of comment of the others in the group. "Jagger, mayor!" shouted Fesler. "I'd rather vote for John Wilkes Booth!"

Morgan waited a moment until the idea had been thoroughly assimilated, then he went on, "Fesler, you're the newest man in this town——"

"What's that got to do with it?" cried Fesler. "You ain't been here so long yourself. We're all new."

"I'm stepping out," Morgan said. "I want no office. I've made my talk. I want no public office. I will, however, go along with you, support you to the limit. On one condition . . . that you elect Joe Jagger mayor of Pawnee City."

"Don't you try dictating to us," blustered Fesler. "You're as bad as Jagger."

Buffington said, "No, Charles, I won't go along with that. Mr. Morgan is right. Regardless of what we think of him personally, Joe Jagger did start Pawnee City. The office of mayor is more or less honorary. The supervisors will have the real authority. Since Mr. Morgan is willing to forego office, I think the least you can do is step down—into a supervisor's post. I say, let's have Mr. Jagger head our ticket——"

The others listened carefully to Alfred Buffington, and Fesler, sensing the trend, looked around the group. His eyes remained longest on the face of Judson Drake. The lawyer nodded slightly.

"All right," growled Fesler, "I think it's a mistake, but if that's what you want, I'll go along."

At that point, Morgan left the meeting.

Outside, he walked back to the real-estate office. It was getting dark. He looked for a long moment at the lights in the hotel, then shaking his head, went inside.

He struck a match, found a wall lamp and lighted it. It was then he saw the white envelope on the realtor's desk. He picked it up. His name was on it and he tore the envelope open.

There was a short note inside: *"Mr. Morgan: Please call at the hotel at your earliest convenience, for the purpose of dissolving the firm of Jagger & Morgan."*

There was no signature, but the note appeared to have been written by a woman.

Morgan was not surprised.

Chapter Twenty-Four

Morgan turned down the lamp and started for the door. Before he reached it he turned back and went to his cot at the rear of the room. He opened his carpetbag, reached into it and brought out the Navy gun that he had carried throughout the war, and during his trip to Texas the winter before. He stuck it behind the waistband of his trousers and again went to the door. Then exclaiming angrily, he took the gun and carried it back, tossing it on his bed.

He went outside and walked swiftly to the hotel.

The night clerk had just come on duty, but there was a light on in the office behind the desk. The door was ajar. Morgan crossed to it, saw that Helen Jagger and Joe were in the room.

"Come in, Mr. Morgan," said Helen coolly. "My brother has asked me to speak for him."

Morgan closed the door. Helen sat behind the rough desk, Jagger on a chair beside her. Jagger's face was as puffed and bruised as Morgan's own, possibly cut a little more.

He did not look at Morgan. He kept his eyes focused on a ledger before Helen.

"My brother," Helen went on, "does not care to discuss any other topic than the one for which we summoned you here. Namely, the dissolving of the firm of Jagger & Morgan."

"Ask your brother," Morgan said, feeling ridiculous even as he spoke, "how the firm can be dissolved? Does he expect me to buy him out, or does he intend to buy my share?"

"My brother is not in a position to buy your half interest in the firm," Helen Jagger said stiffly, "and since I am the

keeper of the records, I know that you are not in a position
to buy him out."

"Just what *is* my position?"

"I will read you the figures." She dropped her eyes to
the books. "Assets:

"Item 1. The townsite of Pawnee City, or as much of it
as still remains unsold, consisting of business
and residential lots. Value $200,000."

"Bought," said Morgan, "for twenty dollars and two
bottles of whiskey."

Jagger uttered a hoarse exclamation and half rose from
his chair, but then he caught himself and sat down again.
Helen continued as if there had been no interruption.

"Item 2. Approximately 1,000 acres of prairie land ad-
jacent to Pawnee City. Value $10,000.
"Item 3. Five thousand acres of prairie land, recently
purchased, value $50,000."

"I'll be damned!" exclaimed Morgan. "When did we ac-
quire that?"

"Mr. Jagger purchased it as an investment for the firm
of Jagger & Morgan.

"Item 4. The Drovers Hotel, value $25,000.
"Item 5. The Longhorn Saloon, value $25,000.
"Item 6. The Pawnee City Bank, value $50,000.
"Item 7. Stockyards and loading pens, value $50,000.
"Item 8. Six business buildings, vacant or leased, value
$50,000."

Helen paused to take a deep breath. "Total assets, $460,-
000." She picked up another sheet of paper: "Liabilities,
$31,650 owed various firms in Kansas City, from building
of property in Pawnee City. Various and sundry miscel-
laneous bills, $12,550.62."

Morgan said, "Well, I put up twelve thousand, five hundred in cash. I'll sell out my interest for fifty thousand
cash——"

"I have already told you," Helen said patiently, "that Mr. Jagger is not in a position to buy you out. He prefers to *divide* the assets——"

"And the debts?"

"Since he took the responsibility of incurring them, he will assume them."

"All right," Morgan said, "how do we divide? Straight down the line? He takes the hotel, I take the bank—and so on?"

"Mr. Jagger will take the bank," Helen declared. "He will also take the hotel——"

"And the shipping pens and stockyards?"

"Mr. Jagger will take them, since he alone knows how to operate them."

"Oh, fine," said Morgan. "My partner gets the assets that produce a revenue. I suppose he will also take The Longhorn Saloon?"

"Tell Mr. Morgan that I've had enough of this talk," snarled Joe Jagger.

Morgan drew a deep breath. "All right, Miss Jagger, suppose *you* tell me how Mr. Jagger wants to divide."

"The hotel," Helen said, "the saloon, the bank, the stockyards and loading pens AND the six business buildings have a total value of $200,000. Mr. Jagger says he will accept these assets and assume the bills and debts. He believes he is being more than fair in permitting you to have the unimproved property in Pawnee City, the six thousand acres of farmland, with a total valuation of $260,000."

"Tell Mr. Jagger I accept his generous offer," Morgan said tautly. "He can have the papers drawn up."

"Very well, Mr. Morgan," Helen said. "You may consider the partnership dissolved, as of today. We understand that a lawyer is now a resident of Pawnee City and I will have him prepare the necessary papers tomorrow."

She closed the ledger. "Good evening, Mr. Morgan."

"Good evening," said Morgan coldly. He went to the door, then with his hand on the knob, he turned. "Will you tell your brother that I also wish him a pleasant evening?"

"Damn!" swore Jagger, leaping to his feet.

Morgan went out.

In midafternoon of the following day, Judson Drake came to the real-estate office, where Morgan had now established himself. "Mr. Morgan," he said, "I am here as the representative of Mr. Joseph Jagger. May I have a few minutes of your time—privately?"

"Get yourself a beer, Hackett," Morgan told the realtor.

The man went out and Judson Drake produced two sheets of folded foolscap. "You understand, Mr. Morgan, I am acting merely as Mr. Jagger's representative. It is not within my province to say that I approve or disapprove of any of the terms of this document. I was informed that you had agreed to them and——"

"Where do I sign?"

"Here," said Drake, indicating. "But aren't you going to read it?"

"I'll read my copy later," said Morgan. He caught up a pen and scrawled his name on the pages.

Judson Drake picked up the sheet and stowed it away in his pocket. "May I now say privately, Mr. Morgan, that I highly approve of your attitude in the matter we had under discussion last night?"

"Does Jagger approve?" Morgan asked thinly.

"He has accepted the office of mayor."

"I thought he would," said Morgan drily.

Chapter Twenty-Five

Joe Jagger and the slate of candidates were elected on August first. Which was no surprise to anyone in Pawnee City, since there had been no opposition slate. The vote was very light, for no one aside from the businessmen had any interest in the election.

The day following, a Texas cowboy galloped his horse up and down the street. Of course he also discharged his revolver a number of times. He aimed mainly at the blue sky but he was rather drunk and one of his shots went wild and struck a horse tied to the hitchrail in front of The Longhorn Saloon.

The horse happened to be a newly purchased mount, belonging to Wild Jack Mason, who spent about four hours every afternoon and about the same time every evening, playing faro in The Longhorn. He also spent a few hours in between at The Texas Saloon.

Someone told Wild Jack that his horse had been wounded by a stray bullet. Wild Jack waited until the faro dealer had gone through the deck, from soda to hock, then went out and examined his injured horse. He found that the bullet had gone through a leg of the animal, crippling it.

Wild Jack, being a man of mercy, sent a bullet crashing through the head of his horse. Then he went up the street and found the cowboy who had shot his horse, reeling into The Texas Saloon.

Wild Jack called him some names. The cowboy went for his gun and Wild Jack placed a bullet neatly between his eyes.

Friends of the dead cowboy gathered within a half hour. They formed a posse and searched the three saloons and a number of stores, but Wild Jack had somehow disappeared from his regular haunts and the cowboys were unable to find him. They compromised by galloping up and down the street, en masse, and smashing virtually every window on the street. The cowboys were mostly sober and their marksmanship was rather good.

They finally rode out of town, with the body of their dead comrade sprawled across his horse.

Wild Jack reappeared later that evening, and won two hundred dollars playing faro.

Chad Morgan knew nothing of the events of the day, for he had been out on the prairie riding until late afternoon when he returned to the office and found every pane of the front window shattered. Hackett, the real-estate man, then recounted the happenings of an otherwise quiet day.

Two days later, a crew of workmen began constructing a building of heavy planking, the Pawnee City Jail. It was to be of two rooms; the one in the rear was to have a small, barred window and would serve as the jail for the prisoners. A small room in front would be the marshal's office, for it developed that the new constitution of Pawnee City provided for a paid marshal. Otherwise, how could the justice of the peace fine prisoners if there was no one to bring him prisoners? The jail building, it also developed, was to be of two stories, the upper one to be the chambers and courtroom of the justice of the peace, Judge Judson Drake.

The marshal, the constitution said, was to be employed by the mayor. The constitution had been drawn up when it had appeared that the first mayor of Pawnee City would be Charles Fesler.

The next issue of *The Pawnee City Lance* carried an article, announcing the appointment of the new city marshal. His name was Jack Mason, commonly known as Wild Jack Mason.

"Mayor Jagger," the article said, "realizes that one must use fire to fight fire. The rowdy element in Pawnee City has become completely out of hand and a man of strength is required for the important post of city marshal. Wild Jack Mason is such a man. His fame and reputation are far-reaching. After a brilliant career as a soldier and scout in the Union Army, Wild Jack comes to Pawnee City——"

That was as much as Chad Morgan ever read of the article.

Chapter Twenty-Six

And then it was September.

No rain had fallen in the vicinity of Pawnee City since mid-April. The bed of the river contained mere inches of water that was churned and muddied by the thousands of Texas steers that grazed the short, curled buffalo grass both north and south of the river.

The herds were still coming from Texas. One a day, sometimes two and three. There was no end to them. Cattle poured through the stockyards, were loaded onto cars, eighty and a hundred to a train.

Dan Hastings, who had brought the first herd into Pawnee City, driving through the quagmire, returned with a second trail herd of over three thousand scrawny cattle. He had a dozen cowboys with him.

Chad Morgan, riding south of Pawnee City, saw the Hastings herd making the easy river crossing and recognizing Hastings, rode up to greet him.

Hastings shook his hand, but there was no pressure in his handshake. "We been hearin' some strange stories on the trail, Mr. Morgan," he said. "I don't know what to believe. First of all, is it true that you and Joe Jagger are no longer partners?"

"That's right, we decided to disagree."

"I'm sorry to hear that," Hastings said. "I thought you made a good team. Tell me, is it also true that you've got a city marshal now . . . and that Wild Jack Mason is the said marshal?"

"That also is true."

"And has he killed six men since putting on the badge?" cried the cattle drover.

"Well," said Morgan, "he may have killed four men

since I left town a half hour ago. Wild Jack is mighty handy with a six-gun, but up to a little while ago, his record was but two men killed. Since he became marshal. He killed a man *before* he was appointed marshal." Morgan smiled without humor. "Of course, I am not counting the men he merely wounded. That might bring the total up to six."

"I don't like it, Mr. Morgan," said Hastings, shaking his head. "The word's gone up and down the trail that Wild Jack hates all Texas people. We need to sell our steers, Mr. Morgan, but Texans is proud folks. They don't take kindly to being mauled and shot by men like Wild Jack, peace officers or no."

"Why don't you speak to Mr. Jagger about it?"

"I aim to do just that!"

Leaving Dan Hastings, Morgan continued along the north bank of the river until he came to a frame farmhouse with a sod roof. This was the farm of Axel Turnboom, to whom Morgan had sold the first farm in the area. A brother of Axel's now had the farm just west and several other relatives of Turnboom had farms elsewhere.

He found Turnboom plowing a long straight furrow with a team of sturdy horses. The farmer was glad to rest when Morgan rode up.

"This is good eart'," Turnboom said, wiping his forehead with a large bandana.

"It's awfully dry," Morgan said. "There hasn't been a drop of rain since you settled here." He looked around. "You didn't raise a crop this year."

"I don't try," said Turnboom. "On'y the veg'table garden. I dig well and we get a little water from it for veg'tables. Now, I plow and maybe early next month, I plant the wheat—"

"Wheat?" exclaimed Morgan. "At this time of the year?"

"Winter wheat," replied Turnboom. "We plant it in the fall back home in Sweden, where the summer is too short for good summer crop."

"I don't understand," said Morgan. "I thought the winters were extremely cold in Sweden."

"Yah, that is true, but cold do not hurt the wheat. So long as she begin to sprout in the fall before it get too cold. Snow is good, keep ground warm and in the spring make it plenty wet. Wheat get early start and in June, maybe July, we cut. Plant in the spring, summer too short, maybe too dry. Winter wheat is good. The eart' here very rich. I get maybe forty bushel to acre——"

"Be damned," said Morgan, "and all this time I felt badly about selling you this farm because I thought you would not be able to raise anything because of the heat and lack of water."

"I raise good crop next year," said the farmer with satisfaction. "Maybe next year I buy more land from you, raise more wheat."

Riding back to Pawnee City, Morgan saw a horse-drawn buggy approaching him. He had been daydreaming and was within a hundred feet of it when he saw that the occupant of the buggy was a woman.

Helen Jagger.

He could not retreat, could not avoid passing her within a few feet. He let his horse continue on its even gait and when he reached the buggy, he touched the brim of his flat-crowned Stetson.

Helen Jagger looked at him and looked through him. She did not speak, did not nod.

Morgan rode on into Pawnee City.

Cowboys in Pawnee City never trotted their horses. They knew only one gait, a terrific gallop coming into town, leaving town and even when going merely from one saloon to another.

Morgan, by contrast, rode his horse at a steady, even walk. Oliver Wakeman, moving merchandise from a wagon into his store, called to him.

"Afternoon, Mr. Morgan!"

Morgan gave him a half salute. A short distance beyond Wakeman's store, an attractive redhead, wearing a rich silk dress, smiled at him from demurely lowered eyelashes.

"Hello, Mr. Morgan," she murmured.

Morgan nodded to her.

Alfred Buffington was arranging a display of rakes, hoes and garden spades in front of his store when Morgan came along. He stepped to the edge of the sidewalk, looked quickly over his shoulder and said, "Wild Jack shot a man a few minutes ago."

"Dead?"

"They carried him to Doctor Sykes's office."

"I suppose," Morgan said slowly, "the man was creating a disturbance."

"Oh, sure," said Buffington. "He was drunk in The Longhorn and interfered with the marshal's faro playing."

"Is there a city ordinance forbidding the marshal to play cards?"

Buffington gave Morgan a look of disgust. "Our marshal keeps the peace of this town. With a gun."

"Can't the board of supervisors—of which you're a member—do something about Wild Jack Mason?"

"Judge Drake says no. The Mayor has the sole authority to hire and fire the marshal. Judge Drake's office is a fee office. He gets one-half of all the fines imposed in the justice court. Wild Jack arrests a good many persons in Pawnee City. None has ever been acquitted. All have been found guilty and paid fines."

"Didn't the publisher of *The Pawnee Lance* bring Judge Drake to Pawnee City?"

"He did, but they are no longer the close friends they once were."

"Sometimes," said Morgan, "friends fall out."

He rode on to the real-estate office, where he tied his horse to the rail. Hackett was out of the office. He had left a note for Morgan, saying that he was showing a farm property to a prospective purchaser.

Later in the cool of the evening, Morgan stood outside his real-estate office. A thin cheroot was in his mouth, but he had forgotten to light it.

People passed back and forth on the street, on the sidewalk in front of Morgan. A pair of cowboys came galloping along the street, Yip-Yip-Yaying, but for a wonder, not shooting their guns at the moon.

Morgan looked toward the hotel. There were many lights in many windows, the lobby was brightly lighted and he could make out people passing in and out of the hotel.

Mayor Joe Jagger was probably in his office, totting up the day's receipts from his shipping pens and stockyards, his hotel, his bank and saloon. No, the saloon receipts would not come in until the early hours of the morning. Jagger's bookkeeper, his sister, would probably enter those sometime during the forenoon.

Morgan threw away his unlit cigar and turning, walked up the street.

Helen Jagger stood on the veranda of the Drovers Hotel, catching a bit of the evening breeze. She wore a dress of soft, wine-colored silk. A lace shawl was draped over her shoulders. A light puff of wind blew a wisp of soft hair over her eyes and she brushed the hair away.

There was a step behind her, but Helen did not turn. A whiff of cigar smoke assailed her nostrils and her brother spoke then: "Still thinking of him, eh?"

Helen gave a start, then said indignantly, "I was thinking of the new bank that's going to open next week and whether it would hurt our own bank very much."

"The faro bank at The Longhorn makes more profit than the Pawnee Savings Bank," said Jagger. "I heard a rumor today that Morgan's put money into the new bank."

"It's inconvenient, I imagine, banking by mail in Kansas City."

"It's a wonder he's got any money to bank," growled Jagger. "The prices he's getting for good city property."

"He must be selling quite a few lots, however," said Helen. "There seems to be more building activity going on than ever before."

"Pawnee City's growing. Two hundred thousand Texas longhorns have passed through my yards and I figure the figure'll go over two hundred fifty thousand before the end of the season." He puffed at his Havana cigar a moment.

"Things are easing up a bit. Why don't you take a trip

to Kansas City? Or maybe St. Louis. You had a lot of friends there."

"Joe," Helen said, "I'm not mooning over Chad Morgan. Believe me, I'm not."

"Who said you were?"

"Isn't that what this talk is all about?"

Jagger was silent a moment, then chuckled easily. "You don't miss much, do you, Sis?"

"I miss a lot," she said with sudden warmth. "If you must know, I miss Chad. I miss him a hell of a lot."

And with that unladylike remark, Helen Jagger turned and went into the hotel.

Jagger stood for a moment puffing at his cigar, then suddently exclaiming angrily, threw the cigar over the veranda rail and walked down the steps and up the street.

Chapter Twenty-Seven

For a change, Marshal Wild Jack Mason was playing poker. Also, for a change, he was patronizing The Texas Saloon instead of his favorite place, The Longhorn.

Dan Hastings, newly arrived from Texas, was in the game, as were Judge Drake and Chad Morgan. It was a modest game, but Wild Jack had lost a few dollars and was not in the best frame of mind.

"Let's stop this penny-ante stuff, gentlemen," he said when Judge Drake's three sevens beat his two pair.

"I haven't got a lot of money," said Dan Hastings. "Won't have until I sell my herd tomorrow."

"Mr. Pillsbury will honor your IOU, I'm sure," said Wild Jack. "I propose a few rounds of table stakes. How about it, Judge?"

"Is eighty dollars enough?" asked the judge.

"It'll do for a starter."

Morgan picked up his discarded hand and tossed it to Wild Jack, who was to be the next dealer. "Deal me out," he said.

"Not much of gambler, are you?" Wild Jack asked thinly.

"I play cards for fun," retorted Morgan. He pushed back his chair and was about to get to his feet when he became aware that Joe Jagger had come into the saloon and had stopped behind Judge Drake.

"The mayor," said Wild Jack. "Care to sit in, Your Honor? The game's too stiff for Mr. Morgan."

"Don't mind if I do," said Jagger, drawing up a chair.

Morgan, instead of rising to his feet, hitched up his own chair. "I'll play awhile," he said.

His eyes flickered across the table and he caught Jagger

looking at him. His former partner quickly averted his eyes, however.

"I suggest we ante a dollar," Wild Jack said, as he shuffled the cards.

No one objected, so five dollars were plunked into the pot. Wild Jack dealt swiftly, put down the pack of cards and looked at his hand.

"I pass," said Hastings, the cattle drover.

"I'll open," said Jagger. "How about five dollars for a beginner?"

"Guess I'm sucked in," said the judge.

Morgan tossed in a five-dollar greenback.

"Dealer stays," said Wild Jack.

Hastings also contributed five dollars and drew two cards. Jagger smiled wolfishly. "One card."

"Three for me," exclaimed the judge. He looked at the three cards that Wild Jack dealt him and promptly threw them down. "I'm out."

Morgan had picked up three queens to begin with. He had not raised the opening bet in order not to reveal his strong hand. He now drew two cards, which indicated that he might have three of a kind, or more likely, a high pair and an ace for a kicker.

He drew a fourth queen and a king.

"Dealer takes one," said Wild Jack, smiling thinly.

Very carefully he dealt himself the single card.

"I should pass," remarked Jagger, "but we'll see where the pikers are. Table stakes? Very well, I'll bet thirty dollars."

Morgan counted out thirty dollars and added another thirty. "And thirty."

"Well, well," said Wild Jack, "things are picking up. I'll match the sixty and double the bet. A hundred and twenty to you, Mr. Hastings."

"Somebody's got more than kings and aces," declared Hastings. "I pass."

He had inadvertently revealed to Morgan that none of the other players could be holding three aces or more than a pair of kings.

Jagger coolly counted out ninety dollars. He hesitated, then fished out a hundred dollars from his stack of money and tossed it into the center of the table.

"Your bet, Marshal, and another hundred."

It would cost Morgan a hundred and sixty dollars to call. Both Jagger and Wild Jack had drawn a single card. They could have been drawing to straights or flushes, which if they had connected, would give them a strong hand—but not as strong as Morgan's four queens. Most likely, both had gone in with two pairs. One or the other could be bluffing. If not, both had drawn to their two pairs and now held full houses. Very strong hands. But not strong enough to beat four queens.

Morgan put out his money and said, "I'll just call."

A faint smirk of satisfaction flitted over Wild Jack's face and Morgan knew that the marshal had a full house, stronger than either a flush or a straight. And the fact that Morgan merely called indicated that his hand was not too strong.

Wild Jack said, "Well, Mr. Jagger, poker's going up. I call your hundred and raise you two hundred and fifty."

Jagger's eyes narrowed quickly. He dropped them to his hand, squeezed the cards and examined them once more. He began counting out money, built up a stack of two hundred and fifty dollars and again examined his hand. "I've got a pretty good hand here," he observed, "but I didn't expect to sit in a table stakes game this evening and came without too much cash. I would like to raise you two hundred and fifty dollars."

"Your Honor," laughed Wild Jack, "you've got a bank. Your credit is good—as good as the Pawnee Savings Bank."

"Then I raise you two hundred and fifty dollars."

Morgan took a slip of paper from his pocket, wrote quickly on it: "IOU, $1,000." He scrawled his name on it.

"I call and raise the pot five hundred dollars," he announced.

Chagrin spread over Wild Jack's face. "Damme, to fall for that! You fooled me, letting that last bet go by. You've got four of a kind."

"Perhaps I'm bluffing."

"It'll cost me seven hundred and fifty dollars to find out." Wild Jack hesitated, then spread out his hand. "You're beating three sixes and a lousy pair of treys."

Morgan and Jagger alone remained in the game. A little ripple of muscle played along the line of Jagger's jaw. Until now, he had not spoken to, had not recognized the presence of Morgan in the game. But things had narrowed down. He was left in the game, alone with his erstwhile partner. Moreover, he had already invested a considerable sum of money in the pot. He had raised it two hundred and fifty dollars on credit, had been raised five hundred. He could drop out and lose what he had already put in the pot, or he could call Morgan's five-hundred-dollar bet . . . with an IOU, or credit.

He did not look at Morgan. Instead, he half turned his chair away from the table.

"Mr. Pillsbury!" he called.

The owner of The Texas Saloon came over. "Mr. Pillsbury," Jagger said, "I find myself temporarily short of funds. Do you have seven hundred and fifty dollars in your safe?"

"I reckon so, Mr. Jagger," said Pillsbury. "I might even have a little more."

"Do you have a thousand dollars more?"

Pillsbury winced. "I'm sure I do not."

"See what you have."

Pillsbury went off. The game was temporarily suspended. Pillsbury was gone for a full two minutes, then returned with a black tin box. He set it on the table before Jagger.

"Help yourself."

Jagger opened the box, counted out seven hundred and fifty dollars in greenbacks. There were only a few bills left in the box, but there were a considerable number of gold coins, even some silver dollars and half dollars. Jagger began to count out the coins.

"You win," said Morgan suddenly.

He thrust his cards under the discards on the table, riffled them together. A hush fell upon the group around the table.

Morgan pushed back his chair, got to his feet. "I'll make good that IOU in the morning."

Jagger stared at him.

Morgan walked around the table and left the saloon.

"Be damned!" exclaimed Wild Jack. "He was bluffing all the time."

"Morgan never bluffed in his life."

"Then he lost his nerve!"

Jagger, starting to rake in the huge pot, stopped. "Don't ever believe that, Marshal!"

Wild Jack suddenly picked up the discards and began to riffle through them. "Marshal!" exclaimed Dan Hastings. "Is that the thing to do?"

"You can judge a man's character by the way he plays poker," said Wild Jack coldly. "I want to see what kind of man Mr. Morgan is——"

He separated the cards, suddenly riffled out four of them and exposed them on the table. "Four queens," he said slowly. His eyes went across the table. "He had a cinch hand!"

"I have a jack high straight," said Jagger slowly. "I was open on both ends and drew a seven."

"I don't get it," exclaimed Wild Jack.

"Damndest poker I ever saw," rumbled Judge Drake.

Chapter Twenty-Eight

And then it was October. Two herds came in during the early days of the month. Another came in on the sixteenth and then for days the faro dealers in the five Pawnee City saloons played solitaire. The flow of whiskey across the bars was a mere trickle.

Wild Jack Mason was scarcely earning his salary and for a full week Judge Mason pocketed not a single fine. The cattle season of 1867 seemed to be over. Two of the saloons shuttered their windows. Merchants began to take inventory of their stocks, figured their profits for the season and found them very good. There would be five months, however, during which they would take in very little cash money. The winter would be cold and long.

Yet the spirit of optimism still prevailed and a group got together and had Charles Fesler print a few large placards, which were scattered about the town. The cards read:

FRIENDS—NEIGHBORS

To celebrate the end of the great cattle drives of 1867, the merchants and business men of Pawnee City will hold, Saturday evening, November 1, 1867——

A GRAND BALL

Everyone Invited. *Refreshments*

Tickets $1.00

November first was a crisp, autumn day. The sky was overcast and it was possible that the first snow of the season might fall before night. A raw wind began to blow from the north during the afternoon. The snow held off, but the thermometer dropped to fourteen degrees above zero, very cold for Kansas so early in the season.

Toward evening, a farmer coming into town to do his shopping for the week, reported that a herd of Texas cattle was making the river crossing south of town.

No one paid any attention. The last trail herd had come in two weeks ago; there would be no more. It was too late in the year.

Morgan had had a partition built in the real-estate office, reducing the size of the office, but giving him a private compartment at the rear, which was twenty feet wide and ten feet deep. He still used the cot, but had bought a couple of chairs, a small table and a washstand on which stood a pitcher and bowl. There was a small mirror on the wall above the washstand and he was standing before this, shortly after seven, stripped to the waist, shaving, when the street door banged.

"Hey, damnyank!" cried a voice. "I'm back!"

Morgan exclaimed in sudden pleasure, and whirling away from the washstand, stepped toward the door leading to the front. He forgot, for the moment, that there was lather on his face, that he held a razor in his hand and that he was stripped to the waist.

"Reb!" he cried.

"*Yippee!*" shouted Cass Simcoe, as she sprang toward him.

She was wearing Levi's, boots, a wool shirt and a warm jacket. Her cheeks were icy cold, but there was warmth in her body. She threw her arms about Morgan, hugged him with her young strength.

"Bet you didn't think we'd make it!" she cried. "We got a late start, but better late than never. Dad wanted to hold off until spring, but I wouldn't let him. I told him I *had* to see you again."

Her arms suddenly rose from about his body, wound themselves about his neck. Her chapped, roughened lips pressed Morgan's quickly, almost hungrily.

Then she stepped back. Morgan, shaken, became aware of his lack of dress.

"Sit down, Reb," he said, "sit down out here while I get dressed——"

"You takin' me to the dance?" cried Cass. "I saw the signs plastered all around town. Don't worry—we came with a chuck wagon this time. I got a dress, you damnyank. I got *two* dresses."

"Reb," said Morgan, "I'll be proud to take you to the dance."

"I gotta go then," she said quickly. "I gotta go get fixed up and washed. I got cow manure all over me and if they got a bathtub at the hotel I might even take a bath, winter or not. Come and get me, Yankee. Eight o'clock!"

She was off then, running through the door and slamming it behind her, before Morgan realized where she had told him to pick her up.

Morgan had not been inside the Drovers Hotel since he and Jagger, rather he and Helen Jagger, had dissolved the firm of Jagger & Morgan.

Morgan finished his shaving, put on a clean white shirt and a heavy sack coat. He tied a knot in a black tie and got his hat. He consulted his heavy watch and discovered that it was still only twenty minutes after seven.

Cass would need all of an hour to get dressed for the dance, possibly more time, if she was able to take a bath.

He left the office, stood outside for a moment, then looked toward the door of The Longhorn Saloon, conveniently near. A gust of cold wind caused him to shiver a little and he buttoned up his coat and walked to the door of The Longhorn.

The faro dealer was dealing to two players, but the bar was doing a fair business. Standing by it was General Simcoe, in a long gray overcoat from which gold braid had been removed. Several cowboys were also lined up.

"General," said Morgan, as he came up, "it's a pleasure to see you again."

"Ah, Mr. Morgan, I was hoping you would stop by. You will drink with me?"

"Certainly."

"Thank you. This is Sam Acres, my foreman and trail boss."

A leathery-faced cowboy gripped Morgan's hand. "It's just about a year since you come to the ranch. I 'member we was doin' some target shootin' when you rode up."

"You mean," said Morgan, chuckling, "you were teaching Miss Cass how to draw and fire a Navy gun without aiming. Just pointing."

Sam Acres grinned. "Mr. Morgan, she can outdraw me today. And outshoot me."

"Yes, Cassie's a fine marksman," agreed General Simcoe. "She's also very good at breaking horses and riding herd. She knows little of the things a woman should know, however. And that is why she is not going back to Texas with me."

"I don't understand."

"I'm sending her to St. Louis. She takes the train tomorrow and will spend the winter at a school for young ladies. The school has been highly recommended to me, by an old army friend of mine, who has two daughters there now."

Cass had not told Morgan.

He drank his whiskey and was putting down the glass when a man came into The Longhorn and approached the bar.

"Mr. Morgan," he said.

It was Tom Alder, wearing a long bearskin overcoat. He had his hands thrust in his pockets and apparently had no intention of shaking Morgan's hand.

"How are you?" Morgan said quietly.

"Not good, not bad. I went down to Texas and got together a little herd of my own. Five hundred head. I got here with under three hundred."

"The Comanches raided us in the Panhandle," explained the general. "There was virtually no water in the Indian Nations and we were stampeded twice by Indians. We left the home ranch with five thousand steers and we reached here with about thirty-five hundred head, not counting Mr. Alder's."

"You came together?"

"We threw our herds together, after the Comanche raid," said General Simcoe. "Well, I learned one thing. Not to drive cattle this late in the season. Our beef is about as scrawny as you ever saw it. Not much more'n hide and bones."

Morgan drew out his watch again. "General, I'm taking a young lady to the dance this evening. I have to pick her up at the hotel. Miss Cass——"

The general's face showed sudden pleasure. "Why, that's fine, Mr. Morgan. I will, perhaps, stop in myself and will see you there."

"Can anybody go to this-here dance, Mr. Morgan?" asked Tom Alder.

"Anyone with a dollar," Morgan replied.

There was no one on the veranda of the Drovers Hotel as Morgan climbed the steps, but in the hotel lobby a drummer, making probably his last visit to Pawnee City of the season, was talking idly with the hotel clerk.

The door of the office behind the desk was open, but the room was dark. Morgan breathed a little easier.

He looked at his watch again. It was five minutes after eight.

Heels clicked on the uncarpeted stairs leading to the second floor of the hotel and then Cass appeared.

Her face was scrubbed so that it glowed, her hair was shiny and soft and looked the color of rich taffy. She was wearing a green velvet dress that revealed bare, golden shoulders and a bodice that was anything but flat.

"She's a young woman," Morgan thought.

She saw Morgan and stopped on the bottom step. "The general took me to Austin," she said. "I'm going to live in St. Louis this winter and he thought—well, he said I had to learn how to wear women's clothes."

"You're beautiful, Cass!"

"I'm not," declared Cass, coming toward him. "I'm a scrawny cowhand from Texas, that's all."

"You'll be the prettiest girl at the ball," Morgan insisted.

She had a cape over her arm and Morgan took it and

helped her on with it. Cass looked at him shyly, then slipped a hand under his arm.

"I can dance," she said, "a little, anyway. Mammy showed me how——"

"Ah, she's back with you!"

"No," said Cass, her face falling. "We looked for her in Austin, but we couldn't find her. Somebody said she'd gone to New Orleans and the general wrote to General Beauregard there, but General Beauregard couldn't find her. We don't know where she is."

Chapter Twenty-Nine

Six weeks before, Morgan had sold a man from Kansas City two lots. The man had hired a building crew and they threw up a frame building forty feet wide by fifty deep. It had been completed only two weeks before, then the owner of the building had decided that he would wait until spring before stocking the store with a line of low-priced furniture.

The building was vacant, therefore, and since it was ideal for the purposes of the grand ball, it was being utilized for that. A four-piece band had been imported from Kansas City for the occasion and it was playing a noisy tune when Morgan and Cass Simcoe entered the "ballroom."

There were about thirty people already in the room, more than two-thirds of them men, for men still outnumbered women by at least four to one in Pawnee City.

The orchestra had apparently just completed a dance tune and the several couples who had danced remained together, talking. There were also several small groups of men on the sidelines, engaged in conversation.

When Morgan entered with Cass Simcoe, he found Fesler, the newspaperman, seated at a small table just inside the door. Behind him stood Wild Jack Mason.

"Two dollars, Mr. Morgan," said Fesler cheerfully.

Morgan gave him the money. While he was doing so, Wild Jack let his eyes run up and down Cass Simcoe.

Wild Jack smirked at Morgan, closing one eye in a wink. "You got a gun on you, Morgan?"

"Of course not," snapped Morgan.

"On'y asking. This is one place I aim to keep the peace and I figure best way's to have the customers check their hardware when they come in." He winked. "The folks made

153

up some punch and it's got a touch of something strong in it. Don't drink too much."

Morgan took Cass's elbow and moved her on into the big room. There was a table against the wall on which were deposited coats and hats. Cass dropped her cape on it and whispered to Morgan, "Golly, I'm scared all of a sudden. Maybe I don't know how to dance."

"Then we'll learn together," said Morgan. "It's six-seven years since I"—he almost faltered, then continued strongly —"since I danced."

His eyes had gone to the far end of the room and taken in Helen Jagger, who was standing there, talking to her brother and Judge Judson Drake.

Cass was aware that Morgan was looking past her and started to turn to follow his eyes, but just then the orchestra began playing a lively number and Morgan took her hand in his left and putting his arm about her, began to dance.

He had told Cass the truth; he had not danced since mid-summer of 1861, but he found now that he had not forgotten the steps. And, while Cass had been afraid of her limited dancing ability, he found that she followed him perfectly, her natural sense of grace and rhythm making up for her lack of practice.

For a moment or two, Morgan kept his eyes on the top of Cass's taffy-colored hair as he concentrated on the steps, but then his eyes flickered away from his partner and he gave a slight start as his eyes met those of Helen Jagger less than six feet away.

She was dancing with Judge Drake.

She wore a wine-colored velvet evening gown that fitted her perfectly. She had done something to her hair and it was shimmering gold. She was the loveliest thing Morgan had ever looked upon.

His dance partner suddenly looked up at him. "Am I— am I dancing all right?" she asked.

"Excellent," he murmured.

Then she almost collided with Helen Jagger, who had moved closer with her partner. Helen's hand dropped upon Cass's shoulder.

"Cass, my dear! I'm glad to see you again."

Cass almost jumped, then recognized Helen. "Miss Helen," she exclaimed. "We just got in from Texas and I—I"—she floundered, gulped and said, lamely—"I don't know how to dance!"

"You're doing marvelously," said Helen. Her eyes suddenly met Morgan's. "Good evening, Chad."

Morgan nodded. "You're looking well, Helen."

"Evening, Mr. Morgan," said the judge. "I don't believe I've met your young friend."

"Forgive me," exclaimed Helen. "Cass, this is Judge Drake. Judge, Miss Cass Simcoe of Texas. She's General Simcoe's daughter."

"Delighted, ma'am," exclaimed the judge. "You'll save a dance for a middle-aged man who doesn't know his right foot from his left?"

"Golly," said Cass, then winced and added in some confusion, "Yes, sir, Your Honor."

Helen laughed merrily and the two couples moved apart. "She's beautiful!" Cass whispered to Morgan. She suddenly looked up at him. "I—I know about you and Mr. Jagger having a fight. It broke your engagement to Miss Helen——"

Morgan grimaced. "You've heard all this since you got in town this afternoon?"

"Oh, no! I knew it back home. I've known it for a long time. How you and Mr. Jagger had a real, dragdown fist fight and you licked him. There's always folks dropping in who've been up The Trail. We keep right well posted on what's going on up North." She exclaimed, "There's the general—dad!"

Morgan looked toward the door and saw General Simcoe standing at Charles Fesler's table. With him were Tom Alder, still wearing the long bearskin overcoat, and the Simcoe trail boss, Sam Acres.

At the table, the general was paying for himself, Alder and Acres. They were about to go on farther into the room when Wild Jack tapped the leathery-faced Sam Acres on the shoulder.

"Your hardware, cowboy," he drawled. "You leave it with me."

Acres looked at him in astonishment. "Why should I give you my gun?"

"Because I'm telling you." A row of nails stuck in the wall and Wild Jack indicated that several guns already hung there.

Acres was still loath to remove his revolver, but the general spoke to him. "Give the marshal your revolver, Sam."

Acres gave Wild Jack his revolver with ill grace. The marshal looked at Tom Alder.

"You carrying a gun under that coat?" Wild Jack asked.

"No," retorted Tom Alder, even as he gripped the butt of a revolver in the pocket of the bearskin coat.

"Mind showin' me?" continued the marshal.

Alder unbuttoned his coat, flicked it open to show that he was not wearing a gunbelt, then without even looking at Wild Jack again, followed General Simcoe and Sam Acres.

Alder's eyes searched the faces of the dancers. He found Cass Simcoe dancing with Chad Morgan. General Simcoe had also located his daughter and said, almost as if remarking to himself, "The child has grace . . . and charm——"

The music stopped and Cass, seeing her father only a short distance away, left Morgan and ran to him.

"I'm going to dance the next dance with you!" she cried.

"My dear," murmured the general, "it is so long since I've danced."

"That's just what Chad—Mr. Morgan said," Cass flashed. "And he danced beautifully . . . !"

Morgan came up, smiling. "I'll surrender her to you for the next turn, General Simcoe. But after that, I don't know. She's such a fine partner I may keep her the rest of the evening."

Cass flashed him a smile, then she saw Tom Alder. "Tom," she cried, "ain't you—aren't you going to take off that horrible overcoat?"

"What for?" asked Alder laconically. "I'm not going to dance."

"Why not?"

"I don't dance," Alder said after a brief pause. His eyes met Morgan's, "I never learned how."

"I'll teach you," volunteered Cass, who a few moments ago had been afraid of her own dancing ability. "I'll dance with you right after the general."

Tom Alder started to shake his head, but was saved by the arrival of Joe Jagger, who had come across the room.

"General Simcoe!" he cried, catching the general's hand and pumping it. "I heard you were in town and I've been hoping to see you. But first things first . . ." He turned, bowed to Cass. "Miss Simcoe, might I have the pleasure of this dance?"

"Golly," cried Cass. "I just promised the general and then——"

"No-no," General Simcoe said hastily. "I'm glad to get out of it. You dance with her, Mr. Jagger."

He exclaimed in relief as the music started and Jagger bowed to Cass. Cass shot a desperate look at Morgan, then allowed herself to be led away.

There were more couples on the floor now than there had been during the previous dance, as several more persons had come into the ballroom. Morgan saw Alfred Buffington dancing with Mrs. Buffington, a heavy gray-haired woman.

Harlow Tarbox was dancing with his wife, and a man with a shiny, bald spot on his head, Amos Leach, Pawnee City's barber, a little man no more than five feet five, was dancing with a woman fully six inches taller than he was. He was swinging along very well, too.

Then Morgan let his eyes flicker away from the dancers. They went to the far corner of the room to where Helen Jagger, not dancing, was talking animatedly with a woman in her early thirties, the wife of Charles Fesler, who was custodian of the door and could not, therefore, dance.

A voice said in Morgan's ear, "If I could dance, I'd be dancing with her."

Morgan shot a quick look over his shoulder at Tom Alder, who had moved up beside and behind him. Alder was looking across the room at Helen Jagger.

Morgan said, "You're sure you can't dance, Alder?"

"You calling me a liar?" asked Alder mockingly.

"You're from Missouri. I never heard of a Missourian who couldn't dance."

"Maybe so," said Alder, "but I come from the brush country. Bay County." A sardonic smile twisted his mouth. "What you-all think I done before the war, Mr. Morgan? Before I joined up with the bushwhackers to give the Yankee boys hell?"

"I've no idea," replied Morgan, "but I somehow doubt that you're quite the cracker you're now trying to tell me you are. For one thing, I'm sure you know how to dance."

"Well, maybe I just don't feel like dancing," Alder went on, more gregarious than Morgan had ever known him to be. "My kid brother, he was the dancer of the family. Right smart, light on his feet. . . . Didn't know I had a brother, did you?"

"Alder," said Morgan evenly, "I know practically nothing about you. You're not a man who talks very much about himself."

"What's there to talk? Your folks put out some posters on me during the big fuss. Said more about me than I ever knew myself. . . ." He paused only briefly. "My brother wore a gray suit. He was in the State Guard when the war started and he stayed with Pappy Price all through it. He even stayed on, after. He was killed in 'sixty-five."

"Sorry, Alder," Morgan said, then could not resist adding, "In Mexico?"

"Close. Texas. He was with Shelby's rear guard when the Sixteenth Illinois cut them to pieces." Alder exhaled lightly. "He was studying law when he went off with the State Guard."

Morgan knew now why Alder had become talkative. He said, "And you? What did *you* do before the war?"

"I *was* a lawyer," Alder replied bleakly. "For that matter, Charley Quantrill was a schoolteacher. And we even had a preacher . . . Skaggs, I seem to recall his name was. The only man we lost at Lawrence. I hear tell they dragged him up and down the street and finally poured coal oil over him and set fire to him."

"That," said Morgan coolly, "was after your bunch murdered some one hundred and seventy-nine men."

Alder bared his teeth slightly. "Guess it's too soon for Johnny Rebs and Yanks to get together and talk about the war." He inclined his head and dropped his voice, "Here comes *your* war!"

Alder faded backwards and Morgan, raising his eyes, saw Helen Jagger coming toward him. Her head was held high, her eyes were determined.

She said, as she came up, "We never danced, Chad. I'm not going to spend my old age wondering what it would have been like if we *had* danced."

"I'm sorry," said Morgan awkwardly.

She held up her arms and he took her and they glided away.

Morgan could feel the pulse pounding in his temples; there were words in him he wanted to say, but he could not say them.

Helen, too, even though she had taken the initiative, was silent for a complete circuit of the dance floor. Then, her eyes watching Cass and her brother nearby, she said, "She's growing up quickly."

Morgan's eyes followed her. "She's all of nineteen, but I suppose a girl is considered grown up at that age."

"She's as old as she'll ever be," Helen replied cryptically. She was silent a moment, then: "Too bad she lives so far away."

From the direction of the door Wild Jack Mason's voice rose above the music: "Damn you, cowboy, when I tell you something, you listen."

There was a sharp yelp of pain, a hoarse cry of rage and as Morgan released Helen and turned toward the door, the sickening smack of something striking flesh.

Morgan, moving swiftly toward the door, almost collided with Tom Alder, who was rushing toward Wild Jack, ahead of him.

A cowboy was down on the floor, blood welling from a bad cut on his forehead. Wild Jack Mason, a revolver in his fist, stood with his back against the wall, beside a white-faced Fesler. The gun was pointed at a second cowboy a few feet away.

The cowboy's hands were slowly rising to shoulder level.

Wild Jack said nastily, as Alder and Morgan descended upon him, "Go back to your dancin', folks. This is marshal business . . . can't have drunken cowboys bustin' in on respectable folks."

Sam Acres came up, running. "It's Billy Carr!" he cried. He started for the guns hung from the nails on the wall. "Gimme my gun."

Wild Jack thrust out his left hand to fend off Acres. "Touch iron, Mister," he snarled, "and I won't waste time buffaloing you——"

"Put down that gun, Mason!" snapped Morgan. "There's no call for gunplay here."

"Ain't there, Mister Morgan?" sneered Wild Jack. "You were one of the original hollerers for law and order. Well, I'm keepin' order here and no Texas cowboys can run a shindy on me."

A crowd was gathering behind Morgan's back. General Simcoe appeared beside him. "Marshal," he said sharply, "I'll be responsible for these men. They work for me."

"Then pay their fines in the morning," snarled Wild Jack, "and get them out of town. I don't stand for any nonsense in my town."

Tom Alder said softly, very softly, "Put up your gun."

Wild Jack's bloodshot eyes focused angrily on Alder. "You talkin' to me?"

"Come outside," Alder said ominously. "I've been hearing about you for a long, long time, Mr. Wild Jack. Maybe you're as good as they say you are . . . and maybe you're a damn-fool bluffer."

Wild Jack became oddly alert to Alder to the extent that no one else facing him seemed to matter.

"I couldn't place you for a minute," he said, "but I remember now. You're Tom Alder."

"The bushwhacker," sneered Alder. "I usually shoot my men from the brush, but I'll make an exception in your case. We'll go out on the street where it's nice and open. That's the way you like it, isn't it?"

"This isn't your affair," Wild Jack said, turning sullen.

"What if I make it my business? So . . . ?" Alder's hand came out of his pocket and there was a Navy revolver in his fist. "Well, Wild Jack?" he taunted. "I've got a gun in my hand."

General Simcoe took a quick step forward, thrust his body between the two men. At the same time Morgan reached out, gripped the hand of Wild Jack that held the gun.

"Put it down," he said.

"You, Morgan," the marshal said thickly, "I don't like your damn——" He broke off.

Morgan, exerting sudden pressure, pushed down on Wild Jack's hand. Mason resisted for a fraction of a second, then suddenly yielded, let his hand be knocked down to his side.

Joe Jagger came up. "Marshal, I think you'd better call this off. This is a friendly get-together and we want no violence."

"Whatever you say, Mayor," Wild Jack said nastily. "I was only doing my duty."

"You've done it. Take this man over to Dr. Sykes's place. Wait—the doctor's here."

Dr. Sykes came through the crowd, bent over the man on the floor. The cowboy was stirring and suddenly a loud groan came from his lips. The groan was followed by some fine expletives.

Sam Acres bent down. "Easy does it, Billy! There's ladies present."

That was all there was to it. Acres and the other Simcoe cowboy helped their companion out of the dance hall. Dr. Sykes went along with them and, after stopping at the door and glaring at everyone within range, Wild Jack also left.

Tom Alder started to follow, but General Simcoe caught his arm and began talking earnestly to him. Morgan, knowing that the crisis was over, turned to look for his dance partner.

He could not find her immediately and then Cass Simcoe came to him.

"I want to go home," she said. "I mean, the hotel."

"Of course, Cass. I'll take you."

He led her to the table where the wardrobe had been piled and fished out her cape from under some others. He helped her into it. "Sorry your evening was spoiled," he said into her ear.

"It wasn't spoiled, Chad. Honest. Only I—I'm tired." She flashed him a wan smile. "I was riding all day, you know."

"Of course," said Morgan. "Well, shall we go?"

He took her arm and steered her toward the door and then Morgan saw that they would pass Helen, who was standing near the guns on the wall, watching them.

She smiled as they came up. "You're leaving already?"

"I've got to get up early," said Cass Simcoe. "I'm taking the train to St. Louis."

"So soon? I'd hoped you were going to stay awhile."

"Can't. We took too long coming up The Trail. Got to be in St. Louis day after tomorrow."

"Then, I'll say goodbye, Cass. Until your next visit to Pawnee City."

She held out her hand to Cass Simcoe.

As they reached the steps leading up to the veranda of the Drovers Hotel, Cass Simcoe stopped.

"Chad," she said, low, "I'm sorry I'm such a poor sport."

"Nonsense, you've had a rugged day of it. The excitement wore you out."

She said miserably, "I lied. I'm not tired at all. I could dance all night and all day tomorrow. If only . . ." She stopped.

"Yes?" said Morgan after a moment.

"Goodbye," she cried, and suddenly buried her head against his coat.

He put his arm gently about her. "I'll see you at the depot in the morning."

"No," she said quickly. "I—I don't want you. Dad'll be

there and I—I don't want to see you then. I don't want him to know——"

"Know what?"

"This," she said, and rising up on her toes, kissed him on the mouth.

She was gone, then, running up the steps, into the hotel.

Chapter Thirty

It snowed the next day. Winter had come to Pawnee City. General Simcoe sold his herd for the lowest price anyone had received during the entire year: eleven dollars a head. The cattle were terribly thin and would have to be fattened at the Kansas City or Chicago stockyards.

Tom Alder's small herd was bought along with the Simcoe steers. He remained in Pawnee City for a few days after the general started back down The Chisholm Trail, but then he, too, disappeared. No one saw him go.

Several more stores and all the saloons except The Texas Saloon and The Longhorn shuttered their windows. The rutted street became hard and brittle.

Most of the rooms at the Drovers Hotel were vacant.

Joe Jagger, going into his and his sister's office, found her standing by the window. She turned as she heard him enter the room.

"I think I'll take that vacation now, Joe."

"Wonderful, Sis. Go to St. Louis. Spend some money. Buy anything your heart desires."

"Diamonds?"

"Why not? You can afford them. If it takes diamonds to make you happy——"

"Once," Helen said, "I wanted diamonds more than anything else in the world. Oh, not just because they were expensive, but—because they were a symbol of the things I wanted. Respectability, wealth . . . power. Now——" She paused.

Jagger gave her a sharp glance. "You danced with Chad Morgan the other night. That's what's bothering you! You never got over him."

"I liked him," Helen said. "I liked him that first time I met him, when you brought him into Nathan Foss's office.

164

I liked him even better when he took me to dinner in St. Louis and I thought I loved him by the time I came to Pawnee City. I didn't, though. I didn't love him then, or . . . or later. I only thought I did. I loved myself more. And now . . . now, when it's too late——"

"Too late? He'd come running any time you snapped your fingers."

"That's where you're wrong, Joe."

"The man isn't worth your little finger."

"I'm not worth *his*. I'm shallow, selfish. I've got a diamond, a big cold diamond for a heart."

"Stop it, Helen! Chad Morgan ought to be glad that you'd even look at him." Jagger snorted. "Hell, if he means that much to you, I'll make it up with him. I'll take him back into the partnership."

"He wouldn't come."

"More fool he." Jagger suddenly cocked his head to one side. "Now, wait a minute, it isn't that little Texas tomboy . . . what's her name . . ." Jagger stared at his sister. "Be damned! So he's fallen for *that* little fluff. Why, she's scarcely more than a kid."

"She's old enough."

"But she wears pants?"

"She didn't at the dance. And she didn't last summer when I loaned her my dress. He saw her then as a woman, and I—I made it possible."

Helen Jagger went to St. Louis. She even went to Chicago and there bought a railroad ticket to New York. But she did not go to New York. She returned, instead, to Pawnee City, Kansas. And there she remained throughout the winter.

It was a cold, blustery day in January when Morgan, his head buried deep in the turned-up sheepskin collar of his overcoat, rode along the river and turned in to the farmstead of Axel Turnboom. He found the farmer in the barn, mending harness.

"How's that winter wheat coming along?" Morgan asked, after the greetings were over.

"Good, good."

"You're sure? The ground's frozen hard as stone. I got to thinking about it in town this morning, and I thought I'd just run out and see this wheat."

"Can't see nottin' now," said Turnboom, "but don't worry about the wheat. She grow in the spring."

"What about the sleet we had before Christmas? The ground was solid ice, mixed with a little frozen mud, for two weeks——"

"Sure, here, too. But don't hurt winter wheat. I plant him good and deep."

"Deep, eh?"

"Five-six inch. Protect little wheat germ, little sprout. . . . Let 'm rain, snow, ice . . . don't hurt wheat . . . !"

A shawl about her shoulders, Helen Jagger stood in the lobby of the Drovers Hotel by the closed front door. There was frost on the panes, but in the center of each rectangle of glass the frost had melted away sufficiently so she was able to look through and see the street of Pawnee City. There was a drift of snow two feet high in front of the hotel and eddies of brittle, white snow were blown here and there about the street.

A lonely horse was tied to the hitchrail in front of The Longhorn Saloon. Farther down the street, in front of The St. Louis Store, stood a buckboard to which was hitched a team.

Outside of the three horses, there was no other living creature on Pawnee City's Main Street.

The first week in February, Chad Morgan sold a business lot. On February twelfth, he sold a sixty-foot residential lot to a man who also bought a double lot on Main Street.

Within a week he sold four other lots to newcomers who came in on the train.

It was the weathervane to what was to follow. Eighteen sixty-eight would be a boom year for Pawnee City.

No one waited more impatiently for the beginning of the cattle season than Joe Jagger. During the winter the bank had not paid the expenses of the single employee Jagger kept there during the off-season. The Longhorn Saloon lost money, although Marshal Wild Jack Mason did his best to keep the place prosperous, but he made no arrests for a period of sixty days and his own income was sadly curtailed. He could not spend money he did not have.

The hotel cost Jagger a great deal even during the winter months.

There had been no income whatever from the stock-yards and shipping pens since November second. Fortunately, they required no salaried employees.

From the overhang of his door at the real-estate office, Chad Morgan, on a day in March, watched the rain pour down upon the street before him. It had rained for three days and there was no sign of its abating in the least.

It was too muddy to show lots. There were buyers at the Drovers Hotel, but they would not sludge through a foot of mud to see a twenty-foot wide pool of mud. It would stop raining one day. It had always stopped raining.

Morgan looked toward the hotel.

They were getting ready there for the first trail herd, the return of the roaring prosperity of the year 1867.

A new year had come, a new season was ahead.

Helen Jagger would once more be in her element, taking in the receipts of the far-flung enterprise. Jagger would add to his wealth. The faro bank would soon be operating at full capacity. Jagger wouldn't need the small revenue of his bank across the street.

A dollar a head for every steer processed through the Pawnee City stockyards, or was it a dollar and a half now? Five dollars for every carload of livestock shipped from Pawnee City. A thousand a week and more from The Longhorn; the revenue of the hotel, which would soon be operating at capacity.

It was what she wanted. Wealth. Power. Joe Jagger had both.

Chapter Thirty-One

The first herd came sloughing through the mud on the second of April. It had a hard time crossing the swollen river, but it was sold to a buyer before the steers were within a mile of the stockyards. The cattle buyers vied with one another for the privilege of shipping the first longhorns of the 1868 season to their packing houses in Kansas City and Chicago.

The steers, fat from the rich buffalo grass of the Indian Nations, sold for an average of thirty-four dollars per head.

The 1868 cattle season opened with a bang—the bang of Marshal Wild Jack's .44.

He killed a Texas cowboy that first day and then he disappeared into a secret hiding place, while Texas cowboys sloshed through the mud of Main Street, searching for the kill-crazy city marshal. They couldn't find Wild Jack, so they vented their rage upon the town itself. Windows were smashed in half the stores on the street and there were now more than two full blocks of stores.

Eighteen sixty-seven had been a Sunday-school picnic compared to 1868. The word had gone around in Texas, on The Chisholm Trail between Texas and Pawnee City, Kansas.

Pawnee City had a city marshal who was the fastest draw west of the Mississippi, the best pistol shot in the country. A Yankee who hated Texas and all things Texan.

Well, fine, fine! Texas men hated the Yankee carpet-baggers who made their lives miserable in their native habitat. Even more they hated all things north of the Red River, Indians in the Indian Nations, saloonkeepers who sold them rotgut whiskey for fancy prices, faro dealers

with trick card boxes, shortchange artists . . . and city
marshals who killed Texas men, or buffaloed them and
caused them to be fined by the justice of the peace of
Pawnee City, Kansas.

They hazed their steers north, they rode herd at night,
swam swollen rivers, rounded up stampeded cattle and
shivered when it rained and sweated when the sun burned
them.

They came into Pawnee City looking for trouble. They
sought it out and welcomed it. They smashed furniture in
the saloons, they broke mirrors and glasses. Much glass-
ware. Windows in the stores. They shot up the town and
now and then they tried to tree the town, take it over
completely and hold sway over it for an hour, or two
hours. Then they started back down The Trail with little,
if any, money in their pockets. Hang-overs and headaches
were usually all they had left of their weeks of toil.

And bitter memories.

"TEXAS MEN TREE PAWNEE CITY" was the headline
spread across Charles Fesler's *Pawnee City Lance*.

The fiery editor of Pawnee City's newspaper pulled no
punches. He called a spade a spade and he castigated the
city marshal of Pawnee City. He demanded that Mayor
Jagger fire him. He even suggested that the mayor was too
busy with his many and sundry enterprises to be a proper
mayor. He called upon the voters to nominate a new
mayor who would bring law and order to Pawnee City, who
would bring a semblance of peace to the newest county in
Kansas, Drake County, which had, that winter, been sev-
ered from its neighbor and formed into a county fifty miles
wide by seventy deep.

The sheriff, John Hampson, was merely an interim
sheriff. Everyone knew that he would serve only until the
July elections and Hampson himself, an appointee of the
governor, knew that he would not be elected. He did
nothing during his brief tenure of office.

The supervisors of Pawnee City had two meetings in
June, one a private one, in the back of Buffington's store,

attended by the supervisors only, and another in the court-room over the jail and marshal's office. Mayor Joe Jagger presided over this second meeting.

He directed his opening remarks at Publisher Charles Fesler. "I'm fed up with your newspaper's policies," he said angrily, "and I don't mind telling you that I resent your continual insinuations about me. I'm making it clear, right here and now, that I'm heading no ticket that includes your name."

"Mr. Mayor," interrupted Fesler, "you're expressing my personal sentiments precisely. I won't allow my name to be on the same ballot with yours. I'm going to let the others speak for themselves, but I can tell you, we're wasting time right now. Pawnee City's become a blot upon the map of Kansas."

"Hold your tongue, Fesler!" roared Joe Jagger. "I'm in charge of this meeting and I'll let you know when it's time for you to talk. That'll be when everyone else is through and then I'm not going to sit here and listen to your blather. I've read it in your lousy newspaper, all I'm going to take from you."

He stopped and looked around at the faces of the board of supervisors. There was no approval on the faces of Alfred Buffington, John Thompson, Harlow Tarbox or Charles Fesler. Only Justice of the Peace Judson Drake nodded his head in approval. And he stopped nodding it the moment he realized that he was registering approval of Joe Jagger.

"All right," said Jagger. "I'll listen to the rest of you now. Tarbox, say your piece."

"I pass," said Tarbox.

"What do you mean, you pass?" snapped Jagger.

"Alfred Buffington'll talk for me."

"Buffington?" Jagger said sharply. "You and Tarbox seem to have talked things over between you."

"We have," said the hardware store man calmly. "I think we're pretty much in agreement. Conditions in Pawnee City have become impossible."

"Have they, now?" sneered Jagger. "Have you gotten so rich in one year that you just want to sit in your rocking chair at your store and have the customers dump their money into your hat? You object to the noise of the Texas cattlemen's gold and silver?"

"Mr. Jagger," Buffington said patiently, "I take in more money from the farmers than I do from all the Texas cattlemen put together. I don't need the trade of the cattlemen and I don't want it."

"You're selling plows to the sodbusters who are ruining the graze of the county," snapped Jagger. "But what about the rest of the businessmen in Pawnee City? They depend on the cattle trade."

"Not me," said John Thompson. "I don't sell glass. If I did, I'd make a fortune selling windowpanes to the people who replace those broken by your cowboys."

Jagger fixed the last speaker with a cold look, then shifted his eyes back to Alfred Buffington.

"All right, Buffington," he said ominously, "finish your piece."

"I've said it. I want a quiet town. Law and order."

"Mr. Jagger," suddenly said Judge Drake, "I am wondering if I do not have the answer to the problem that is bothering some of our good friends. During recent weeks, I have heard considerable criticism of our city marshal. I have even heard it said that he is worse than the illness— ha-ha! the remedy is worse than the ailment! I would like to suggest, with all due respect to everyone concerned, that the services of Marshal Mason be dispensed with." He stopped, shot a quick look around at the supervisors, then finished lamely, "A good deputy marshal might also be the answer."

"Is that what this is about?" demanded Jagger. "You want me to fire Wild Jack Mason?"

"We want you to step out as mayor!" shouted Fesler.

Jagger winced almost as if the newspaperman had struck him with his fist.

"Is that what you've all decided upon? You want me to step down?" Jagger waited any protest that might be made. None came and the flush faded from Jagger's cheeks.

He got up from the chair behind the table, walked heavily to the door. There he stopped a moment as if about to turn back and say more on the subject, but he apparently changed his mind, for he went out without another word.

His feet were still sounding on the stairs outside when Judge Drake rose.

"Gentlemen, I want to make one more suggestion. We're going to have to send a man to the state legislature next month. I would like to propose the name of, ah, our mayor, Mr. Joseph Jagger. The office is not a particularly important one, but it has considerable prestige. You might say that we were—ah—kicking him upstairs." He looked around at the few faces watching, saw that there was no response to his suggestion whatever. He said, "Well, *somebody* has to go to the legislature!"

Fesler got to his feet. "Gentlemen, before we decide upon a candidate for the state job, let's settle our biggest problem right here. The office of mayor. Last year you honored me by suggesting me."

"No," said Harlow Tarbox promptly. "You talk too much. You keep everyone stirred up all the time."

Fesler opened his mouth to blast the owner of The St. Louis Store, then remembered suddenly that Tarbox was the biggest single advertiser in the *Pawnee City Lance*. He closed his mouth again.

"We haven't discussed this among ourselves," Tarbox went on, "but I'm sure we all know the one man for the job. Chad Morgan."

Buffington sprang to his feet. "I second the motion."

"And I," cried Oliver Wakeman.

John Thompson bobbed his head.

Charles Fesler let out a heavy wheeze. "All right, all right, I'll go along with that."

"And now about the legislature," pursued Judge Drake.

"You want that job?" asked Buffington.

The judge turned red. He hesitated, then nodded. "It would be a privilege to serve the citizens of the county that bears my name."

Harlow Tarbox and Alfred Buffington went to call on Chad Morgan. They found him alone in the real-estate office, reading a book on agriculture. His realtor was out, showing some property to a potential buyer.

"Morgan," said Tarbox, "neither Alf or I know how you're going to take this. As your oldest friends in Pawnee City, we hope you'll agree to what we're about to propose to you." He drew a deep breath. "We want you to be our next mayor!"

Morgan closed his book, put it down on the desk and looked from Buffington to Tarbox, then back to Buffington. "What about Joe?"

"He's not going to run."

"You decided that for him?"

"If you want to put it that way."

"I see." Morgan drew a deep breath. "I think both of you know me well enough by now to know that it isn't a job I want and *I* know that you're ready with a lot of arguments . . . it's my duty, et cetera."

"It is," declared Buffington.

"I know it is," admitted Morgan. "I'm one of the founders of this town and I will never get over the feeling of responsibility. I have a pretty fair idea that this isn't going to make me awfully popular with some of the people in this town, but"—he shrugged—"it can't be helped, I'll take the job."

"Chad," exclaimed Tarbox, "all I can say is . . . thanks."

Morgan made a wry face. "This may be the last word of thanks I'll get from anyone." He got to his feet. "What about our fine judge? Do I get him?"

"No," said Buffington.

"Good!"

"He's going to the legislature," blurted out Tarbox. "He kind of squirmed into that, but he may be all right in that job. He's got friends at the capital and—he'll be out of your hair."

"A lawyer named Carmichael hung up his shingle a few weeks ago," suggested Buffington.

"I know. I sold him his office. I think he'll be an improvement over Drake."

Chapter Thirty-Two

That same afternoon Pete Mossman rode into Pawnee City. He had with him his towheaded trail boss, Brog, and a round dozen of the most disreputable-looking Texans that had ever come to Kansas. Several of them had been with the towhead trail boss the year before when they had given Pawnee City the worst hurrahing of the 1867 season.

Mossman and his men brought a herd of five thousand longhorns with them, the largest herd to reach Pawnee City thus far.

The cowboys visited The Longhorn Saloon, had a drink or two apiece, then wandered about town. They were strictly under wraps, having been given explicit and positive instructions by their employer, Pete Mossman, not to cut loose.

Not until the herd was sold, the money in Pete Mossman's saddlebags. Then the men were on their own.

Wild Jack Mason sought out Joe Jagger, at the Drovers Hotel.

"Pete Mossman's in town."

"I know it."

"He's brought with him twelve-fifteen men. I've been hearing it all around town; they've got a grudge against this town and they figure to hurrah it to hell and back. What am I supposed to do against that many men?"

"Mason," said Jagger, "I don't give a damn what you do. I'm through trying to run this town."

"But you're the mayor," protested Wild Jack.

"Not any more. My time's up in a few weeks, but I'm not sticking out my neck any more. You go talk to that blather-mouthed newspaper publisher, Fesler. He wants to run this town. You can tell him for me to go ahead. I'm not waiting until next month. I'm quitting right now."

"Fesler hates my guts," said Wild Jack bitterly. He was silent a moment, then he grunted. "Well, I guess that's the way the cards fall. If you're out, I'm through. I might as well hand in my badge."

"Give it to Fesler," snapped Jagger.

"This is a good time for me to quit," suddenly grinned Wild Jack. "Let 'em handle Mossman's crowd." He pursed up his thin lips. "Talk is that the cowboys are going to give it to Chad Morgan. Somebody said something about him having a run-in with Mossman last year."

"Not Mossman, his trail boss. I don't know what his name is——"

"Brog. Supposed to be quite a revolver man."

"Morgan caught him drunk and ran him out of town."

"I heard that, but I didn't believe it. Faced them down, took away their guns." Wild Jack scowled at an unpleasant memory. "I got a bone to pick with Morgan myself."

Jagger looked sharply at Wild Jack. "You and Morgan have trouble?"

"The dance last winter. He sided with that bushwhacker, what's his name, Alder, Balder——"

"I'd almost forgotten Alder," Jagger said. "Whatever became of him?"

"Alder? Who knows? On the dodge, I imagine. Probably joined up with his old friends. That whole Missouri bunch have turned outlaw, I hear. The Youngers, Frank James, his kid brother, Jesse. They say they've been robbing banks over in Missouri. Well, old Allen Pinkerton will be catching up with them pretty soon and I wouldn't be a bit surprised if this Alder fella isn't grabbed along with the others."

"I was under the impression that Alder had made Texas his home. Didn't he come up with General Simcoe last fall?"

"How should I know? Texas?" Wild Jack wrinkled his nose in disgust. "Well, I might as well mosey over to this newspaperman and hand him my tin star."

Mason went out of the hotel, passing Helen Jagger

coming in. She turned to look after him, then frowning, came toward Jagger.

"Is it true, Joe?" she asked worriedly. "About you—and Chad?"

"Me and Chad?" exclaimed Jagger. "What are you talking about?"

"A silly report that you had been—that you weren't going to run for re-election as mayor and that Chad was taking over."

"Morgan!" cried Jagger aghast. "Who told you that?"

"Mrs. Fesler said it was all arranged. I didn't know whether to believe it or not."

"Chad Morgan," said Jagger dully. "So he's beaten me again!"

"I don't believe it. Chad has no personal ambitions, not of that nature. He doesn't *want* to be mayor."

"The hell he doesn't," snarled Jagger. "He's been scheming against me ever since last year. He wanted the job, then——"

"That's not true, Joe. I—I happen to know that it was he who insisted they make you mayor. He said he would fight them if they didn't elect you."

"Don't give me that," said Jagger angrily. Then he shifted to the attack. "Still standing up for him? The way things are you'll soon——" He caught himself.

"I'll soon what?"

"I'll tell you just this much. For old times' sake. For *his* sake. Tell him to get out of town and stay out for the next day or two. Pete Mossman's men are gunning for him and, as of just about this moment, there's no city marshal to protect him. Wild Jack's quit his job. And so have I. Mr. Chad Morgan can handle the grief right now. He doesn't have to wait until his gang railroads him into office next month."

Morgan had not known that Mossman's outfit was in Pawnee City. A man had stopped at the office within an hour after Morgan had consented to become mayor. He wanted to look at some farm property and Morgan had gone out to show him a parcel of land, an eighty-acre tract some five miles from Pawnee City.

The errand took a considerable time, the prospect asking many questions, stopping every few dozen feet to sample the soil. He had finally told Morgan that he would think things over, and Morgan had let him go back to Pawnee City alone.

Morgan himself rode to Alex Turnboom's place. He had caught a distant glimpse of the wheat on the way out and he wanted to look at it close. He found the Swede, aided by two growing sons, building a fence on the river side of the farm.

"Damn cowboy," swore Turnboom, as Morgan came up. "They don't watch their cows and they trample my wheat. Them damn Texas cows too lazy eat grass, like better wheat."

Morgan looked around the growing wheat field. As far as he could see the light green stalks, just beginning to turn brown, spread across the landscape.

"I guess I'll have to believe you now," he said thoughtfully. "The cold weather didn't kill it."

"I tell you it don't. I raise winter wheat in old country." The farmer broke off a stem of wheat, felt the husk of kernels between his thumb and forefinger. "Good, fat kernel. This eart' very fine loam. Raise forty bushel wheat to acre——"

"Forty bushels an acre and wheat is selling now for around ninety cents!"

"Go down when harvest come," Turnboom said.

"Your cousins," Morgan went on. "How's their wheat?"

"All same. Very good. We keep cows away two-three more week, we all right. Thrash wheat then and don't care about cows."

"Will this fence hold them off?"

"This fence and maybe bullets," scowled Turnboom.

"No," Morgan said, "don't use your gun. You're a good farmer, Axel, and you know a lot about wheat. But guns are the business of the Texas men. They cut their eyeteeth on them. Go to the sheriff, if they get too bad. I'll talk to the cattlemen myself." He hesitated. "I'm running for mayor of Pawnee City next month."

The farmer's eyes lit up. "You, mayor? Is good. Very good. I vote for you."

"I don't know if you're eligible," laughed Morgan. "It's a city election. You can, however, vote for the county offices, which will be filled at the same time."

"I like vote for you," persisted Turnboom.

Chapter Thirty-Three

Artie Puffpaff struck the spark that started the fire that became the holocaust. Brog, the towhead, and his baker's dozen of cowboys were still under wraps. They coursed the street, up and down, back and forth. They dismounted now and then to get a drink at one of the seven Pawnee City saloons. They made no overt moves. They talked quietly, they had their periodic drinks, but they sought no trouble.

They were ready to resist any that came to them.

Artie Puffpaff, having cadged his normal complement of drinks about the town, came out of The Longhorn Saloon and started wobbling across the street. The tail end of Brog's men were trotting by on their horses. Puffpaff, who seldom looked where he was walking, reeled into the back end of one of the broncs.

He was knocked aside, going down to a sitting position in the dust of the street.

"You goddamned bastards!" he shouted. "Why don't you look where you're going?"

Puffpaff, at that instant, had only moments of life left. He may have known it. It had been a miserable life.

The Texas man whose horse had knocked Puffpaff over swiveled in his saddle.

"Watch that tongue of yours, sodbuster," he growled back.

Puffpaff bounced to his feet. "What'd you call me, you goddam Johnny Reb? We licked you bastards a few years ago and we can do it again. . . ." He added insult to injury by waving his fist.

The cowboy swore angrily, whirled his horse back. He probably had no other intention than to give Puffpaff, at close range, a blast of verbal invective, but the little squat-

179

ter, in his usual drunken condition, yelled and lurched forward into the path of the onrushing bronc. The Texas man cried out, jerked his mount to such an abrupt stop that it reared up on its hind legs.

Its front legs came down—crushing the skull of Artie Puffpaff.

The cowboy, fighting to control his horse, was aghast at what had happened to Artie Puffpaff. His companions came swirling back.

"You've done it, Crocker!" snarled Brog, the towhead.

"Damn, damn, damn!" swore the man whose horse had killed Puffpaff.

He drew his revolver and, in a blind rage, fired it at the window of Morgan's real-estate office. The glass had scarcely crashed than the other Texas men had their guns out and were blazing away in all directions except at the harmless sky.

Windows crashed, horses screamed and plunged at the tie-rails. A team of horses, in front of The St. Louis Store, went wild and, rushing away with the farm wagon they were pulling, overturned the wagon.

The Texas men galloped down the street in a solid phalanx. Most of them were more sober than drunk and their aim was deadlier than customary for hurrahing cowboys. Windows crashed with monotonous regularity.

At the end of the street, they wheeled their horses and came back.

Chad Morgan heard the shooting as he neared Pawnee City. He guessed instantly that cowboys were trying to free the town, but he did not know that the men were his own personal enemies, that he was their actual target.

He was unarmed, however, and knew that it was folly to ride blindly into the midst of indiscriminate shooting. He turned his horse to the left and started it down the alley behind the west row of business buildings. When he reached the rear of Buffington's store, he dismounted and tied his horse to a plow handle.

He crossed quickly to the rear door of the store, whipped it open and entered.

A clerk rose up from behind a counter where he had taken refuge. Buffington and a second clerk were at the front of the store, crouched and peering out through a broken window.

They were so intent on watching the street that they did not hear Morgan approach until he spoke.

"What's the matter with the marshal?" Morgan asked.

Buffington whirled, saw Morgan and exclaimed in relief. "He's quit! Joe Jagger resigned as mayor and Wild Jack handed his badge to Charlie Fesler." He suddenly winced. "Those are Pete Mossman's men out there."

"So they're back!"

"It's worse than that." Buffington hesitated. "They're after *you*."

"Well, I can't say that I haven't expected it," replied Morgan.

Buffington's face showed concern. "They're not drunk this time. It won't be the same as last year. They're fighting mad—and they've already killed Artie Puffpaff."

Morgan exclaimed, "Why'd they pick on that harmless old coot?"

"No one's going up to ask the cowboys," retorted Buffington.

The spiteful crack of a rifle came in from the street. Glass crashed somewhere and a raucous voice shouted, "Come on out, Morgan, wherever you are!"

Morgan stepped to the window. Through a broken pane he picked out the Texas men. There were a full dozen or more of them. Half were sitting their horses, the others were gathered in a close group around the mounted men.

They were on the far side of the street, up three or four doors, making the total distance from the front of Buffington's store about two hundred feet. A fairly long range for a revolver, short for a rifle.

Morgan turned to Buffington. "Have you got a gun?"

Buffington gave a start. "You're not going out there——"

"Not this time, but I'm going to do something I should have done last year. Kill that towhead."

The rear door of the store banged and the men at the window whirled and saw Charles Fesler dashing forward.

"Here you are, Morgan!" cried the newspaperman. "It's about time. You've told him, Buffington?"

The hardware man nodded. "I've told him that Jagger's quit, yes."

"And the marshal?"

"Good riddance," snapped Morgan. "He wouldn't go up against that bunch, anyway."

"You will?"

"Fesler," cried Buffington, "this isn't the same. Those men are sober, they've already killed one man."

"It's his job," persisted Fesler. "He's the new mayor."

"Not yet," Morgan reminded.

"Yes, you are. The board of supervisors appointed you interim mayor, until the election. It's up to you to keep the peace of this town."

Morgan said bitterly, "I was a fool to let myself in for this."

His eyes picked out a rack of Winchester rifles high on the left wall of the store. Leaving Fesler and Buffington, he strode toward the rack. When he saw where Morgan was going, Buffington followed hurriedly.

"Don't do anything foolish, Morgan," he warned again.

"Anything's foolish at this stage," snapped Morgan. He tore down a Winchester, worked the pump lever and saw that the gun was clean and in good operating condition. "Where do you keep your cartridges?"

"In the counter there." Buffington winced, then, "I mean, I don't know where."

It was too late, Morgan had already located the Winchester cartridges. He took out a box, ripped it open and began stuffing shells into the rifle.

He loaded it and took a great handful of shells and dropped them into his pocket.

He looked at Fesler then. "Am I going into this alone?"

"Alone? Why—why"—the newspaperman gasped— "*I'm* no gunfighter."

"Neither am I," snapped Morgan. "You wanted this mayor's job so bad, what would *you* do in a case like this?"

"What could I do? I—I'd leave things to the law enforcement body. The marshal——"

"There's no marshal."

"The sheriff . . ." Fesler snatched at that. "Yes, the sheriff. He's supposed to step in when the town marshals are unable to perform their duties. . . . John Hampson's the sheriff." He whirled to Buffington. "Where is he?"

"Hiding, I suppose. Like everybody else with any sense."

Out on the street, two quick rifle shots sounded. One of the bullets zinged through the wood of the front door, crashed into a stack of galvanized pails, scattering them.

"They're getting close," Morgan said grimly.

He drew a deep breath and turned toward the front of the store.

"Wait!" cried Fesler hysterically. "You can't bring them here. I—they'll riddle this place and kill us all." He sent a frightened look around, saw the rear door of the store and scuttled for it.

"A good idea," growled Morgan. "Buffington, get your men and clear out."

Buffington replied by reaching for a rifle on the rack. "You and me, Morgan," he said grimly, "we're original settlers. We both had a hand in making this town and I guess it's up to us to hold it. We can't let a bunch of killers take it away from us."

"Come, then," snapped Morgan.

Buffington followed him to the front, stuffing shells into his Winchester.

Reaching the door, Morgan stooped and peered through a broken pane. The cowboys were not in as compact a group as previously. They had become restless. Two or three of the mounted men had spread out. A man on foot, with a rifle, was bent low and moving forward across the street.

Morgan gave him but a quick glance. He was searching for the towhead Brog.

He found him, one of the mounted men, moving away from the main group. Morgan raised his Winchester, thrust the muzzle through the hole in the window and took quick aim.

He pulled the trigger.

The towhead seemed to rise high in the saddle. He fell over backwards, hitting the earth heavily. He never moved once he hit the ground.

For one moment there was a stunned silence on the street of Pawnee City. Then a Texas man cried out, "The hardware store! It come from there——"

Buffington's store was instantly the cynosure of hostile eyes. Guns began to fire, but before they opened up, Morgan had pumped a fresh cartridge into the chamber of the Winchester and taken a second shot . . . at the rifleman crossing the street.

Two men down!

There was a mad scramble now. The unmounted Texans vaulted into their saddles. The mounted ones converged, began rushing the hardware store. Bullets smashed glass, tore through wood.

Buffington's gun spoke. Morgan fired a third time and a horse screamed and, rearing up, threw its rider. Buffington brought down the cowboy as he was scrambling to his feet.

The charge of the cowboys came almost to the front door of the hardware store. One horse even reached the wooden sidewalk, skidded and jolted his rider so that the cowboy, virtually thrusting a revolver into Morgan's face, missed his fire. The man threw away his gun in sudden fright, and scurried away on hands and knees.

The charge broke them.

There was no leader, no unity among the cowboys. They scattered, firing wildly and blindly in all directions.

And then it happened. Faces peering from doors and windows up and down the street had seen the towhead dropped with a single shot, had seen and heard the firing from the shelter of the hardware store.

Wakeman, one of the supervisors, sprang out of his livery stable with a revolver in his hand. He began firing at the scattering cowboys. The bald barber produced an old dragoon pistol, sent a crashing shot in the general direction of the cowboys.

A third businessman appeared with a shotgun that

boomed over the other firing. Even Harlow Tarbox, the owner of The St. Louis Store, joined in the firing, producing a gun from behind his counter.

Morgan and Buffington appeared in front of the hardware store. Both men pumped cartridges into rifle chambers and fired, coolly and methodically.

In moments there was no one left at whom to fire.

The businessmen of Pawnee City, amateurs though they were at armed warfare, had dispersed and completely routed the men who lived by the gun.

The score was: three dead cowboys, two badly wounded. Undoubtedly, two or three others carried wounds away with them.

None of the townsmen had been wounded. Only Artie Puffpaff lay in the dust of the street in front of Morgan's office.

Chapter Thirty-Four

Alfred Buffington stared at Chad Morgan. "You're serious? A hundred plows?"

"And twenty harrows."

"Good lord, how much land are you going to work?"

"I own forty-six hundred acres," Morgan said. "I'm planning to put it all in wheat."

"That'll cost you a fortune."

"Every cent I can beg, borrow or steal. I've given Wakeman orders to find me a hundred of the best teams of horses in the country. I'm sending to Kansas City for a hundred and fifty farm laborers. I've got to feed them, build bunkhouses."

"You're risking all this on wheat?"

"You're in touch with the farmers, Buffington," Morgan said; "you know how good their crops were this summer. Axel Turnboom averaged forty-two bushels of wheat to the acre. He sold it at eighty-six cents a bushel——"

"I know," Buffington said. "I was surprised myself at how well the winter wheat did. Still, forty-six hundred acres——"

"It's the big gamble, the biggest one I've ever taken in my life. If I lose, I'm sunk for good. If I win——"

"You've made history." Buffington stared at Morgan. "You may change the entire economy of this section of the country. The cattle trade——"

"Pawnee City doesn't need it. The only ones who profit by it are the saloonkeepers."

"And Joe Jagger."

Morgan frowned. "I can't help that."

"I know. Jagger's fought us every step of the way. He's been interested only in the things that bring him money. The stockyards and loading pens, The Longhorn Saloon

. . . his hotel. . . . We can't go on with shootings and killings, living in continual terror. If I had my way about it, I'd refuse to let a cattleman or a cowboy come into Pawnee City."

Morgan regarded Buffington thoughtfully. "You'd back me up in that?"

Buffington looked at him sharply. "You've got something up your sleeve?"

Morgan nodded. "I'm planning to make a proposal to the board of supervisors at the meeting tomorrow night."

A smartly dressed young woman stepped down from the train at the Pawnee City depot. The conductor who had descended before her, piled her boxes and bags on the platform: two hat boxes, a valise and a carpetbag.

"It's been a pleasure having you as a passenger," he said warmly.

"Thank you," replied Cass Simcoe. "I enjoyed the train ride."

The station agent hurried forward as Cass looked around. It was September, almost ten months to the day she had left Pawnee City.

Pawnee City had changed, although Cass was not sure it was for the better. But perhaps it was the change in Cass herself. She wore a suit of fine material, a hat with a small curled ostrich feather. Her hands were soft, smooth. There had been no callouses on them for some months now.

Her hair had grown, was smartly coiffured.

Cass Simcoe looked exactly like a young lady of fashion, stepping out of a handsome carriage on Fifth Avenue in New York in front of Tiffany's jewelry store.

An idle thought flitted through her mind. What would it be like to straddle a bucking bronc with her legs—limbs —that had grown soft from disuse?

The station agent was saying, "Ma'am, I'll get someone to carry these bags for you. Where do you want 'em taken?"

"The hotel."

Helen Jagger was relieving the day clerk at the desk when Cass entered the lobby. Helen was working on a ledger and did not look up immediately—until her nostrils caught the perfume.

Her eyes widened and a flicker of alarm came and went in them as she recognized Cass Simcoe.

"Cass!" she exclaimed. "Where in the world have you come from?"

"St. Louis. I just stepped off the train."

Helen continued to stare at her. "I almost didn't recognize you. Are you *sure* you're Cass Simcoe?"

"Have I changed that much?"

"Is day night? Does a longhorn have *short* horns?"

Impulsively, Cass reached out and caught Helen's hand. She squeezed it, then let go of it, embarrassed, lest it seem that her newly won sophistication was only veneer thin.

"Has my father gotten in?" she asked.

"I haven't seen him this year. We were wondering just the other day why he hadn't made a drive."

"He's only making the one this year—a big one. He wrote me six weeks ago and said they were leaving. He wanted me to meet him here."

"Then I imagine he'll be along any day. You want a room, of course. Or two?"

"One will be ample."

"Where's your luggage?" Then Helen saw a man coming into the hotel. He was laden with the hat boxes, the valise and the carpetbag. "Don't tell me all of that is yours."

"I'm afraid it is."

"You mean," Helen asked mischievously, *"I'll* be borrowing a dress from you this time?"

"You can have anything I own!" exclaimed Cass. She stopped, turned and looked around the lobby as the man with the luggage came up and piled it before the desk.

"Thank you," she said. She fumbled in her haste to open her purse and bring out a scented greenback. She pressed it upon the man, who seemed loath to accept it.

"It was a pleasure, ma'am."

"And now," Helen said, writing Cass's name on the hotel ledger, "you want to know what is new in Pawnee City ——"

"Everything. I—I feel almost as if this is home now."

"Perhaps it will be . . . one day," said Helen in a low tone. Then she raised her face and smiled at the flushed young woman facing her. "We've a new mayor."

Cass winced. "I know. Dad wrote me." She smiled wanly. "I get my news—most of it—from Texas. Everybody down there knows what's going on in—in Kansas. Dad writes me twice a week. He told me that—Mr. Morgan had been elected mayor. I—I don't know what to say."

"About Mr. Morgan? Or—my brother losing the office?"

"Mr. Jagger. I—I imagine he didn't want to be mayor any more."

"Oh, he wanted to be, all right. The town didn't want him . . ." Helen faltered. "I suppose you've heard the rest, then, of Ch— Mr. Morgan's cleanup."

"His fight with the cowboys? His no-gun-toting ordinance?"

"I can see there's very little I can tell you."

"Yes, there is." Cass looked at Helen bravely, while her color deepened. "How . . . is he?"

"I won't answer that," Helen said, her own face flushing. "He can tell you himself when you meet him."

Dan Hastings, the first Texan to reach Pawnee City with a herd, had arrived in town on his second visit, in 1868. He was an angry man when he went into Chad Morgan's real-estate office.

"Look here, Morgan," he said. "I've got thirty-five hundred longhorns below the river and there ain't enough graze to fill the bellies of a bunch of sick calves. The grass has been worked over too much."

"I know," Morgan said, "too many steers have come to Pawnee City this year. It's gotten so you have to graze out pretty far now."

"Somebody's gone and put a fence around the best graze," Hastings said. "There's miles and miles of fence." He glowered. "Somebody said it was your fence."

"It is, Mr. Hastings. We're going to start plowing there next week."

"Plowing! You?"

"I'm putting in some winter wheat."

"I—I don't understand," said Hastings, puzzled. "You're a cattleman."

"Not any more," said Morgan. "I'm a farmer. But I'll tell you what—you're going to sell your steers pretty soon, aren't you?"

"As soon as I get a decent price for them. I thought I might graze them a few days."

"Graze them on my land. Cut the fence and turn your herd in."

"That's damned decent of you, Mr. Morgan. But I'm still curious. I know that there've been quite a few sod-busters fencing in their places, but it never bothered us— not too much. There was plenty of graze. Only—this place of yours is pretty big. What about next year? Won't you be using your land then?"

"Yes." Morgan inhaled. "The truth of the matter is, Mr. Hastings, Pawnee City has outgrown the cattle trade. There are other, newer towns on the Kansas and Colorado now. They've built shipping pens at Emporia, Wichita. They're actually closer to Texas and you'd save two, three and even five days if you drove your herds there."

"You don't want us here any more?" ejaculated Hastings.

"You, personally. Yes, Mr. Hastings. I count you one of my best friends. Speaking for the town of Pawnee City, we do not want the cattle trade. Not after this season ends."

Hastings got red in the face, but before he could blow off steam, a seventeen-year-old boy, who did odd jobs for the Drovers Hotel, came in. "Mr. Morgan," he said, "here's a letter from the hotel."

Morgan caught a faint whiff of lilac as he started to rip open the square, tinted envelope, then looked at the inscription. Only his name was on the envelope: *Mr. Chad Morgan.*

He opened the envelope and extracted a folded sheet of note paper.

The message read:

Dear Mr. Morgan:
If you do not have a previous engagement, the under-signed would be very happy to have dinner with you. Six o'clock.

(Miss) Cass Simcoe

Morgan exclaimed and got to his feet so quickly he almost knocked over the chair. "Excuse me, Mr. Hastings, something has just come up—something important."

He rushed to the door, then after he had jerked it open, whirled back. "Cut my wire, Mr. Hastings, it's perfectly all right."

He turned away.

Helen Jagger was still behind the desk when Morgan came striding into the hotel lobby. She saw him falter as he approached.

"Room four," Helen said. "That's in the front of the house."

"I know," Morgan said. "I used to live here—once."

"Of course, Mr. Morgan."

Her eyes fell to the ledger over which she had been working. Morgan looked at her a long moment, then stepped closer to the desk. "Still working," he said quietly.

"I'm *always* working," Helen replied with a trace of acerbity. "Isn't that what's wrong with me?"

"No, Helen," he said. "Would you listen to me a moment if I talked?"

"Our guest is waiting." He made no reply and after a moment she said, "I can't stop you from talking. And since I can't leave the desk, I'll *have* to listen to you."

"For what's happened, Helen," Morgan said, "I'm deeply sorry. I—I don't have the words to say any more than that."

"You're saying them very well," said Helen in a low, strained voice.

"The next ones aren't going to be said as well. I just want you to know that what's going to happen *had* to happen. I know, I'll be blamed for it, but Helen, please believe me, it can't be helped. I can't stop it any more

than I could stop the moon from waxing and waning. It's
inevitable——"

She was looking at him. "What are you talking about?
I don't understand."

"You will tomorrow. And you'll probably hate me even
more than you do now."

"Hate you!"

"Joe's an army man. Lord knows he's heard it enough
times. No man's indispensable. No single man. Someone
has to fight in the rear guard for the benefit of the others.
Tell him that—think of it yourself."

Helen's surprise had turned to suspicion. "I don't like
the way you're talking."

"I'm sorry," he said stiffly. He nodded and turned away
from the desk. He started for the stairs, but before he
reached them, he changed his mind and went out of the
hotel.

Cass, looking out of the window of her room, from
which she had watched the boy deliver the message, had
seen Morgan coming toward the hotel and had awaited his
knock on the door. She saw him leaving the hotel now and
a gasp was torn from her throat. Then she whirled and,
sobbing, threw herself on the bed.

Chapter Thirty-Five

Yet, Morgan was waiting for her in the lobby when Cass Simcoe descended the stairs at precisely three minutes after six. Three minutes late—purposely. At the school in St. Louis they had said five minutes.

The words, "Hi, Reb," that Morgan was about to utter died stillborn. An ejaculation was torn from his lips. "Good Lord!" Then he was striding toward her.

He did not kiss her. He wanted to, but the satin evening gown she wore held him off. He gripped her hand savagely and Cass returned his pressure, even though her hand hurt from his grip.

"It's wonderful," she gushed in a restrained sort of a way. "I've been looking forward to this for so long——"

"So was I," said Morgan, "but I didn't know it." He grinned. "Wasn't a day I didn't think about you."

"I thought of you twice a week, Thursday evenings and Sunday afternoons," smiled Cass, then added mischievously, "They kept me at my lessons all the rest of the time."

They went into the dining room and for a while Morgan kept looking toward the door, expecting Helen Jagger to make her appearance; when she did not, he realized that she was purposely keeping out of the way. She was probably having her dinner in her room tonight.

Later, Joe Jagger strolled into the dining room, saw Morgan and left again. They had not spoken a single word to each other since the day Jagger had resigned as mayor and Morgan, propelled into the job, had been forced to fight the Texas men.

The food came and Cass knew the proper knife and fork, the correct spoon. She talked of her school in St.

Louis and said that she was not going back even though
the general had written her that he thought another year
would be only right and proper.

"I'm going home with Dad," she said wistfully. "I'm
going to ride down The Trail with him and the boys and
I'm never going to leave Texas again."

She paused then and it would have been the moment
for the right man to say the right words about changing
her mind. Even if he was the right man, but not quite
ready for those words, the opening had been given him and
he could have said, without committing himself, "Maybe
there's a Yankee, or a Northerner who might make you
change your mind—when he was ready."

Morgan didn't say the words and the animation that had
seeped through Cass's veneer of poise began to draw away
from her. She became nervous and when the dessert had
been eaten and it was close to eight o'clock, Cass was actually relieved to see Morgan take out his watch. Looking at
it, he said, "Cass, this job of being mayor has its draw-
backs. There's a meeting of the board of supervisors at
eight o'clock that I've got to attend. It's an important
meeting."

"Of course," said Cass. "I'm going to bed early, unless
—unless Dad happens to show up this evening."

During the almost two hours they had been together
they had not talked about anything that they could not
have discussed in the hotel lobby with twenty people standing around, all with big ears.

The meeting that evening in the courtroom above the
jail was the most momentous one ever held by the board
of supervisors in its entire existence. The supervisors, already informed by Alfred Buffington, listened with complete attention while Morgan read from a sheet of paper
that he had prepared previously:

*"Resolved: That the city of Pawnee City, Kansas, au-
thorizes the Mayor to prepare and have printed a number
of circulars which are to be distributed during the next
three months, via U. S. Mail, to various persons in the*

*state of Texas. Said circulars are to contain the following
message in essence: To wit: The cattle trade is no longer
desired in the city of Pawnee City, Kansas, county of
Drake. Grazing grounds in and about Pawnee City are no
longer available. The merchants and businessmen of Pawnee City no longer desire the custom and patronage of the
cattlemen. Shipping points, stockyards and loading pens
are now available at points on the Kansas & Colorado
R.R. which are considerably closer to Texas than is
Pawnee City. It is suggested that cattlemen who formerly
drove herds to Pawnee City divert these herds, on and
after January first, 1869, to these other shipping points.*

> *Signed: City of Pawnee City, Kansas.*
> *Chad Morgan, Mayor*
> *Approved by the Pawnee City
> Board of Supervisors, this
> 2nd day of September, 1868."*

When Morgan finished reading the document he looked
at the sober faces of the men facing him.

Alfred Buffington rose to his feet. "I make a motion that
we unanimously approve Mr. Morgan's statement."

"I second the motion," shouted Charles Fesler.

Morgan nodded. "All those in favor, say aye."

"Aye!" said every man in the courtroom.

Fesler then got to his feet. "Do we let Joe Jagger find
this out from reading it in the *Pawnee Lance?*"

Morgan hesitated, then shook his head. "I have made a
copy of this resolution. I am prepared to sign it and I would
like all of you gentlemen to sign it. I will then have the
copy sent over to Mr. Jagger by special messenger."

The board meeting was over by eight twenty. At twenty
minutes to nine a boy brought a letter into the Drovers
Hotel and handed it to Joe Jagger seated in an armchair
near the door, smoking a thin cheroot. He read the contents of the envelope and his face turned as white as the
paper he held in his hand.

He was still staring at the sheet five minutes later when
Helen Jagger came hesitatingly down the stairs. She

glanced toward the dining room, saw the rapt attention her brother was giving the paper he was holding and went over to him.

He looked up at her and then, without a word, handed her the piece of paper that was his financial death warrant.

She read it through, exclaiming even before she finished, "So this is what he meant!"

"Morgan," said Joe Jagger thickly. "He's turned sod-buster. He's bought a hundred plows and he intends to plow up all the land I gave him—*the land I gave him!*"

"Joe," cried Helen, "don't say that. When we dissolved the firm we—we *forced* him to take that land. It had no value then, but it was the only thing we could do because we didn't dare let him know about the bank—about Nathan Foss and the cattle-loading bribe."

Jagger did not even seem to hear her. "He's fought me ever since we came to Kansas. He's gone out of his way to try to hurt me, and now—now he's succeeded. He's ruined me."

"Let's go back to Illinois," pleaded Helen. "I hate this country. I hate what it's done to you—and to me——"

Jagger got up, rocked on his heels a moment, then brushing Helen aside, headed for the door. He went out.

At the loading pens and stockyards, Jagger found the foreman of the night crew. He was a hulking, beetle-browed man who called himself Smith and was probably wanted somewhere in the East under a different name.

"Smith," Jagger said to him, "you've got a tough crew working here and you see a lot of rough men come and go. Do you happen to know a man I could hire for a—a private matter?"

"What's the *matter?*"

Jagger said deliberately: "I want to—take care of a man——"

Smith showed snaggled teeth in a wicked grin. "You don't have to look any farther, Mr. Jagger. Give me the man's name and I'll take care of him myself, personally."

"How much will you want for the job?"

"For a little thing like that? Hell, Mr. Jagger, it'd be

my pleasure. I don't want no pay. Anybody else five bucks, maybe ten. For you, free."

"Ten dollars?" Jagger shook his head. "By taking care of a man, I don't mean—beating him up——"

Air came out of Smith's lungs so swiftly that he whistled. "Gosh, Mr. Jagger, I dunno. Breaking a couple of ribs or maybe a jaw, that's fun. But——the *other* thing——"

"What do you think I mean by—the other thing?"

"I—I dunno. It sounded almost like you meant"— Smith gulped—"you wanted a man taken care of for keeps!"

"You don't know anyone who'd do a thing like that— for a price? A good price——"

"N-no, Mr. Jagger. We're working people down here. We work, we eat and sleep. We get drunk on payday and we maybe fight a little. But we ain't the kind of people you want for that—*that* job." He grimaced. "What you want is somebody like that killin' marshal you had a while back. He'd have cut his grandmother's throat. A lawman like that's worse than——"

He stopped, for Jagger was walking away from him.

Chapter Thirty-Six

In The Longhorn, Jagger called the manager, Blake, to one side. "Where can I get in touch with Wild Jack Mason? Did he tell you where he was headed for when he left here?"

"He didn't tell anyone. He snuck out of town the minute he turned in his star." Blake shrugged. "Somebody said somethin' about seein' him in K.C. a while ago. He was hanging around Chief Speer's place, giving shooting demonstrations." Blake shook his head. "He's a fancy man with a gun. Probably the best in the country."

"Do you think he's in Kansas City now?"

Blake frowned in thought. "It was over a month ago that I hear about him. I doubt if he's still there. He had a bad run of the cards the last two weeks he was here. He must have pulled out with about thirty dollars in his pocket. That wouldn't hold him very long." Blake hesitated. "You wasn't thinking of gettin' him back here, was you?"

"No," lied Jagger. "I—I had something of his I wanted to send on to him."

He turned away from Blake and went to the door. As he went out, he passed a man coming in, a cowboy by his clothing, a gaunt, unshaven man.

Jagger was outside before he realized that the man was Tom Alder and turning, he went back into the saloon.

Alder was already at the bar. Jagger went up to him and said, "Haven't seen you around lately."

"Just came in from Texas with General Simcoe. He's gone on to the hotel to see if his daughter's got there yet."

"She's here," Jagger said briefly. Then: "Something I'd like to talk to you about in private, Alder. I wonder if you could come over to the hotel in a few minutes. I'll be up in

198

my room. Room three. Come right up and we'll have a talk."

"I'd like to have a talk with you," said Alder. "I'd like it a lot."

"It may be to your advantage."

He went out and Alder, pouring out a glass of whiskey, held the glass in his hand for a long moment. He nodded thoughtfully, downed the whiskey in a single gulp and strolled out of the saloon.

There was a light in the back of Morgan's real-estate office, but the front part was dark. Alder stood outside the door a moment, tempted to go in, but he shook his head suddenly and turning, headed for the hotel.

There was no one in the lobby but the night clerk and Alder, giving the man a careless glance, went up the stairs. He found room three and knocked on the door.

As he waited for the door to open, Alder heard a voice in the adjoining room, number five, that he recognized. Cass Simcoe. The general's heavy voice replied to her.

Jagger opened the door, stepped aside for Alder to enter, then closed the door.

"I won't beat about the bush," Jagger said bluntly. "You're the right man for the job I'm about to propose to you. You've killed your man. That's what I want you to do now—kill a man!"

Alder showed no change of expression. His slitted eyes remained slitted and he said, with careless ease, when Jagger concluded, "Who's the man you want killed?"

"I'll tell you when you agree to the job."

The faintest hint of a sardonic smile curled the left side of Alder's mouth. "Mr. Jagger," he said, "that's a very interesting little proposition. And I like the way you made it. Of course you wouldn't come right out like that with anyone else. Kill a man for me. But you're right. I'm a safe man to talk to like that. I'm a former Missouri bushwhacker. I'm a killer. A fugitive who can't go home. The Union Army posted a reward for me. But that was last year. Haven't you heard—the Yankee government in Washington passed a general amnesty bill this summer.

Even us downright die-hard guerrillas can come in now.
We're not outlaws any more. I can go right back to Ray
County, Missouri, and show my face on the street."

"You're still a killer," scowled Jagger. "I intend to pay
you for this job."

Alder nodded in agreement. "That I am. In fact, I'm
going to kill a man in a little while, and I'm not going to
get a white nickel for doing it."

"I'm willing to pay you—enough."

"Maybe you are and maybe you aren't. Mr. Jagger, you
haven't talked to me more than to say hello in the several
times I've been in Pawnee City. You don't know me."

"I know all about you," Jagger said harshly. "Morgan,
my former partner, told me quite a lot about you."

"Before you and he had a fight?" Jagger made a gesture
of dismissal and was about to speak, but Alder continued in
a low, even tone, "Guess where I've been since last November, when I pulled out of here?" He smiled thinly. "I
made some money here. Enough to do a little traveling on
the cars. I even had a little piece to slip a politician in
Washington City, to get me some information that I
wanted."

"Washington?" exclaimed Jagger, startled.

"That's where the War Department is. Your—*our*—
Yankee War Department. They keep some awfully good
records there, all the battles, all the skirmishes, the names
and rank of everyone. You served in the Sixteenth Illinois
Cavalry, Mr. Jagger. A sergeant, weren't you?"

"You didn't have to go to Washington to hear that,"
Jagger said irritably. "You could have learned that right
here in Pawnee City."

"Oh, I knew it before I went to Washington. You and
Sergeant Morgan were both in the Sixteenth and you were
both in a little rear-guard fight down in Texas round about
June twenty-second, eighteen sixty-five . . . when our
bunch was headed for Mexico. You whomped our boys
back there and it bothered us a lot, later on. You got our
supplies . . . and twenty-five thousand dollars in gold coin
that Shelby was counting on."

He paused and Jagger scowled at him. "Wait a minute,

Alder. I know what you're driving at. Morgan told me. You've an idea that it was Morgan and I who got that gold . . . that it's the money we used to build this town."

"That's right."

"Suppose I said that we did come out of the army with, say, twenty-five thousand dollars? That wouldn't prove a thing."

"No, it wouldn't because the army never had a report of anyone picking up twenty-five thousand down in Texas. The funny part of it is, that along about five months ago, General Sheridan *got* twenty-five thousand dollars. It was in greenbacks, but the patriotic citizen who sent it didn't sign his name to the note that came with the money. The note just said that it was some money the sender had captured while serving with the army, that he wanted to make things right."

"Be damned!" exploded Jagger. Then he looked sharply at Alder. "You're lying!"

"Don't call me a liar, Mr. Jagger," said Alder softly. "There's just one more thing I haven't told you. That the Johnny Reb who was guarding that gold was my brother, Jim Alder."

He turned his back deliberately on Jagger and crossing the room, sat down on the edge of Jagger's bed. When he again looked at Jagger, the latter had had time to mask his expression.

"I knew about Jim before I ever came to Pawnee City," Alder went on. "I'd been down in Texas and I'd scouted around. I found the ambulance, the wooden treasure chest . . . and what was left of my brother. You didn't bother to search him. He was just another dead Johnny Reb . . . when you left him."

"Morgan!" cried Jagger suddenly. "Morgan shot your brother."

"Morgan or you. Yes, I know Jim was wearing a gray uniform—not like me—and you were wearing a blue. You were doing the job you had to do and he was doing his. But murder—Mr. Jagger, that's another horse."

"Murder? I—I don't understand."

"I found my brother's bones two years ago," Alder went

on remorselessly. "Then I checked up on things last winter. This summer I went back to Texas for another look-see. My brother was shot through the chest."

"Morgan!" cried Jagger. "I never could hit the side of a barn. But you know about Morgan, he was the best shot we had in the Sixteenth. Some people even thought he was as good as—as you, Alder!"

"I've heard about his shooting."

"We were after your brother, but he was giving us a run for it. Morgan brought down one of the horses while we were on horseback. It was over two hundred yards and he got the horse. That upset the ambulance and we charged your brother. He whanged back at us and Morgan got him with a single shot."

"With what kind of a gun?"

"His carbine."

"And the second bullet? The one through the head?"

"When your brother went down, Morgan ran up. He —he drew his revolver and shot your brother to finish him off."

"While he was lying on his back?"

Alder looked at Jagger for a long moment. Then Jagger played his trump card. He took from his pocket the Resolution he had received from Chad Morgan as Mayor of Pawnee City.

He handed it to Alder, who read it. "Do you know what this does to me?" Jagger asked. "It's utter ruin. When the cattle stop coming here, I'm through. My bank goes bust. I lose the yards, this hotel. I might save the saloon, but I never thought of myself as a bartender, or a saloonkeeper. Do you know now who it is I want you to kill?"

"Morgan!"

"Yes—Morgan. The man who's ruining me. The man who—who murdered your brother. Ten thousand dollars, Alder. Ten thousand in cash paid to you as soon as the job's done." He added, "I could save that ten thousand, Alder, if I could hit a target with a revolver . . . or even with a rifle."

"I'll do it, Mr. Jagger," Alder said slowly. "I would

have done it for nothing, but I'm a man with nothing. I've spent my time and my money on a long chase. And maybe," he added, "I'll take a trip to Europe with the ten thousand. It might—help——"

He crossed the room, opened the door. Jagger closed it from inside.

As Tom Alder walked toward the stairs, the door of room number one opened soundlessly and Helen Jagger looked out. Her eyes followed Tom Alder until he had disappeared down the stairwell.

The walls of the hotel rooms were very thin. A person in one room who was alone, lying quietly on a bed, could hear the conversations in the next room, especially if one strained his, or her, ears—and put one against the wall when she heard certain names.

Chapter Thirty-Seven

Morgan was fully dressed, although he was lying on his cot with the light out, when he heard someone rattling the knob of the front door.

He paid no attention. A drunk. Knuckles rapped the windowpane and he was still unconcerned. But then a voice called, a low, almost frantic voice. "Chad—Chad, are you inside?"

He exclaimed and swung his feet to the floor. He took two quick strides and was through the door that led to the office section of the building. He saw the person outside, close to the glass-paned door and he shot the bolt.

He reached out, caught Helen Jagger's arm and pulled her inside.

"I had to talk to you, Chad," she said, almost sobbing.

"Of course," he replied. He looked over his shoulder, hesitated. "There's no shade here. Do you mind coming in back?"

She flashed him a wan smile. "So nobody will see me in here?" She started for the rear. He was with her, all the way, his hand resting lightly on her arm to guide her in the semidarkness.

They went into his bedroom and he asked, "Shall I put on a light? It can't be seen from the street."

"N-no, I'd rather talk to you in the dark. Chad—I—I saw the Board of Supervisors' Resolution that you sent to Joe———"

"*My* resolution, Helen. That's what I was talking about this afternoon. *I* wrote the resolution—I'll take the responsibility for it. But it had to be, Helen. They would have drawn it up if I hadn't. It was only a matter of—of time. . . . I'm sorry."

His fingers curled around her arm. Helen disengaged

herself gently, stepped forward and sat down on his bed. She did not look up at him immediately. "Chad," she said in a strained, low voice, "don't—don't talk for a minute. And don't touch me. I want to say this clearly without—without hysterics." She laughed shortly, harshly. "Hysterics! A year ago I would have thought that *soft*—something I most certainly was not. . . . I know about Joe, Chad, I know that he's wrong, that he's been wrong all the time. But he's my brother—our parents died when we were both young and before the war he was almost like a father to me—a much older brother. He took care of me and I guess I idolized him. And then, when he was away for all those years, he was the only thing I had to cling to. But now——"

Morgan said gently, "Joe was my friend all through the war. I trusted my life to him. He never let me down."

"The money did it," Helen went on. "The twenty-five thousand dollars that you—you and Joe stole. Yes, I know, Chad. I think I suspected it all along, but I didn't want to know. Then, tonight——"

"Make no mistake, Helen," Morgan said earnestly. "Joe didn't *force* me into it. I went in of my own free will. I *wanted* to get rich as much as he did."

"No, that's not true, Chad. I know it isn't." She stopped and raised her head. "He's going to kill you, Chad! Not Joe—he knows he can't do it himself. But he—he's hired Tom Alder."

"Alder!" exclaimed Morgan. "But it was Tom Alder's——"

"His brother, the man you killed to get the money. Tom Alder knows it. He knew the whole story and what he didn't know, Joe told him—that you—you shot Tom's brother."

In the semidarkness, Morgan stiffened.

Helen went on miserably, "Alder's a gun fighter. I know that much. And—and Joe's promised him ten thousand dollars." A shudder ran through her and she buried her face in her hands. He started to move toward her and she heard his step. "Don't touch me, Chad! I—I feel so terrible. I had to tell you—and I'm being a traitor to Joe——"

Morgan wanted to reassure her and did not have the words for it. But he tried. "It'll work out, Helen."

"How can it?" she cried poignantly. "Everything's wrong."

She got up and Morgan wanted to take her into his arms and couldn't. What had been between them was . . . gone. It had faded into the tears and the heartaches . . . and the mists of time.

"Helen," he said awkwardly.

She was going and he could not stop her. She went out and after a moment he heard the street door open and close. He stood in the darkness for a long moment and then the instinct of self-preservation caused him to go out and shoot the bolt on the street door. When he returned to his room, he sat down on the bed and for a long time did not move. At last he sighed heavily, got up and struck a match.

He lit the lamp and getting down to one knee, reached under his cot and pulled out his valise. He opened it and took from it his Navy Colt. He spun the cylinder, saw that the chambers were loaded and finally dropped the gun on the bed beside him.

Tom Alder stood in front of The Longhorn Saloon. He had been standing there for a half hour before Morgan came out of the real-estate office and saw him in front of the saloon. He stopped.

If this was the moment . . .

Morgan counted mentally to ten and when Alder still made no movement and gave no sign of recognition, Morgan crossed the street and went to the Chinese restaurant. A man had a daily routine to go through, even if it was his last day on earth.

While Morgan was in the restaurant, Tom Alder remained outside The Longhorn Saloon. He saw Joe Jagger come from the direction of the hotel, was aware that Jagger was casting furtive glances at him, but Alder gave him no sign of recognition.

Jagger went into the Pawnee Savings Bank and a few minutes later, Alder caught a glimpse of him peering through the window.

A chuck wagon came lumbering down the street and stopped before The St. Louis Store. Sam Acres, the Simcoe trail boss, who was as close to Tom Alder as any man, jumped down from the chuck wagon and went into the store, scowling at a long sheet of paper he carried in his hand. A list of things they would take back to Texas.

General Simcoe and Cass came along a few minutes later. Cass had changed from her smart city clothes to something more serviceable. Calfskin boots, a tan skirt and waist, a jacket.

She saw Tom Alder and came up quickly. "It's good to see you again."

"How are you, Miss Cass?" Alder asked easily. "You'll be going back to Texas pretty soon."

"How did you know?" exclaimed Cass. "I've been arguing with Dad all through breakfast."

"Guessed it," said Alder. "One year at school was all you'd stand."

"It was too long."

"A Texas lady has to learn things," General Simcoe said, trying to look stern.

"Oh, fiddlesticks," replied his daughter. She took her father's arm. "That's our chuck wagon over by the store. Since we're so rich, I'm going to load it to the top and if there isn't enough room, we'll buy another wagon, Tom— I'll see you later."

"Perhaps," said Alder to himself. "Perhaps."

The general continued on with his daughter and after a moment they cut diagonally across the street. They reached the far sidewalk in front of the restaurant, but did not look inside. They continued on to The St. Louis Store and entered.

Tom Alder took a thin cigar from his shirt pocket and sticking it in his mouth, put a match to it. He drew deeply on the smoke and looked at his hands. He held them out, the fingers spread apart. They were steady.

Alder knew what he could do.

Well, so did Chad Morgan, for that matter. He had not been afraid of Wild Jack Mason. He had backed down Brog and his drunken cowboys when a wrong move or the slightest hesitation would surely have caused his own death.

He had finally killed Brog, the towhead trail boss.

Alder did not underestimate Chad Morgan.

He looked across the street and Morgan had come out of the restaurant. He was standing there, looking carelessly up the street. In a moment or so he would be coming back to his office and would pass near Tom Alder.

Alder drew on his cigar and kept his slitted eyes turned toward Morgan across the street.

He heard the quick, light footsteps on the wooden sidewalk, knew that it was a woman, a woman in a hurry who was coming along. He did not turn his eyes away from Morgan, however.

Then Helen Jagger was beside him.

"Mr. Alder," she said tautly. "Please . . . you mustn't."

Alder took his eyes from Morgan, but he did not look at Helen Jagger. He said wearily, "Please go away, Miss Jagger. You can't stop this."

"You mustn't," said Helen, choking on the words. "My brother lied to you. *He* killed your brother."

"This isn't a thing for a woman to see," Alder said evenly. "Go inside. . . ." There was a taut moment, then he said, "He's coming."

Helen cried out softly and reached for his left arm. He half turned away with a brushing movement.

Morgan was coming across the street, was less than thirty yards away now. Alder called, "Have you got a gun, Morgan?"

Morgan came to a full halt. "Yes," he said, "I've got a gun."

"Use it, then!"

Morgan saw Helen Jagger only a few feet from Tom Alder. She stood on the wooden sidewalk, petrified with fear. Morgan knew that she had pleaded with Alder, had tried to stop the impending tragedy. He knew, too, that she had failed.

Morgan wore a coat that was open. His gun was thrust behind the waistband of his trousers. It was not a good draw, he knew, but—would a good draw save him against Tom Alder?

He said tonelessly, barely loud enough for Alder to hear across the distance, "I'm going to kill you, Alder. You may get me, but you'll die yourself. You know that, don't you?"

"If that's the way of it, that's the way of it," said Alder.

Across the street, Joe Jagger had been unable to bear the suspense and had opened the bank door and stood in the open doorway. Morgan did not see him and Alder himself was only vaguely aware of Jagger.

Morgan had guts. He was a man and Alder felt an odd regret that this had to be.

There was no question here of the code, of the other man letting you draw first. Alder was the professional, Morgan the amateur. It was kill or be killed.

Morgan reached for his gun. His hand gripped the butt firmly, whipped the gun out and up as smoothly and swiftly as he could, his thumb pressing back the hammer even as he drew.

Morgan drew as fast as he could draw, yet Alder's gun thundered before Morgan's was even thrust out.

An invisible bolt smashed Morgan's right forearm. He looked down in astonishment at his Navy Colt, which suddenly lay at his feet. Was this the best Alder could do? Shoot him in the arm?

Morgan started to stoop to pick up the gun with his left hand, to put one bullet into Tom Alder before the former guerrilla could give him the *coup de grâce*.

A scream split the air even as Morgan started to bend over. It didn't come from Helen Jagger. It came from behind Morgan.

Cass Simcoe, who had been in the doorway of The St. Louis Store, when Alder's gun had spoken, was running forward now. "No, no!" she cried. "Don't!"

But Morgan was committed. He had reached for the gun in the street and he had to go through with it. Instinct told him what to do. Stoop, lunge for the gun, throw yourself to the ground, roll away and come up . . . shooting.

He did all those things. He heard a roar and thunder, as

his fingers closed on the revolver. Momentarily, he expected the stunning blow of the bullet and he exerted every ounce of his will to continuing the roll . . . bringing up the gun . . . and pulling the trigger.

He won.

Prone in the dust, only his head and gunhand raised a few inches, the gun bucked his fist once, twice.

And Alder was down!

Shocked by the victory, Morgan got to his knees, started to push himself up. A man came flying from the direction of the bank. Joe Jagger.

A gun was in his hand. It lanced fire and thunder at Morgan and a bullet kicked up dust, inches from Morgan's foot. A second bullet whizzed by his ear.

Joe Jagger could not hit the proverbial barn door.

He jerked back the hammer of his gun for a third shot . . . and at that instant, Cass Simcoe leaped in front of Morgan, her arms thrown wide, as if to protect him.

Joe Jagger's third and final bullet was his best shot. It was aimed true and would have struck Morgan . . . except that Cass was now in front of him. Morgan heard the bullet thud into her body, heard her cry out and saw her fall. Morgan dropped his gun, lunged for her, but missed her. Cass fell to the street on her face.

Alder, down on the ground, fired one last shot. There was just enough life left in him for it. The bullet went to Joe Jagger. Jagger was dead before he hit the ground. In the last moment of his life, Alder had known the truth. That Morgan was not the kind of man that Jagger had said he was. It was Jagger who had put that last bullet into Jim Alder's head; Tom Alder knew that as he fired.

Morgan was down on his knees. Gently, he turned Cass Simcoe over. The left side of her shirt was stained with blood, but her eyes were open.

"What'd you have to kill him for?" she wailed. "Tom Alder liked you."

"I liked him," said Morgan, "but he was trying to kill me."

Chapter Thirty-Eight

The golden wheat spread out, acre upon acre, mile upon mile. A sea of golden, waving grain, dotted here and there by the reaping machines, the thrashers, the growing shocks of stacked sheaves.

It was fine wheat, the stalks containing full heads of fat kernels. It would make good bread.

This was the future of Kansas.

Wheat.

Yesterday, the longhorn had grazed here and become fat on the buffalo grass. The day before, the buffalo alone had been supreme.

The buffalo had gone. The longhorn had gone.

And now wheat was king.

Chad Morgan was in the field that lay beside the road running along the river. It was June and he was stacking up the sheaves of bound wheat into shocks. He was new at this work and he performed the task usually given to the youths and the women of the wheat growing countries.

Still it was hard for him. The sun was hot, the day had started early and he was tired, hot and hungry. Sweat ran down his face.

His eyes went to the road and he was glad when he saw a horseman galloping toward him. He needed a rest.

The horseman was coming at a furious pace. When still some distance away, the horse left the road and came diagonally across the stubbled field toward Morgan.

And then Morgan saw that the rider was a girl, a girl wearing man's shirt, Levi's, cowboy boots.

It was Cass Simcoe.

"You damnyank!" she cried.

"Reb!"

"I rode all the way from Emporia since sunup and it's fifty-some miles."

"You came alone?" Morgan asked inanely.

"From Emporia. Dad and the boys brung—brought—a herd up The Trail and I thought while they was dickerin' to sell, I'd take a run over here. . . . I had some business," she finished defiantly.

"Of course," said Morgan.

"It don't concern you," retorted Cass. But her eyes could not meet his steady look. She made a sweeping gesture toward the wheat. "That—there's wheat, the stuff you sodbusters raise?"

"That's wheat," Morgan said quietly, "from which you make your bread."

"We eat biscuits back home, not bread." She sniffed. "Can they raise this stuff in Texas?"

"I think so. Why? Were you thinking of turning farmer?"

"Me? Are you crazy? I wouldn't be a farmer for all the—all the longhorns in Texas. Well, I gotta go now. I only stopped by here to tell you that I'm gettin' married soon."

"Married? Who'd be marrying *you* . . . ?"

She flared. "Lots of men'd marry me. Good Texas men. Why there's a rich cattleman near Denton——"

"Cass," Morgan said, "you're telling a whopper."

"All right, what if I am? And what about *you?* You're marrying—or maybe you've already married—Miss Jagger."

Morgan shook his head. "Helen Jagger went away last fall. She took her brother to be buried at their old home town, Bloomington, in Illinois. She never came back. She sold the hotel. I had a letter from her a couple of months ago. She was on her way to Europe."

"Europe?" sniffed Cass. "Why'd anyone want to go to Europe?"

"Why does anyone want to live in Texas when they can live in Kansas?"

Her eyes flashed and her mouth opened wide to blast

him, but Morgan, grinning, suddenly stepped toward her horse. She grabbed up the reins, started to whirl the horse away and it did turn, but Morgan's arms shot out and swept her from the saddle.

He held her in a tight embrace and their lips met in a fierce kiss.

Then suddenly Cass pulled her head away.

"Do I *have* to be a damnyank?" she wailed.

ABOUT THE AUTHOR

FRANK GRUBER had been editor of various trade magazines when, in 1934, he began to devote all his energies to writing. A most prolific writer, Mr. Gruber published 250 stories in more than forty magazines during the next five years. From 1939 to 1941 Mr. Gruber tried his hand at novels and published sixteen in quick succession. Though most noted for his westerns, Mr. Gruber was also author of such screenplays as *Mask of Dimitrios, Northern Pursuit, Johnny Angel* and *The Kansan,* and also several well-known mystery series.

★ WAGONS WEST ★

A series of unforgettable books that trace the lives of a dauntless band of pioneering men, women, and children as they brave the hazards of an untamed land in their trek across America. This legendary caravan of people forge a new link in the wilderness. They are Americans from the North and the South, alongside immigrants, Blacks, and Indians, who wage fierce daily battles for survival on this uncompromising journey—each to their private destinies as they fulfill their greatest dreams.

☐	22808	**INDEPENDENCE!**	$3.50
☐	22784	**NEBRASKA!**	$3.50
☐	23177	**WYOMING!**	$3.50
☐	22568	**OREGON!**	$3.50
☐	23168	**TEXAS!**	$3.50
☐	23381	**CALIFORNIA!**	$3.95
☐	23405	**COLORADO!**	$3.50
☐	20174	**NEVADA!**	$3.50
☐	20919	**WASHINGTON!**	$3.50

Buy them at your local bookstore or use this handy coupon: